ALEXANDRE DUMAS

The Courtship of
Josephine and Napoleon
And
Other Stories

by

Alexandre Dumas

Fredonia Books
Amsterdam, The Netherlands

The Courtship of Josephine and Napoleon and
Other Stories

by
Alexandre Dumas

ISBN: 1-4101-0192-4

Reprinted from the 1927 edition

Fredonia Books
Amsterdam, The Netherlands
http://www.fredoniabooks.com

In order to make original editions of historical works
available to scholars at an economical price, this
facsimile of the original edition of 1927 is
reproduced from the best available copy and has
been digitally enhanced to improve legibility, but the
text remains unaltered to retain historical
authenticity.

Table of Contents

Introduction

ALEXANDRE DUMAS was born at Villers-Cotterets, Aisne, France, on July the 24th, 1802. His mother was Marie Labouret, the daughter of a tavern-keeper. His father, who died in Alexandre's childhood, was General of the Hercules Guards (Strong Men) of the Republican Army of Napoleon Bonaparte. The General's mother was a negress of San Domingo named Louise Dumas, who had married Count Alexandre Davy de la Pailleterie, a white.

The youth loved reading and books. He learned Italian and German and, inspired by ambition to become a famous writer, tramped to Paris, earning his way by shooting game.

With the aid of General Foy, he entered the household of the Duc d'Orleans as a clerk. His leisure time was spent in reading and writing. In 1827, after seeing a picture at the Salon of Christina of Sweden, he wrote a play Christine, meeting with success. In 1828 Henri III. of France, a drama, appeared. A powerful genius was demonstrated when we remember that this performance restored romance to the Parisian stage. The Committee of the Theatre Français gave their approval, which was usually reserved for much older or more experienced writers.

The Revolution of 1830, which overthrew the Bourbons, changed the dramatist into a fighter, and, remembering his father's gigantic exploits, Alexandre flung himself into the frenzied flow of blood,—marched to Soissons, single-handed and alone seized a store of gunpowder and brought it to the Revolutionary party. The mighty stories of Trigaud and Porthos bear a striking resemblance to Dumas himself and his father.

Alexandre's old master, the Duc d'Orleans, now became King Philippe, and his clerk was Librarian of the Household. However, old ties do not always endure in new dwellings, and, displeased with court functions and political disturbances, the romancer's quill became wet again. The interference revigorated the natural giant energy.

This Vulcan of fiction hammered out volumes as an ordinary author would write a chapter. He reminds us of the huge negro sledge-swingers who smile and sing in rhythm to their monster task, and as the hours increase the song grows louder and the blows re-bellow.

Although Dumas had many collaborators, their name has been forgotten, yet some of them doubtless were men of talent.

He won high recognition from the French Government when they selected him from among all the writers in France to visit Algeria and describe it to the French people for furtherance of colonization.

In 1860 Alexandre's powerful nature and brave blood demanded action. Garibaldi welcomed him to his forces in Italy and then made him Superintendent of the Naples Museum and Excavations. The Memoirs of Garibaldi give the reader an idea how well Dumas knew the subjects of his writings.

Later he fell into disfavor with Victor Emanuel, due to articles which appeared in a journal under his editorship, and he returned home to Paris.

The Neapolitan stories, such as Lady Hamilton and Admiral Nelson, Gaetano, the Gorger, and An Historic Banquo, are inflamed with the vengeful fire that Alexandre felt for the foul treatment of his father, the General, by the English and Italian court conspirators, which he had vowed some day he would expose to the world.

We may here remark the literary secret of Dumas. His characters of the Three Musketeers, D'Artagnan, Porthos, and Athos were real swordsmen whose exploits were recorded in a book of Memoirs. The magic hand of Dumas has made them walk out of the pages into real life again.

Unlike many authors, Dumas was not an idle desk romancer. Whatever town, district or country offered its citizens as romantic heroes, he journeyed there and lived for a long period, learning its private and public history, breathing its atmosphere and uniting himself to the people's faiths and fervors. This energy explains why every story seems to jump right out of the page and every suffering character is so furiously defended.

He united two qualities sometimes found in muscular men of poetic spirit. For example, he believed in the Revolution of France, but believed also in the glorious heroes of Royalty whom that Revolution considered as food only for the Guillotine.

His plan of writing is simple. The day or night is described in one word. One, two or three people are seen doing something — traveling, for instance. Their actions are always in some way out of the ordinary. They talk to each other. Their name and brief history is given (generally a person of an important historical era). The reader's imagination awakes at the first sentence. His human nature begins to stir in the next. His curiosity is aroused in the third, and in the fourth he is a prisoner at once of the delights of romantic fiction about real people.

Had Dumas written an Epic, Homer would have a French twin.

He read memoirs, histories, private papers, public documents, chronicles, and we marvel at the historical news of his stories. But he is not like many modern romancers. He has no swollen Dumas. He never stops the narrative to vaunt his vast knowledge, but keeps to the story.

He is huge. He covers the sixteenth to the nineteenth century. A king is as natural with him as a peasant. He overwhelms us with exploits and conquests. His beautiful women are real, yet his raptures are always poetic. He paints like Titian, but no unfleshly damsel beyond the touch or the eye. No two are alike. Diana de Castro has no similarity to Helen von Chandroz, Emma Hamilton to Mme. Dubarry. His description of Mary Stuart as a maiden is sublime and glorious (see The Tenth Muse).

A fighter himself, the duels and battles are full of real sword-thrusts, pistol shots and strategic manœuvres of real heroes upon historic battle grounds.

A lover of laughter, he is not witty or humourous in only single instances or small quantities. He is full of mirth and fun. To laugh at the beginning of a tale would be infantile. The comedy must increase and increase in joyful confusion to the end.

INTRODUCTION

Patriot—his ardor for France will reach eloquence in a single short passage and never out of place in the story. We would be surprised if he omitted it. Moreover, his patriotism is astounding for its intelligent practical truth.

Man of hard struggles and common sense,—he despises equally those who mock heroes and those who rant their praises but never tell what they did.

Unearthly in aim and nerveless in zeal, he treads the region of the supernatural and the mystic with firm and sure feet. In *Terra Daemoniorum* he has found his own comrades and exults in their invisible and occult pastimes. Where Poe analyzed, Dumas adventured.

Lover of animals, a little dog is often the perfect completion of a great tragedy and appears at the corner of the scene as we behold in some of the great masters of painting.

Dumas was too big-minded to be small either in subjects, language, treatment, plots or number of works. His generosity or profluence of mysteries, exciting scenes and great personages make the reader wonder whether he is not receiving ten-fold the delights that should belong to one story.

In 1864 he built a mammoth theatre (just his nature) in Paris, the Theatre-Historique. Financially it was not a success. Friends and money are never bound by nature, and Alexandre Dumas had the habit of generosity not uncommon to chevaliers of the drama and stage.

A few years later at a fatal period of French history, overwork having outworn the restless, burning brain, Alexandre, the son (author of Camille), removed his father to an estate near Puys in Dieppe. Here on December the 5th, 1870, the pen left the mighty hand forever.

His works conservatively number one thousand volumes. The dramas have not endured but the heroes and heroines of his stories are as living to-day as they were in actual life. D'Artagnan is almost accepted as Napoleon.

That wonderful name demands pause. The stories of Napoleon in this volume (no matter what lives or accounts have been read before) will show you the Corsican Cæsar in action, not as he sometimes is in myth. You will see the business-like Believer of a Boundless Vision supported by a beautiful Faith. And you will know why that great Believer failed. Napoleon could have ended like Washington. The author explains the mystery.

Dumas has won his crown. To give him a royal title, he is another world conqueror in a different realm. He is another Alexander the Great.

G. W. B.

The Courtship of
Josephine and Napoleon
And
Other Stories

The Courtship of Josephine and Napoleon

WHEN artillery has roared down public boulevards and blood has flowed in the streets of a capital city, society always suffers an upheaval for a long period before calm is restored.

The 14th Vendémiaire of the year 1795 in Paris removed both the traces and bodies of the terrible conflict in which the tottering Convention, namely, the Revolution and its leaders, had come out victorious and in complete control over their enemies the Sectionaries. But the people still agitated the struggle.

The Convention dismissed the officers of the National Guard, broke up the chasseurs and grenadiers, and placed Barras or in reality his young associate, Bonaparte, the active leader, at the head of the National Guard.

Stories of that bloody day which was to remain indelible upon the Parisian soul, never ended. The thrilling words of heroism from the mouth of the wounded or better from the wounds themselves were told over and over again.

They praised Barras for choosing his second with such unerring judgment at the first glance, and that second, who, unknown to them on the previous evening, had burst upon them like a god from the midst of thunder and lightning and led the Republican victory. Bonaparte remained general of the interior; and to be within reach of the staff, who had their headquarters on the Boulevard des Capucines, in what had formerly been the Ministry of Foreign Affairs, he took two rooms in the Hôtel de la Concorde, Rue Neuve-des-Capucines.

A young man was introduced into the room which he used for a study, under the name of Eugene de Beauharnais.

Although he was already besieged by petitioners, Bonaparte had not yet reached the point of drawing a sharp line as to whom he would or would not receive. He therefore gave orders that the young man was to be admitted.

He was a handsome young man of sixteen or seventeen years of age. He had large eyes, thick black hair, red lips, white teeth, and aristocratic hands and feet—a mark of distinction which the general immediately noticed—and apart from the embarrassment inseparable from a first interview, he had that attractive modesty which is so becoming in youth, above all when its possessor appears as a supplicant.

From the time he entered the room Bonaparte watched him attentively, which did not tend to lessen Eugene's timidity.

But suddenly shaking the feeling off as if it were unworthy of him, he raised his head, and, drawing himself

1

up, said: "After all, I do not see why I should hesitate to proffer a request which is both pious and loyal."

"I am listening," said Bonaparte.

"I am the son of the Vicomte de Beauharnais."

"Of the citizen-general," corrected Bonaparte gently.

"Of the citizen-general, if you prefer," said the young man, "and if you insist upon Republican forms."

"I insist upon nothing," replied Bonaparte, "save that which is clear and concise."

"Well," resumed the young man, "I come to ask at your hands, citizen-general, the sword of my father, Alexandre de Beauharnais, who was a general like yourself. I am sixteen years old, and my military education is almost completed. It is for me to serve my country now. I hope some day to wear at my side the sword which my father wore. That is why I have come to ask you for it."

Bonaparte, who liked clear, precise replies, was much prepossessed by this firm, intelligent language.

"If I should ask you for more information concerning yourself and your family, citizen," asked Bonaparte, "would you attribute the request to curiosity or to the interest with which you have inspired me?"

"I should prefer to think that the report of our misfortunes had reached your ears," replied the young man, "and what it is to that I owe the kindness with which you have received me."

"Was not your mother, Josephine de Beauharnais, a prisoner also?" asked Bonaparte.

"Yes, and she was saved almost by a miracle. We owe her life to citizeness Tallien and to citizen Barras."

Bonaparte reflected a moment. "How does your father's sword happen to be in my hands?"

"I do not say that it is in your hands, but you can have it restored to me, though. The Convention ordered the disarming of the Section Le Peletier. We are living in our old house in the Rue Neuve-des-Mathurins, which the general had restored to us. Some men came to my mother and asked for all the weapons in the house. My mother gave orders that they should take a double-barrelled hunting gun of mine, a single-barrelled rifle which I bought at Strasbourg, and finally my father's sword. I regretted neither the double-barrelled gun nor the rifle, though I took pride in the memories which they recalled. But I regretted, and I confess still regret, that sword which fought so gloriously in America and France."

"If you were to see the weapons which formerly belonged to you," said Bonaparte, "you would probably recognize them."

"Beyond doubt," replied Eugene.

Bonaparte rang and a sub-officer entered.

"Accompany citizen Beauharnais to the rooms where they have put the arms belonging to the Sections," said Bonaparte. "You will allow him to take those which he will point out to you."

And he held out his hand to the young man, the hand which was to lift him so high. Ignorant of the future, Eugene darted toward it and kissed it gratefully.

"Ah, citizen!" said he, "my mother

and sister shall know how good you have been to me, and, believe me, they will appreciate it as much as I do."

Just then the door opened and Barras entered without being announced.

"Ah!" said he, "here I am on ground with which I am doubly familiar!"

"I have already told citizen Bonaparte how much we owe you," replied Eugene.

"Well," said Barras, "the bad days are over and the good ones have returned. What has brought you here, my young friend?"

Eugene told Barras the reason of his visit.

"Why did you not come to me," asked Barras, "instead of disturbing my colleague?"

"Because I wished to meet citizen-general Bonaparte," replied Eugene. "It seemed to me that it would be a good omen if he returned me my father's sword."

And, bowing to the two generals he went out with the officer, much less embarrassed than when he had come.

The two generals were left alone. Both had followed the young man with their eyes, each one inspired with different thoughts, until the door had closed upon him.

"That boy has a heart of gold," said Barras. "Just think, when he was only thirteen years and a half old—I did not know him then—he went to Strasbourg alone in the hope of finding some papers there which would justify his father before the revolutionary tribunal. But the revolutionary tribunal was in a hurry. It cut off the father's head while it was waiting for the papers the son was collecting. It was time anyway for Eugene to return, for had

it not been for Saint-Just, whom he met there, I do not know what might have happened to Eugene. He attacked Tétrell, one of the leaders, who was twice as big as he, in the midst of a play at the theatre. If the people, who had seen him during the day when he was fighting against the Prussians, had not taken his part boldly, the poor boy would have been badly singed."

"I suppose," said Bonaparte, always precise, "that you did not put yourself out to come here for the purpose of discussing this young man, since you did not know that he had come to see me."

"No," said Barras, "I came to make you a present."

"Me?"

"Yes, you," said Barras. And going to the door of the antechamber, he opened it and made a sign. Two men entered. They were carrying an immense piece of rolled canvas on their shoulders as two carpenters would carry a beam.

"Goodness! what is that?" asked Bonaparte.

"You have often spoken to me of your desire to make a campaign in Italy, general."

"You mean," interrupted Bonaparte, "of the necessity which will some day arise for France to decide the Austrian question."

"Well, for some time Carnot, who is of your opinion, has been occupied in making the most complete map of Italy which exists in the world. I asked for it at the Ministry of War, and although they were inclined to refuse, they finally gave it to me, and I give it to you."

Bonaparte seized Barras's hand, and

said: "This is indeed a present, especially if it is given to me as the man who is to make use of it. Open it," he continued, addressing the men who were carrying it.

They knelt down and untied the cords, but when they tried to unroll it they found that the room was not half large enough to hold it.

"Good!" exclaimed Bonaparte; "here I am forced to build a house to hold your present."

"Oh!" replied Barras, "when the time comes for you to use it, you may be living in a house which is large enough for you to hang it between two windows. In the meantime look at the part which is unrolled. Not a hill, not a brook is wanting."

The porters opened the map as far as the space permitted. The portion which they uncovered extended across the Gulf of Genoa, from Ajaccio to Savona.

"By the way," said Bonaparte, "is that not where Schérer, Masséna, and Kellermann are—here at Cervoni?"

"Yes," replied Barras, "we received word to that effect only this evening. How could I have forgotten to tell you! Augereau has won a great victory at Loano. Masséna and Joubert, whom Kellermann kept in his army despite the order of their dismissal which the Committee of Public Safety forwarded him displayed magnificent courage."

"It is not there, it is not there," murmured Bonaparte. "What do blows aimed at the limbs amount to? Nothing! They should aim at the heart. Milan, Mantua, Verona, those are the places to strike. Ah! if ever—"

"What?" asked Barras.

"Nothing," replied Bonaparte. "Because battles are not won with a map, a pair of compasses, and red, blue or green-headed pins. It needs instinct, an unerring glance, genius. I should like to know if Hannibal had plans of the battles of Trebbia, of Lake Trassymene, and of Cannes sent him from Carthage. I snap my fingers at your plans! Do you know what you ought to do? You ought to give me the details which you have received concerning the battle of Loano; and, since this map is unrolled at that very place, I would be interested in following the movements of our troops and the Austrians."

Barras drew from his pocket a note written with the laconism of a telegraphic despatch and handed it to Bonaparte.

"Patience," said he; "you have the map, and the command will follow perhaps."

Bonaparte read the despatch eagerly. "Good!" said he. "Loano is the key to Genoa, and Genoa is the magazine of Italy." Then, continuing to read the despatch, he said: "Masséna, Kellermann, Joubert, what men! and what could not a man do with them! He who could bring them together and make the most of their diverse qualities would be the veritable Olympian Jove with the thunderbolt in his hand!" Then he murmured the names of Hoche, Kléber and Moreau, and, with a pair of compasses in his hand, he stretched himself out upon the great map, of which only one corner uncovered. There he began to study the marches and counter-marches which had led up to the famous battle of Loano. When Barras took his departure, Bonaparte scarcely noticed it, so absorbed was he in his strategic combinations.

"It cannot have been Schérer," he said, "who devised and executed this movement. Neither can it have been Carnot; there is too great an element of the unexpected about it. It was doubtless Masséna."

He had been lying upon this map, which was never to leave him, for about half an hour when the door opened and a voice announced: "The citizeness Beauharnais."

Bonaparte, in his abstraction, thought he heard the words, "The citizen Beauharnais," and, imagining that it was the young man whom he had already seen who had returned to thank him for the favor which he had just granted him, he exclaimed: "Let him come in, let him come in!"

As he spoke, there appeared at the door, not only the young man whom he had already seen, but also a charming woman of about twenty-seven or eight years of age. He half rose in his astonishment, and it was thus with one knee on the ground, that Bonaparte first saw Marie-Rose-Josephine Tascher de la Pagerie, the widow of Beauharnais.

Bonaparte paused as if smitten with admiration. Madame de Beauharnais, about twenty-seven years of age, of indisputable beauty, with a charming grace of manner, exhaling from her whole person that subtle fascination which resembles the perfume which Venus gave to her chosen ones to inspire love.

Her hair and eyes were black, her nose was straight, her mouth a smiling curve; the oval outline of her face was irreproachable. Her neck was set gracefully upon her shoulders, her figure was flexible and undulating, her arm was perfectly shaped, and her hand beautiful beyond comparison.

Nothing could have been more attractive than her Creole accent, of which she had retained only sufficient trace to betray her tropical birth.

As her maiden name indicated, Madame de Beauharnais belonged to a noble family. Born at Martinique, her education, like that of all Creoles, was left entirely to herself; but rare qualities of mind and heart had made of Mademoiselle Tascher de la Pagerie one of the most cultivated women of any age. Her kind heart had taught her early in life that, although they had wool on their heads, the negroes were more to be pitied than other men, since, through the power and cupidity of the whites, they had been torn from their own country and transferred to a land where they suffered constantly, and not infrequently were killed by cruelty.

The thing that attracted her attention was the plight of these unhappy men. All their family ties were sundered, but brothers in toil they stood with bent backs, toiling beneath the rays of the sun, delving in a soil which their blood and their sweat fertilized, but not for themselves.

She asked herself in her youthful intelligence, why these men had been placed beyond the pale of the law? Why they should vegetate, naked, without shelter, without property, honor, liberty? and she herself found the answer—that all this was to enrich avaricious masters, who, from infancy, condemned this race to a life of hopeless and unending torture. And young

Josephine's pity had influenced her parents, at least, to make an earthly paradise for the slaves.

They were still white and black; but almost to the extent of being free, these blacks shared in all the advantages and some of the pleasures of life. And, while nowhere in the island were the negroes sure of marrying the women of their choice, marriages for love rewarded with affectionate and faithful service more surely their young mistress Josephine than was the case with any of the other slave owners.

She was about thirteen years old when a young officer of great merit and noble birth arrived at Martinique, and became acquainted with her at her Aunt Renaudin's house.

This was the Vicomte de Beauharnais.

The one possessed in his person everything calculated to please. She possessed in heart everything destined to inspire love. They loved each other therefore with all the ardor of two young people who have the delight of realizing their dreams of kindred souls.

"I have chosen you," said Alexandre, pressing her hand tenderly.

"And I have found you," replied Josephine, holding up her forehead to him to kiss.

Her Aunt Renaudin felt that it would be opposing the decrees of Providence to forbid the loves of the two young people. Their relatives were all in France. Their consent was necessary in order to consummate this marriage to which Aunt Renaudin saw no obstacle. Obstacles were raised, however, by Messieurs de Beauharnais, the father and uncle of the young man. In an access of fraternal affection they had once promised each other that their children should marry each other. He whom the young Creole already regarded as her husband was therefore the destined spouse of another, and that other his cousin.

Alexandre's father yielded first. When he saw the despair into which his refusal had plunged the young people, he himself agreed to go to his brother and tell him of the change which threatened to upset their plans. But the latter was less kindly in disposition, and informed his brother that while he might be willing to break his word, a thing unworthy of a gentleman, he, the brother, would not acquiesce in any such arrangement.

The vicomte's father came away in despair at having quarrelled with his brother, but he not only renewed his promise to consent, he actually did consent.

It was then that the young Josephine, who was later to give the world an example of such heroic self-sacrifice and absolute devotion, sounded the prelude as it were to the great divorce scene. She insisted that the vicomte should sacrifice his passion for her to the tranquillity and welfare of his family. This the noble vicomte refused to do.

And the count, with tears in his eyes, took the hands of the two young people and said:

"Never were you more worthy of one another than when you renounced your hopes of mutual happiness. You ask my final decision. It is that you shall marry, and it is my earnest wish that you may be happy."

A week later Mademoiselle de la

Pagerie became the Vicomtesse de Beauharnais.

Nothing happened to disturb the happiness of the young people until the Revolution began. The Vicomte de Beauharnais ranged himself among those who favored its adoption; only he made the mistake of thinking that the avalanche could be directed as it rushed on, carrying all before it. He was swept in its wake to the scaffold.

On the evening preceding the day on which he was to die, the Vicomte de Beauharnais wrote his wife the following letter. It was his final farewell:

"Night of the 6th and 7th Thermidor. "At the Conciergerie."

"Yet a few moments to give to love, to tears, and to regrets, and then every thought shall be devoted to the glory of my destiny and to the great dreams of immortality. When you receive this letter, oh, my Josephine, your husband, in the words of this world, will long have ceased to exist; but already in the bosom of his God, he will have tasted of the joys of real life. You see therefore that you must not weep for him. The wicked men, the senseless ones who survive him, should have all your tears, for they do evil and cannot repair it.

"But do not let us blacken with their guilty image these last moments. I would, on the contrary, brighten them by thinking that, beloved by an adorable wife, the short day of our wedded life has passed without the slightest cloud. Yes, our union has lasted but a day, and that reflection draws a sigh from me. But how serene and pure was that day which has vanished like a dream; and how grateful ought I to be to that Providence which must have you in its keeping! To-day that same Providence is taking me away before my time, and that is another of its favors. Can a good man live without grief, and almost remorse, when he sees the whole universe in the clutches of the wicked? I should therefore be glad to be taken away from them, were it not for the feeling that I am leaving to their tender mercies lives which are so precious and dear to me. If, however, the thoughts of the dying are trustworthy presentiments, I feel in my heart that these butcheries are soon to cease, and that the executioners will follow their victims to the scaffold. . . .

"I resume these incoherent, almost illegible lines after being interrupted by my keepers. I have just undergone a cruel formality which, under other circumstances, I would rather have died than endure. But why cavil at necessity? Reason teaches us to make the best of it.

"After they had cut off my hair, I bethought me of buying back a part of it, in order to leave my dear wife and children unequivocal proofs and tokens of my dying remembrance. . . . I feel my heart breaking at this thought, and my paper is wet with tears.

"Farewell, all that I love. Love me, speak of me, and never forget that the glory of dying a victim of tyrants, and a martyr to the cause of liberty, makes the scaffold illustrious!"

Arrested in turn, the vicomtesse wrote to her children, just before she was to die, in the same strain. She ended a long letter, which we have before us, with these words:

"For my part, my children, as I am about to die, as did your father before me, a victim to the mad excesses which he always opposed, and which finally devoured him, I leave this life with no feeling of hatred for his executioners and for my own whom I despise.

"Honor my memory even as you share my sentiments. I leave you for an inheritance the glory of your father and your mother's name, which some poor wretches have blessed—our love, our blessings, and our regrets."

Madame de Beauharnais was finishing this letter when she heard shouts of "Death to Robespierre! Long live Liberty!" in the courtyard. It was the morning of the 10th Thermidor.

Three days later Madame de Beauharnais, thanks to the friendship of Madame Tallien, was free; and a month later, through the influence of Barras, such of her property as had not been sold was restored to her. The house in the Rue Neuve-des-Mathurins, No. 11, was a part of this property.

When her son, who had not told her of his intention, returned with his father's sword in his hand, and told her of the circumstances attendant upon its return, in the first burst of enthusiasm she left her house, and, having only the boulevard to cross, hastened to thank the young general, who was much astonished at her appearance.

Bonaparte held out his hand to the beautiful widow, more beautiful than ever in the mourning robes which she had worn ever since her husband's death. Then he made a sign to her to step over the map and take a seat in that part of the room which was not encumbered by it.

Josephine replied that she had come on foot and that she did not dare to put her dainty little shoe upon the map for fear of soiling it.

But Bonaparte insisted, and with the assistance of his hand, she sprang over the Gulf of Genoa, the toe of her shoe making a mark where it touched the little town of Voltri.

An arm-chair was standing on the other side. Josephine seated herself in it, and Bonaparte, who had remained standing near her, partly from respect and partly from admiration, put his knee on another chair and leaned with his arms on the back.

Bonaparte was at first embarrassed. He was not accustomed to society, and had rarely talked with women; but he knew that there are three things to which their hearts are always alive— country, youth, and love. He therefore talked to Madame de Beauharnais of Martinique, of her relatives, and of her husband. An hour slipped by, which, clever mathematician that he was, seemed no longer than a few minutes to him.

They spoke little of the present state of affairs, but Bonaparte noticed that Madame de Beauharnais seemed to stand in close relations with all those who were in power, or who seemed likely to attain to it, her husband having been a prominent exponent of the reactionary opinions which were then in high favor.

For her part, Madame de Beauharnais was too clear-sighted a woman not to detect, for all his innate eccentricity, the powerful intellect of the victor of the 13th Vendémiaire.

This complete and rapid success had made of Bonaparte the hero of the day. He had often been mentioned in Madame de Beauharnais's presence; and curiosity and enthusiasm had prompted her, as we have said, to pay him this visit. She found that Barras's protégé was intellectually far beyond what Barras had claimed for him, so that when her servant came to tell her that Madame Tallien was waiting for her at her house, to go, she knew where, as they had planned, she exclaimed: "But our appointment was for five o'clock."

"And it is now six," said the lackey, bowing.

"Heavens!" said she in surprise; "what shall I say to her?"

"Tell her, madame," said Bonaparte, "that your conversation charmed me so greatly that I prevailed upon you with my entreaties to give me another quarter of an hour."

"That is bad advice," said Josephine; "for in that case I should have to say what is not true in order to excuse myself."

"Let me see," said Bonaparte, anxious that she should prolong her visit for a few moments, "was Madame Tallien contemplating another 9th Thermidor? I thought the days of Robespierre were gone forever."

"If I were not ashamed to make the confession, I would tell you where we are going."

"Tell me, madame. I shall be delighted to share a secret with you, especially one which you are ashamed to confess."

"Are you superstitious?" asked Madame de Beauharnais.

"I am a Corsican, madame."

"Then you will not make fun of me. Yesterday we visited Madame Gohier, and she told us that when she was passing through Lyons ten years or more ago, she had had her fortune told by a young woman named Lenormand. Among other predictions which this fortune-teller made her, she said that she would love a man whom she could not marry, and would marry a man whom she did not love, but after this marriage she would become very much attached to the man she had married. That has been precisely what has happened. Now she has heard that this sibyl, named Lenormand, is living in Paris in the Rue Tournon, No. 7. Madame Tallien and I were curious to see her; and she agreed to come to my house, where we are to disguise ourselves as grisettes. The appointment was, as I have said, for half-past five; it is now a quarter-past six. I must go and make my excuses to Madame Tallien, change my dress, and, if she still wishes it, go with her to Mademoiselle Lenormand's. I confess that we flatter ourselves, thanks to our disguise, that we shall be able to mislead the prophetess completely."

"You have no use for a companion, a locksmith, a blacksmith, or a gunsmith, I suppose?" said Bonaparte.

"No, citizen," said Madame de Beauharnais, "I regret to say we have not. I have already been indiscreet in telling you of our plan. It would be far more so to permit you to accompany us."

"Your will be done, madame, on earth as it is in heaven," said Bonaparte.

And giving her his hand to lead her to the door, this time he avoided letting her step upon the beautiful map, upon which her foot, light as it was, had left its trace.

As she had told the young general, Madame de Beauharnais found Madame Tallien waiting for her.

Madame Tallien (Thérèse Cabarus) was, as everybody knows, the daughter of a Spanish banker. She was married to M. Davis de Fontenay, a councillor of the parliament of Bordeaux, but was soon divorced from him. This was at the beginning of '94, when the Terror was at its height.

Thérèse Cabarus wished to rejoin her father, who was in Spain, in order to escape the evils of which proscription was the least. Arrested at the gates of the city, she was brought before Tallien, who fell passionately in love with her at first sight. She made use of this passion to save a great number of victims. At this time love was the most powerful opponent of its rival, death.

Tallien was recalled, and Thérèse Cabarus followed him to Paris, where she was arrested; from the depths of her prison she brought about the 9th Thermidor, after which she was free.

Her first care had been to secure the liberty of her companion in prison, Josephine de Beauharnais.

From that time the two women had been inseparable. One woman only in Paris disputed the palm of beauty with them; and that woman was Madame Récamier.

This evening, as we know, they had decided to go to the fashionable sibyl, Mademoiselle Lenormand, disguised as maids, and under assumed names. In a twinkling the two great ladies were transformed into two charming grisettes.

Their lace caps fell over their eyes, and the hood of a little silk mantle hid the head; clad in short dresses of India muslin, and bravely shod with shoes with paste buckles and stockings embroidered with pink and green, which their skirts did not hide, they jumped into a hired carriage, which they had ordered to stop at the great gate of the house No. 11, Rue Neuve-des-Mathurins. Then, in a trembling voice, like that of all women who are doing something out of the ordinary, Madame de Beauharnais said to the driver: "Rue du Tournon, No. 7."

The carriage stopped at the place indicated, the driver got down from his seat, opened the door, received his fare, and knocked at the house-door, which was opened at once.

The two women hesitated an instant, as if their hearts failed them at the critical moment. But Madame Tallien urged her friend on. Josephine, light as a bird, alighted upon the pavement without touching the step; Madame Tallien followed her. They crossed the formidable threshold, and the door closed behind them.

They found themselves under a sort of porte-cochère, the arch of which extended into the court. At the further end, by the light of a reflector, they saw these words written on an outside shutter: "Mademoiselle Lenormand, book-seller."

They advanced toward this light, which revealed a short flight of four steps. They went up the four steps and came to a porter's lodge.

"Citizeness Lenormand?" inquired Madame Tallien, who, although the younger of the two, seemed on this occasion to take the initiative.

"Ground floor, left-hand door," replied the porter.

Madame Tallien went up the steps first, holding up her already short skirt, which discovered a leg that might vie with a Greek statue in shape, which had, nevertheless, condescended this evening to the grisette's garter tied below the knee. Madame de Beauharnais followed, admiring her friend's free and easy manner, but unable to emulate it. She was still only half-way up the steps when Madame Tallien rang the bell. An old servant opened the door.

The new arrivals, whose faces were more of a recommendation than their attire, were examined with the most scrupulous minuteness by the lackey, who bade them sit down in a corner of the first room. The second, which was a salon, and through which the lackey had to pass to reach his mistress, was occupied by two or three women whose rank it would have been difficult to determine, all ranks at that time being practically merged into that of the bourgeois. But to their great astonishment, the door of the second salon opened after a few moments, and Mademoiselle Lenormand herself came and spoke to them, saying:

"Ladies, be good enough to enter the salon."

The two pretended grisettes looked at each other in astonishment. Mademoiselle Lenormand was supposed to make her predictions in a state of somnambulism. Was this true, and had she, by reason of her second-sight, recognized, even without seeing them, the two ladies of rank in the supposed grisettes whom the lackey had announced?

At the same time, Mademoiselle Lenormand signed to the ladies in the first salon to pass into the second room, where she told fortunes.

Madame Tallien and Madame de Beauharnais began to examine the room in which they had been left. Its principal ornaments were two portraits, one of Louis XVI. and the other of Marie-Antoinette. Notwithstanding the terrible days that had passed, and the fact that the heads of the originals had fallen upon the scaffold, the portraits had not left their places, and had not for an instant ceased to be treated with the respect which Mademoiselle Lenormand entertained for the originals.

After the portraits, the most remarkable thing in the room was a long table covered with a cloth, upon which sparkled necklaces, rings, and pieces of silverware elegantly wrought; most of the last dating from the eighteenth century. All of these trinkets had been given to the sibyl by persons to whom she had doubtless made agreeable predictions which had been fulfilled.

The door of the cabinet opened shortly, and the last person who had arrived before the two ladies was called. The friends remained alone.

A quarter of an hour passed, during which they conversed in subdued tones, then the door opened again, and Mademoiselle Lenormand came out.

"Which of you ladies wishes to come in first?" she asked.

"Can we not go in together?" asked Madame de Beauharnais quickly.

"Impossible, madame," replied the sibyl; "I have sworn never to read the cards for one person in the presence of another."

"May we know why?" asked Madame Tallien, with her customary vivacity, and we may almost say her usual indiscretion.

"Because in a portrait which I had the misfortune to draw too near to life one of two ladies whom I was receiving recognized her husband."

"Go in, Thérèse; go in," said Madame de Beauharnais, urging her friend.

"So I am always to be the one to sacrifice myself," said the latter. And then, smiling at her friend, she said: "Well, so be it; I will risk it." And she entered.

Mademoiselle Lenormand was at that time a woman of from twenty-four to twenty-nine years of age, short and stout in figure, and vainly endeavoring to disguise the fact that one shoulder was higher than the other; she wore a turban adorned with a bird of paradise. Her hair fell in long curls around her face. She wore two skirts, one over the other; one was short, scarcely falling to the knees, and pearl-gray in color; the other was longer, falling in a short train behind her, and was cherry-red.

Beside her on a cushion lay her favorite greyhound, named Aza.

The table upon which she made her calculations was nothing but a common round table covered with a green baize cloth, with drawers in front, in which the sibyl stowed her various apparatus. The cabinet was as long as the salon, but narrower. An oak bookcase ran along the wall on each side of the door, filled with books. Facing her seat was an arm-chair for the person who was consulting her.

Between her and the subject lay a steel rod, which was called the divining-rod. The end, pointing toward the client, was tipped with a little coiled steel serpent; the other end resembled a riding-whip.

This was what Madame de Beauharnais saw during the brief moment that the door was open to admit her friend.

Josephine took up a book, drew near to the lamp, and tried to read; but her attention was soon diverted by the sound of a bell and the entrance of another person. It was a young man dressed in the fashion adopted by the incroyables (Beaus of the Revolution). Between his hair, which fell to a level with his eyebrows, his dog's-ears falling over his shoulders, and his neckcloth, which reached to his cheekbones, one could scarcely distinguish a straight nose, a firm and resolute mouth, and eyes as brilliant as black diamonds.

He bowed without speaking, twirled his gnarled stick three or four times around his head, hummed three false notes, as if he were just finishing a tune, and sat down in a corner.

But although this griffin's eye, as Dante would have said, was hardly visible in the corner, Madame de Beauharnais was beginning to feel uncomfortable under its stare, although the incroyable was seated at one end of the salon and she at the other. But just then Madame Tallien came out.

"Ah! my dear," she said, going straight to her friend, without seeing the incroyable, who sat in the shadow— "ah! my dear, go in quickly. Mademoiselle Lenormand is charming; just guess what she has predicted for me?"

"Why my dear," replied Madame Beauharnais, "that you will be loved, that you will be beautiful until you are fifty years of age, and that you will have love-affairs all your life—"

And as Madame Tallien made a

movement as if to say, "No, not that," she continued: "And that you will have a tall footman, a fine house, beautiful carriages, and white or bay horses."

"I shall have all that, my dear; and, furthermore, if our sibyl is to be believed, I shall be a princess."

"I congratulate you sincerely, my beautiful princess," said Josephine; "but as I do not see that there is anything left for me to ask for, and as I shall probably never be a princess, and my pride already suffers at being less beautiful than you, I will not give it further cause for envy, which might make us quarrel."

"Are you in earnest, dear Josephine?"

"No; but I will not expose myself to the inferiority which threatens me on all sides. I leave you your principality; let us run away."

She made a movement as if to go away, and to take Madame Tallien with her; but just then a hand was placed lightly on her arm, and a voice said: "Remain, madame, and perhaps when you have heard me, you will find that you have nothing to envy your friend."

Josephine greatly desired to know what was in store for her that would exalt her so that she would have no need to envy a princess. She therefore yielded, and entered Mademoiselle Lenormand's cabinet in her turn.

Mademoiselle Lenormand motioned to Josephine to seat herself in the chair which Madame Tallien had just vacated, and then she drew a fresh pack of cards from a drawer—probably that the destinies of one should not influence the other. Then she looked fixedly at Madame de Beauharnais.

"You sought to deceive me," she said, "by coming to consult me in vul-

gar attire. I am a clairvoyant, and I saw you leave a house in the centre of Paris; I saw you finally in the anteroom when your place was in the salon, and I came to look for you. Do not seek to deceive me; answer my questions frankly, and since you have come in search of truth, tell the truth."

Madame de Beauharnais bowed.

"If you care to question me I am ready to reply."

"What animal do you like best?"

"The dog."

"What flower do you prefer?"

"The rose."

"What perfume pleases you the best?"

"That of the violet."

The sibyl placed before Madame de Beauharnais a pack of cards almost double the size of ordinary ones. These had not been invented more than a month, and were called the "great oracle."

"Let us see first where you are placed," said the sibyl.

And, turning over the pack, she separated the cards with the wand and found the consulting client; that is to say, a brunette in a white dress with a broad, embroidered flounce, and a cloak of red velvet with a long flowing train. She was placed between the eight of hearts and the ten of clubs.

"Chance has placed you well, as you see, madame. The eight of hearts has three different meanings in as many different rows. The first, which is the eight of hearts itself, represents the conjunction of the stars under which you were born. The second, an eagle carrying away a toad from a pond, over which he is hovering. The third, a female near a tomb. This is what I see, madame, in the first card. You were born under the influence of Venus and the moon. You have recently had a very satisfactory experience, almost in the nature of a triumph. Finally, this woman dressed in black near a tomb indicates that you are a widow. On the other hand, the ten of clubs promises success in an undertaking which has just begun, and of which you are scarcely cognizant. It would be impossible to find a more fortunate throw of cards."

Then, taking up the pack and shuffling them, Mademoiselle Lenormand asked Madame de Beauharnais to cut them with her left hand, and to draw fourteen cards, which she was to place in any order she chose beside the brunette, from right to left, as Orientals write.

Madame de Beauharnais obeyed, and cut and arranged the cards as requested.

Mademoiselle Lenormand followed them with her eyes, more attentively than Madame de Beauharnais, as the latter turned them.

"In truth, madame, you are fortunate," said she; "and I am convinced that you did well not to be frightened by the prediction which I made to your friend, brilliant though it was. Your first card is the five of diamonds; beside it I find the beautiful constellation of the Southern Cross, which is invisible to us here in Europe. The main subject of the card, a Greek or Mohammedan traveller, indicates that you were born either in the East or the colonies. The parrot, or the orange tree, which forms the third subject, makes me incline to the colonies. The flower, which is a veratrum, very common in Martinique, would almost jus-

tify me in saying that you were born in that island."

"You are not mistaken, madame."

"Your third card, the nine of diamonds, makes me think that you left the island when still very young. The convolvulus, which figures on the lower part of the card, and which is the symbol of a woman seeking for something to cling to, would indicate that you left the island to be married."

"That is also true, madame," said Josephine.

"Your fourth card, which is the ten of spades, indicates the loss of your hopes; but the fruits and flowers of the saxifrage which are on the same card suggest that the disappointment was but momentary, and that a happy conclusion — probably a marriage — succeeded fears which amounted even to loss of hope."

"If you had read in the book of my own life, madame, you could not have seen more clearly."

"That encourages me," said the sibyl; "for I see such strange things in your cards that I should stop short if your denial were added to my own doubts."

"Here is the eight of spades. Achilles is dragging Hector, chained to the car, around the walls of Troy; lower down a woman is kneeling before a tomb. Your husband, like the Trojan hero, must have died a violent death, probably upon the scaffold. But here is a singular thing, on the same card: opposite the weeping woman the bones of Pelops are crossed above the talisman of the moon, which means, 'Happy fatality.' To a great misfortune will succeed good fortune which is even greater."

Josephine smiled.

"That belongs to the future and therefore I cannot answer for it."

"You have two children?" asked the sibyl.

"Yes, madame."

"A son and a daughter?"

"Yes."

"See here on the same card, the ten of diamonds, your son takes a resolution without consulting you, which is of the greatest importance, not in itself, but in its results.

"On the bottom of this card is one of the talking oaks of the forest of Dodona, as you see; Jason is lying in its shade and listening. What does he hear? The voice of the future which your son heard when he decided upon that step which he has just taken.

"The card which follows, the knave of diamonds, shows you Achilles disguised as a woman at the court of Lycomanes. The glitter of a sword will make a man of him. Is there something about a sword that has occurred between your son and some other person?"

"Yes, madame."

"Well, here at the bottom of the card is Juno, crying: 'Courage, young man, help will not be wanting!' I am not sure, but in this card, which is nothing less than that of a king of diamonds—but I think I see your son addressing a powerful soldier, and obtaining of him what he wants.

"The four of diamonds shows you yourself, madame, at the moment when your son is telling you of the fortunate result of his attempt. The flowers growing at the bottom of this card admonish you not to let yourself be overcome by difficulties, and that you will thereby reach the goal of your desires. And finally, madame, here is the eight of clubs, which positively indicates a marriage; placed as it is, next to the eight of hearts, which is the eagle soaring aloft with the toad in his talons, it indicates that this marriage will exalt you above the most eminent ranks of society.

"Then, if we still doubt, here is the six of hearts, which unfortunately is so rarely seen with the eight. Here is the eight and upon it the alchemist watching the transformation of the stone into gold; that is to say the ordinary life changing into one of nobility, honors, and a lofty position. See among these flowers a convolvulus, twining itself around a lily shorn of its blossoms; that means, madame, that you will succeed; that you, who are simply seeking a support, will succeed—how shall I tell you?—to everything that is grandest and most powerful in France, in short to the lily shorn of its blossoms; and, as indicated by the ten of clubs, that you will succeed to all this by passing across battlefields, where, as you see, Ulysses and Diomedes are carrying off the white horse of Rheseus, placed under the care of the talisman of Mars.

"There, madame, you will enjoy the respect and affection of the whole world. You will be the wife of this Hercules stifling the lion of the Nemean forest; that is to say the useful and courageous man who exposes himself to every danger for the good of his country. The flowers with which you are crowned are the lilac, the arum, and the immortelle, for you will represent true merit and perfect goodness."

Then, rising enthusiastically and seizing Madame de Beauharnais's hand as she fell at her feet, she said: "Madame, I know neither your name nor your rank, but I can read your future. Madame, remember me when you are— empress!"

"Empress? I? You are mad, my dear woman."

"What, madame, do you not see that your last card, the one to which the other fourteen lead, is the king of hearts, the great Charlemagne, who holds his sword in one hand and the globe in the other? Do you not see upon the same card the man of genius, who, with a book in his hand and a sphere at his feet, meditates upon the destinies of the world? And, last of all, do you not see on the two desks, placed opposite each other, the Book of Wisdom and the laws of Solon, which proves that your husband will be a legislator as well as a conqueror."

Improbable as was the prediction, the blood rushed to Josephine's head. Her eyes grew dim, her forehead was bathed with perspiration, and a shiver ran through her whole body.

"Impossible! impossible! impossible!" she murmured, and she sank back in her chair.

Then suddenly remembering that this consultation had lasted nearly an hour, and that Madame Tallien was waiting for her, she rose, tossed her purse to Mademoiselle Lenormand without looking to see how much it contained, and darted into the salon. She seized Madame Tallien by the waist and drew her away, scarcely replying to the bow which the incroyable made to the two ladies as they passed before him.

"Well?" asked Madame Tallien, stopping Josephine on the flight of steps which led down to the courtyard.

"Well," replied Madame de Beauharnais, "that woman is crazy."

"What did she predict for you?"

"It is your turn first."

"I warn you, my dear, that I have already become accustomed to her prediction," said Madame Tallien; "she said that I would be a princess."

"Well," said Josephine, "I am not yet accustomed to mine. She said that I would be an empress."

And the two false grisettes got into their carriage.

As we have said, the two ladies, excited over their predictions, had scarcely paid any attention to the young man who was waiting his turn.

During the long session that Madame de Beauharnais had with the sibyl, Madame Tallien had tried more than once to discover to what class of incroyable the young man in question belonged. But he, evidently little inclined to respond to her attempts at conversation, had drawn his hair over his eyes, his cravat over his chin, and his dog's-ears over his cheeks, and had settled down in his chair with a sort of grunt, like a man who would not be sorry to shorten the time of waiting by a short nap.

Madame de Beauharnais's long sitting had passed thus: Madame Tallien pretending to read, and the incroyable pretending to sleep.

But as soon as the ladies had gone out, and he had followed them with his eyes until they had disappeared, he presented himself in turn at the door of Mademoiselle Lenormand's cabinet. The appearance of this new client was so grotesque that it brought a smile to her lips.

"Mademoiselle," he said, affecting the

ridiculous speech of the young dandies of the day, "will you have the goodness to tell me the fortunate or unfortunate vicissitudes which destiny has reserved for the person of your humble servant. Nor will he conceal from you that that person is so dear to him that he will learn with gratitude whatever agreeable presages you may impart to him. He must add, however, that owing to his great self-control, he will listen with equanimity to whatever catastrophes with which you may be pleased to threaten him."

Mademoiselle Lenormand looked at him anxiously for a moment. Did his indifference amount to madness, or was she dealing with one of those young men of the day who took pleasure in mocking the holiest things, and who would, therefore, have no scruple about insulting the sibyl of the Rue Tournon, firmly established though she was in the good opinion of the inhabitants of the Faubourg Saint-Germain.

"Do you wish me to cast your horoscope?" she asked.

"Yes, my horoscope—a horoscope like that which was cast at the birtl of Alexander, son of Philip of Macedon. Without expecting to attain to the renown of the conqueror of Porus, and the founder of Alexandria, I intend some day to make a stir in the world. Have the goodness therefore to prepare whatever may be necessary, and to predict the best of good fortune for me."

"Citizen," said Mademoiselle Lenormand, "I employ different methods."

"Let us hear what they are," said the incroyable, thrusting his stomach forward, and slipping his thumbs into the armholes of his waistcoat and letting his cane dangle from the cord around his wrist.

"For example, I prophesy by the whites of eggs, the analysis of coffee grounds, spotted or algebraic cards, and I sometimes read the future by means of a cock."

"The last would suit me very well," said the young man. "But we should need a living cock, and a glassful of wheat; have you got them?"

"I have them," replied Mademoiselle Lenormand. "I also use catoptromancy at times."

"I am looking for a Venetian mirror; for, as nearly as I can remember," said the young man, "catoptromancy is performed with a Venetian mirror and a drop of water spilled upon it."

"Exactly, citizen. You seem to be well informed concerning my art."

"Bah!" said the young man. "Yes, yes; I take an occasional turn at the occult science."

"There is also chiromancy," observed Mademoiselle Lenormand.

"Ah! that is what I want. All the other practices are more or less diabolical. As much cannot be said for hydromancy, you will concede, citizeness, which has to do with a ring thrown into water; nor of pyromancy, which consists of placing the victim in the midst of a fire; of geomancy, which is performed by tracing cabalistic signs upon the ground; of capnomancy, where poppy seeds are thrown on burning coals; of coscinomancy, in which the hatchet, the sieve and the tongs are employed; nor, finally, of anthropomancy, in which human victims are sacrificed."

Mademoiselle watched her interlocutor with a certain uneasiness. Was he speaking seriously? Was he making fun of her? Or did he conceal beneath his assumed indifference a desire to remain unrecognized?

"Then you prefer chiromancy?" she asked.

"Yes," replied the incroyable; "for with chiromancy, were you the devil himself, or his wife Proserpine," and he bowed gallantly to Mademoiselle Lenormand, "I should not fear for the safety of my soul, since the patriarch Job has said (verse 7, chapter xxxvii.), 'God hath drawn lines in the hands of men in order that each may know his destiny.' And Solomon, the pre-eminently wise king, added: 'Length of life is marked in the right hand, and the lines of the left hand betoken wisdom and glory.' Finally we read in the prophet Isaiah, 'Your hand denotes that you will live a long time.' Here is mine, what does it say?"

As he spoke, the young incroyable took off his glove and extended a hand that was delicate and well-shaped, although thin and tanned by the sun. Its proportions were perfect, the fingers long and smooth; and he wore no rings.

Mademoiselle Lenormand took it and examined it carefully. Then her eyes turned from the young man's hand to his face.

"Sir," said she, "it must have cost your natural dignity much to clothe yourself as you have, and in so doing, you must have yielded, either to a great curiosity, or to the first expression of an unconquerable feeling. You are wearing a disguise and not your accustomed attire. Your hand is that of a soldier accustomed to wield the sword rather than to twirl the cane of

an incroyable, or the switch of a dandy. Neither is this language you now affect natural to you. You know all of these sciences which you have mentioned, but you have learned them while studying others which you deemed more important. You have a taste for occult researches, but your future is not that of a Nicolas Flamel or a Cagliostro. You have asked in jest for a horoscope similar to the one which was cast at the birth of Alexander, son of Philip of Macedon. It is too late to cast the horoscope of your birth, but I can tell you what has happened to you since your birth, and what the future holds in store for you."

"Faith, you are right," said the young man in his natural voice, "and I confess that I am ill at ease in this disguise; neither, as you have said, am I accustomed to this language which I have just now used. Had you been deceived by my language and my attire, I should have said nothing, and would have left you with a shrug of the shoulders. The discovery which you have made in spite of my efforts to deceive you, proves to me that there is something in your art. I well know that it is tempting God," he added gloomily, "to seek to wrest from him the secrets of the future; but where is the man who feels within himself the power to achieve great things, who would not wish to aid, by a knowledge of the future, the events which life holds in store for him? You say that you will tell me of my past life. I ask but a few words on that score, being anxious rather to know the future. I repeat, here is my hand."

Mademoiselle Lenormand's eyes rested for a moment on the palm of his hand, then, raising her head, she said:

"You were born on an island, of a family which, though noble, has neither wealth nor renown. You left your country to be educated in France, you entered the service in a special branch, the artillery. You have gained a great victory, which was of immense use to your country, but for which you were poorly recompensed. For a time you thought of leaving France. Fortunately obstacles multiplied and you remained. You have just forced yourself into notoriety by a brilliant stroke which has assured you the support of the future Directory. This very day—and mark well the date—though it has been signalled by the most ordinary events alone, will become one of the most important landmarks of your life. Do you believe in my art now, and shall I continue?"

"Certainly," replied the pretended incroyable, "and that you may have every facility in your work, I will begin by showing you my real features."

At these words he took off his hat, threw aside his wig, untied his cravat, and revealed that head of bronze, of which it has been said that it seemed to have been modelled from an antique medal. He frowned slightly, brushed his hair from his temples with his hand, and his eye grew stern, resolute, almost haughty, as did his voice; and he said, no longer with the lisp of the incroyable, or the gentleness of a man addressing a woman, but with the firmness of a command, as he presented his hand to the sibyl for the third time: "Look!"

Mademoiselle Lenormand took the hand, which her client held out to her,

with a feeling almost akin to veneration.

"Will you have the whole truth?" she asked, "or shall I tell you only the good and conceal the evil, as I would to one of those effeminate creatures, to whose nervous irritability you are sometimes subject?"

"Tell me all," said the young man briefly.

"See that you remember the order which you have given me," she said, emphasizing the word "order." "Your hand, which is the most perfect of any that I have ever seen, presents all the virtuous sentiments, and all the human weaknesses; it reveals at once the most heroic and the most hesitating of characters. Most of the lines of your palm dazzle by their brilliancy, while others seem to point to the darkest and most painful hours. I am about to reveal to you an enigma more difficult to read than the Theban Sphinx; for even as you will be greater than Œdipus, so will you be more unhappy. Shall I go on, or shall I stop?"

"Go on," he said.

"I obey you," and again she emphasized the word "obey."

"We will begin with the most powerful of the seven planets; all seven are impressed upon your hand, and are placed in their recognized order.

"Jupiter is at the extremity of your index finger. Let us begin with him. Perhaps some confusion will result from this method of procedure, but we will bring forth order out of chaos.

"Jupiter then in your hand is placed at the extremity of your index finger, which means that you will be the friend and the enemy of the great men of this world, and among the fortunate of this age. Notice this sign in the shape of a fan on the fourth joint of this finger; it indicates that you will forcibly levy tribute upon people and kings. See this sort of grafting on the second joint, broken at its seventh branch; that means that you will occupy in succession six positions of dignity, and that you will stop at the seventh."

"Do you know what these positions are?"

"No. All that I can tell you about them is that the last is that of Emperor of the West, which is to-day in the house of Austria.

"See that star under the grating; it betokens that you have a good genius who will watch over you until your eighth lustre, or until you are forty years old. At that time you will probably forget that Providence chose a companion for you, for you will abandon that companion, as a result of a false calculation of human prosperity. The two signs directly beneath that star, which resemble, the one a horseshoe, and the other a chessboard, indicate that after long prosperity you will inevitably fall, and from the greatest height to which man has ever attained. You will fall rather through the influence of women than the strength of men. Four lustres will be the term of your triumph and power.

"This other sign, at the foot of Jupiter accompanied by these three other stars, indicate that during the last three years of your greatness and prosperity, your enemies will be trying to undermine you, and that three months will suffice to hurl you from your exalted position, and that the crash of your fall will resound throughout the East and the West. Shall I go on?"

"Go on!" said the young man.

"These two stars at the extremity of the middle finger, which is the finger of Saturn, indicate positively that you will be crowned in the same metropolis which has witnessed the coronations of the kings of France, your predecessors. But the sign of Saturn, placed immediately below these two stars, and governing them, is of the gloomiest import for you.

"On the second joint of this middle finger there are two signs, which are peculiar in that they seem to contradict each other. The triangle denotes a curious, suspicious man, not at all lavish of his means except to his soldiers, and who during his life will receive three wounds: the first on the thigh, the second on the heel, and the third on the little finger. The second of these signs, a star, denotes a magnanimous sovereign, a lover of the beautiful, forming gigantic projects, which are not only impossible of realization, but which none but he would be capable of conceiving.

"This line, which resembles an S, winding over the middle joint, forebodes, beside various other perils, several attempts at assassination, among which there is a prearranged explosion.

"The straight line, the letters C and X, which extend almost to the root of the finger of Saturn, betoken a second alliance, more illustrious than the first."

"But," interrupted the young man, impatiently, "this is the second or third time that you have spoken of this first alliance which is to protect the first eight lustres of my life. How am I to recognize the lady when I see her?"

"She is dark," replied the sibyl; "the

widow of a fair-haired man who wore a sword and perished by the axe. She has two children, whom you will adopt for your own. In examining her face you will recognize her by two things: one is that she has a noticeable mark on one of her eyebrows, and the second that in talking she frequently raises her right hand, being accustomed to holding a handkerchief, which she carries, to her mouth whenever she laughs."

"Very well," he returned, "now let us come back to my horoscope."

"See at the base of the finger of Saturn these two signs, one of which resembles a gridiron without a handle, and the other the six of diamonds.

"They predict that your second wife will destroy your happiness, and that she, unlike your first wife, will be fair and born of a race of kings.

"The figure representing the image of the sun at the end of the third joint of the ring finger, which is the finger of Apollo, proves that you will become an extraordinary personage, rising by your own merit, but especially favored by Jupiter and Mars.

"These four straight lines, placed like a palisade below this image of the sun, betoken that you will struggle in vain against a power which unaided, will stop you in your career.

"Beneath these four straight lines we find again that serpentine line, in the form of the letter S, which has already twice predicted misfortune for you on the finger of Saturn; if the star, which is below that line, were above it instead, it would indicate that you would continue in the zenith of your power for seven lustres.

"The fourth finger of the left hand bears the sign of Mercury at the end of the third joint. This means that few men will possess such sagacity, knowledge, finesse, exactness of reasoning power and keenness of mind as you. You will bend several nations to your vast projects; you will undertake expeditions which will occasion great wonderment; you will cross deep rivers, ascend steep mountains, and traverse immense deserts. But this sign of Mercury also denotes that you will have a very abrupt and capricious temper; that this temper will create powerful enemies against you; and that in the spirit of a true cosmopolitan, tormented by lust of conquest, you will not be contented anywhere, and that sometimes you will even feel that Europe is too confined a sphere for you.

"As for this ladder which is drawn between the first and third joints of the finger of Mercury, it denotes that in the days of your power, you will carry out immense works for the embellishment of your capital as well as the other cities of your kingdom.

"And now we pass to the thumb, which is the finger of Venus.

"As you see, here is her all-powerful sign on the second joint. It announces that you will adopt children which are not your own, and that your first union will be childless, although you have had, and will have again, natural children. But as compensation, here are the three stars which are dominated by it; this is a sign that, in spite of the efforts of the enemy, surrounded by great men who supplement your genius, you will be crowned between your sixth and seventh lustre, and that the Pope himself, to gain your favor for the Church of Rome, will come from Rome to place the crown of Louis XIV, and

Saint Louis upon your head and that of your wife.

"Beneath the three stars, do you see the sign of Venus and that of Jupiter? Beside them, and on the same line, do you see those numbers which are so lucky when in conjunction—9, 19, and 99? They are the proof that the East and West will clasp hands, and that the Cæsars of the house of Hapsburg will consent to ally their name with yours.

"Below those numbers we find the same sun which we have already seen on the tip of the finger of Apollo, and which indicates that, contrary to the celestial luminary, which goes from east to west, your course will be from west to east.

"Now let us go up from the first joint of this thumb to the O which crosses a bar diagonally. Well, that sign indicates disordered vision, political blindness. As for the three stars on the first joint and the sign which surmounts them, they are only a confirmation of the prediction that women will have a great influence upon your life, and they indicate that even as happiness will come to you through a woman, so will it take flight through a woman.

"As for the four signs scattered about the palm of the hand in the form of an iron rake, one in the field of Mars, another adhering to the line of life, and the remaining two adjoining the base of the mountain of The Moon, they indicate prodigal expenditure of the blood of soldiers, but only upon the battlefield.

"The top of this forked line, divided toward the mount of Jupiter, number 8, denotes extended journeys in Europe, Asia, and Africa. Some of these journeys will be forced ones, as the X at the top of the line of life denotes, overlooking the mount of Venus. Finally, as its branches cross beneath the line of Mars, it is a sure sign of great renown, due to glorious feats of arms. In speaking to you, men will exhaust the whole vocabulary of humility and eulogy; you will be the glorious man, the man of prodigies and miracles. You will be Alexander, you will be Cæsar, you will be even greater than they; you will be Atlas bearing the world. After seeing the whole universe lighted up with your glory, you will see it black as night on the day of your death; and men, seeing that the world is out of joint will ask, not whether a man has just died, but whether the sun has set."

The young man had listened to this prophecy with an air of gloom rather than joy; he had seemed to follow the sibyl to these heights where she had paused, fatigued, to take breath; then with her he had descended into the abyss, where, as she said, his fortune would be sunk.

He remained silent a moment after she had ceased.

"You have prophesied Cæsar's fortune for me," he said, after a pause.

"It is greater than Cæsar's," she said; "for Cæsar did not attain his end, and you will yours. Cæsar put his foot only upon the first step of the throne, and you will take your seat upon it. But do not forget the dark woman who has a mark above her right eyebrow, and who carries her handkerchief to her mouth when she smiles."

"And when shall I meet her?" asked the young man.

"You have met her to-day," replied the sibyl, "and she marked with her foot the spot where your long line of victories will begin."

It was so manifestly impossible that the sibyl could have prepared beforehand this series of undoubted truths which had taken place in the past, and the succession of incredible facts which were still buried in the future, that for the first time the young officer believed thoroughly in what she had told him. He put his hand in his pocket and drew forth a purse containing some gold-pieces; but the sibyl laid a detaining hand upon his arm.

"If I have prophesied lies," she said, "the price is too great. If, on the contrary, I have told you the truth, we can settle our account only at the Tuileries. At the Tuileries, then, when you are Emperor of the French."

"So be it," replied the young man, "at the Tuileries! And if you have told me the truth you will lose nothing by waiting."

On the 9th of the following March, 1796, about eleven o'clock in the morning, two carriages stopped before the door of the mayoralty of the second district of Paris.

A young man about twenty-six, wearing the uniform of a general officer, descended from the first. He was followed by two witnesses.

A young woman about twenty-eight or thirty descended from the other. She was followed by her two witnesses.

The six presented themselves before citizen Charles-Théodore François, civil magistrate of the second district, who asked them the questions usually propounded to matrimonial aspirants, to which they made the customary replies. Then he ordered the following document read to them, which they afterward signed:

"The 19th Ventôse, in the Year of the Republic.

"Contract of marriage between Napolione Bonaparte, general-in-chief of the army of the interior, aged *twenty-eight* years, born at Ajaccio, in the department of Corsica, residing in Paris, Rue d' Antin, son of Charles Bonaparte, gentleman, and Lætitia Ramolini:

"And Marie-Rose-Josephine Tascher, aged twenty-eight years, born in the island of Martinique, in the Windward Islands, residing in Paris, Rue Chantereine, daughter of Gaspard-Joseph de Tascher, captain of dragoons, and his wife Rose-Claire Desvergers de Sanois.

"I, Charles-Théodore François, civil magistrate of the second district of the canton of Paris, after having in the presence of these parties and their witnesses, read:

"1. The certificate of birth of Napolione Bonaparte, which states that he was born on the *5th of February*, 1768, of the lawful marriage of Charles Bonaparte and Lætitia Ramolini;

"2nd. The certificate of birth of Marie-Rose-Josephine Tascher, which states that she was born on the 23d of June, 1765, of the lawful marriage of Joseph-Gaspard de Tascher and of Rose-Claire Desvergers de Sanois;

"The certificate of death of Alexandre-François-Marie de Beauharnais, being taken into consideration, which states that he died on the 7th Thermidor, in the year II., married to Marie-Rose-Josephine de Tascher;

"Also that the certificate of publication of said marriage was duly posted without opposition during the time prescribed by law;

"And also that Napolione Bonaparte and Marie-Rose-Josephine Tascher had declared aloud that they took each other for husband and wife—I did pronounce Napolione Bonaparte and Marie-Rose-Josephine Tascher to be husband and wife.

"And this in the presence of the adult witnesses hereafter named, to wit: Paul Barras, member of the executive Directory, living at the Luxembourg; Captain Jean Lemarrois, aide-de-camp, living in the Rue des Capucines; Jean Lambert Tallien, member of the Corps-Legislatif, living at Chaillot, and Etienne-Jacques-Jerôme Calmelets, lawyer, living in the Rue de la Place Vendôme, No. 207, all of whom have signed with the principals, as I have done, after this reading."

The Drowner

An onlooker, watching the strange procession as it approached from the far side of Moutiers and slowly ascended the hill, would have found it difficult to make out the meaning of the strange jumble of men on foot and on horseback: Whites in the Vendéan costume made sacred by Charette, Cathelineau and Cadoudal, Blues in the Republican uniform, accompanied by women, children and peasants, and rolling along in the midst of this human tide, restless as the waves of the ocean, an unknown machine—unless the spectator had seen one of the placards.

But these placards were for the time being considered merely as one of those gasconades which the parties permitted themselves at this period; and many persons had come from afar, not to see the promised execution—that would have been too much to expect—but to learn the explanation of the promise which had been made them.

Moutiers was the appointed meeting place, and all the peasants in the neighborhood had been waiting in the public square of that town since eight o'clock in the morning.

Suddenly they were told that the procession, which was growing with every step, was approaching the town. Every one at once hastened to the spot indicated; and there they could see the Vendéan chiefs, who formed the advance-guard, half-way up the hill. In their hands they were carrying green branches, as in the old days of expiation.

The crowd which had gathered at Moutiers streamed along the road; and, like two rivers meeting, the two human floods surged against each other and mingled their waters.

There was a moment of confusion and tumult. Every one fought to get near the cart which carried the scaffold and the carriage which contained

Goulin, the executioner and his assistant. But as they were all animated by the same desire, and as enthusiasm was perhaps greater than curiosity, those who had caught a glimpse thought it only right to fall back and give the others a chance to have an equal opportunity.

As they advanced, Goulin grew paler and paler; for he realized that they were making straight for a goal which they would surely reach. Moreover, he had seen, on the bill which had been thrust into his hands, that Moutiers was to be the scene of his execution; and he knew only too well that the town they were approaching at every step was Moutiers. He rolled his eyes around the crowd, unable to fathom this mingling of Chouans and Republicans, who on the previous evening were waging such furious warfare and yet in the morning united in such friendly fashion to form his escort. From time to time he closed his eyes, doubtless in the vain hope of persuading himself that it was all a dream. But then the tempestuous roaring of the crowd and the swaying of the carriage must have carried with it the suggestion of a tempest at sea. Then he raised his arms, which he had succeeded in freeing from their shroud-like wrappings, beat the air like a crazy man, stood up, tried to cry out, and perhaps did cry out; but his voice was lost in the tumult, and he fell back again on the seat between his two gloomy companions. At last they reached the plateau of Moutiers, and then there came a cry of "Halt!"

They had reached their destination. More than ten thousand persons were assembled on this plateau. The nearest houses in the village were crowded with spectators and the trees along the roadside were loaded with human freight.

When the procession had halted, and each person had placed himself as he or she wished to be placed during the execution, Cadoudal raised his hand in token that he wished to speak.

Every voice was hushed, and even the breath seemed to expire upon pale lips. A mournful silence ensued, and Goulin's eyes were fastened upon Cadoudal, of whose name and importance he was ignorant. He had none the less distinguished him from the others as perhaps the man whom he had come from afar to seek—the man who at their first meeting was to change rôles with him, to make of himself the judge and executioner, and of the judge and executioner proper the victim—if an assassin can be described as a victim, no matter what manner of death was reserved for him. Cadoudal, as we have said, had signified that he wished to speak.

"Citizens," said he, addressing the Republicans, "as you see, I give you the title which you give yourselves—my brothers," he continued, addressing the Chouans—"and I give you the name with which God receives you in his bosom—your meeting here at Moutiers to-day, and its object, prove that each of you is convinced of the guilt of this man, who is deserving of the death which he is about to suffer. And yet, Republicans, whom I hope some day to call brothers, you do not know this man as we do.

"One day, in 1793, my father and I were carrying some flour to Nantes. There was a famine in the town. It was scarcely light. Carrier, the infamous Carrier, had not yet arrived at Nantes. Therefore we must render unto Cæsar the things which are Cæsar's, and unto Goulin the things which are Goulin's. It was Goulin who invented the drownings.

"My father and I were going along the Quai de la Loire. We saw a boat on which they were loading priests. A man was driving them into it two by two, and counting them as they went aboard. He counted ninety-seven of these priests, who were bound in couples. As they entered the boat they disappeared, for they were thrown into the hold. The boat left the shore and floated out into the middle of the Loire. This man stood in front with an oar.

"My father stopped his horse and said to me: 'Wait and watch, something infamous is about to happen here.'

"And in fact the boat had a plug. When the boat reached the middle of the stream, the unfortunates in the hold were thrown into the water. As they came up to the surface, this man and his wretched companions struck at these heads, which already wore the halo of martyrdom, and bruised them with their oars. It was that man there who urged them on to the terrible work. Two of the condemned men, however, were too far away to be struck; they made their way toward the bank, for they had found a sandbar which afforded them a foothold.

"'Quick,' said my father, 'let us save those two.'

"We sprang from our horses and slipped down the bank of the Loire with our knives in our hands. They,

thinking that we also were murderers, tried to escape from us. But we cried out to them: 'Come to us, men of God! these knives are to cut your bonds, not to strike you.'

"They came to us, and in an instant their hands were free, and we were on horseback, with them behind us, galloping away. They were the worthy Abbés Briançon and Lacombe.

"They both took refuge with us in the forest of the Morbihan. One of them died of cold, hunger and fatigue, as so many of us have died. That was the Abbé Briançon.

"The other," said Cadoudal, pointing to a priest who tried to conceal himself among the crowd, "recovered, and to-day serves God with his prayers, as we serve him with our arms. That other is the Abbé Lacombe. There he is!

"From that time," he continued, pointing to Goulin, "this man, and always the same, presided at the drownings. In all the slaughter which took place at Nantes, he was Carrier's right arm. When Carrier was tried and condemned, François Goulin was tried at the same time; but he posed before the tribunal as an instrument who had been unable to refuse to obey the orders that were given him. I possess a letter written entirely by his hand."

Here Cadoudal drew a paper from his pocket.

"I wanted to send it to the tribunal to enlighten its conscience. This letter, written to his worthy colleague, Perdraux, was his condemnation, since in it he described his mode of procedure. Listen, you men of hardfought battles, and tell me if ever a war-bulletin made you shudder like this."

And amid solemn silence, Cadoudal read aloud the following letter:

"CITIZEN—In the exaltation of your patriotism, you ask me how I make my Republican marriages.

"When I get ready for the baths, I strip the men and women, and go through their clothing to see if they have any money or jewelry. I put the clothing in a great hamper, then I tie the men and women together, face to face, by the wrists. I bring them to the banks of the Loire; they go aboard my boat, two by two, and two men push them from behind and throw them into the water, head first; then when they try to save themselves we have great clubs with which we beat them back.

"That is what we call the civil marriage.

"FRANCOIS GOULIN."

"Do you know," continued Cadoudal, "what prevented me from sending that letter? It was the intercession of the good Abbé Lacombe. He said to me: 'If God has given this man a chance to escape, it is that he may have an opportunity to repent.'

"Now, has he repented? You see him. After having drowned more than fifteen hundred persons, he seizes the moment when the terror has been revived to ask the favor of returning to this same region where he was executioner, in order to make fresh executions. If he had repented, I also would have pardoned him; but since, like the dog in the Bible, he returns to his own vomit, since God has permitted him to fall into my hands after escaping those of the revolutionary tribunal, it is because God wishes him to die."

A moment of silence followed Cadoudal's words. Then the condemned man rose in his carriage, and cried in a stifled voice: "Mercy! mercy!"

"Well," said Cadoudal, rising in his stirrups, "so be it. Since you are standing there, look around you. There are ten thousand men who have come to see you die. If, among them, a single one asks for mercy, you shall have it."

"Mercy!" cried Lacombe, stretching out his arms.

Cadoudal rose again in his stirrups.

"You alone, father, of us all, have no right to ask for mercy for this man. You extended mercy to him on the day when you prevented me from sending his letter to the revolutionary tribunal. You may help him to die, but that is all that I can grant you."

Then in a voice which made itself heard by all the spectators, he asked for the second time: "Is there one among you who asks for mercy for this man?"

Not a voice replied.

"You have five minutes in which to make your peace with God," said Cadoudal to François Goulin; "and, unless it be a miracle from heaven, nothing can save you. Father," said he, addressing Lacombe, "you may give this man your arm, and accompany him to the scaffold." Then, to the executioner, he said, "Do your duty!"

The executioner, who now saw that his only part in the performance would be the execution of his ordinary function , rose and put his hand on Goulin's shoulder in token that he belonged to him.

The Abbé Lacombe approached the condemned man, but the latter pushed him back.

Then ensued a frightful struggle between the man who would neither pray nor die and his two executioners. In spite of his cries, his bites and his blasphemies, the executioner picked him up in his arms as if he had been a child; and, while the assistant prepared the knife, he carried him from his carriage to the platform of the guillotine.

The Abbé Lacombe went up first, with a ray of hope, and waited for the culprit; but his efforts were vain, for Goulin would not even put his lips to the crucifix.

Then on this awful stage there occurred a scene which is beyond description. The executioner and his assistant succeeded in stretching the condemned upon the fatal plank. It rocked. Then a flash as of lightning. It was the knife which fell. Then a dull thud. It was the head which had fallen. A deep silence followed, and in its midst Cadoudal's voice could be heard saying "God's justice is done!"

The Blood Union

THE map-space now occupied by Austria, outside the actual dukedom, its kernel, consists of Bohemia, Hungary, Illyria, the Tyrol, Moravia, Silesia, the Slavonian district of Croatia, the Vaivody of Servia, the Banat, Transylvania, Galicia, Dalmatia, and Styria.

We do not count four to five millions of Roumanians scattered throughout Hungary, and on the banks of the Danube. Every one of the above districts has its own character, its own customs, language, costume, frontier. Especially the dwellers in Styria, composed of Norica and the ancient Pannonia, have retained their own language, costume, and primitive customs. Before it became included in Austria, Styria had its own separate history and nobility, dating from the time when it was known as the march of Styria, about 1030. And from that epoch Karl von Freyberg dated his ancestry, remaining a great noble at a time when great nobles are becoming rare.

He was a handsome young man of about twenty-seven, tall, straight, slight, flexible as a cane, and equally tough. His fine black hair was cut close, and he had beneath black eyebrows and eyelashes, those dark grey eyes which Homer attributes to Minerva and which shine like emeralds. His complexion was sunburnt, for he had hunted since childhood. He had small hands and feet, unwearied limbs, and prodigious strength.

Alas! War ravages manhood. The Prussian-Austrian battles of 1866 left living wrecks; and woe lay heaviest on the citizens of Frankfort.

A party from the battle-fields were going down the river by boat to Port Offenbach and the city of Frankfort could be seen in the distance silhouetted against the sky. A group on board were carrying a wounded soldier. The boat finally reached the landing place where waited a carriage and close to it a litter. The party left the boat, carrying the wounded man. They put him in the litter and drew the curtains, one a girl, the bodice of her dress stained with blood, wrapped herself in a large shawl and walked beside the litter. People watched her with astonishment and questioned the litter-bearer. When he said it was a fiancée who was following the body of her lover, they recognized Fraulein Helen von Chandroz and stopped back bowing respectfully as the body of Count Karl von Freyburg went by.

Helen von Chandoz belonged to a Frankfort family of French descent, her ancestors having been expatriated by the revocation of the Edict of Nantes. The family now had left only her elder sister Emma, and her aged grandmother (the mother having succumbed to illness recently), called Madame von Beling.

Helen was nearing twenty years of age.

She was worthy of her name. Her hair was of that exquisite blonde tint which can only be compared to the colour of ripe corn. Her complexion faintly tinted with rose had the freshness and delicacy of the camellia. And the effect was almost astonishing when under these fair locks, and upon that countenance of almost transparent pallor, she raised large dark eyes, eloquent of passion, overarched with dark eyebrows and fringed with lashes which gave to their sparkling orbs deep reflections like those of the black diamonds of Tripoli.

One could divine in Helen all the tempestuous future which the united passions of two races held in store.

Helen was a sister of those delightful creations that are to be found on every page of Germany's popular poetry. We attribute great merit to those poetic dreamers who perceive Loreleis in the mist of the Rhine and Mignons in the foliage of thickets, and do not remind ourselves that there is, after all, no such great merit in finding these charming images, because they are not the visions of genius, but actual copies, whose originals the misty nature of England and of Germany sets before them as models weeping or smiling, but always poetical. Observe, too, that on the shores of the Rhine, the Main, or the Danube, it is not necessary to seek these types—in the ranks of the aristocracy, but they may be seen at the citizen's window or the peasant's doorway, where Schiller found his Louisa.

Thus Helen accomplished a deed that seems to us the height of devotion with the most entire simplicity, and never knew that she deserved a glance of approval from man, or even from God.

On the nights when Helen sat up, beside the wounded count, Benedict Turpin, a comrade of war, who relieved in the watching, rested in a room, throwing himself fully dressed upon the bed, so as to be ready at the first call to run to Helen's assistance or to go for the surgeon. His dog Frisk often watched beside him. A carriage ready harnessed was always at the door, and, oddly enough, the further recovery progressed, the more the doctor, who had been called in, insisted that this precaution should not be neglected.

One evening after having watched by Karl, Benedict had yielded his post to Helen, had returned to his room and flung himself upon the bed, when, all at once he thought he heard himself loudly called. Almost at the same moment his door opened, and Helen, pale, dishevelled, and covered with blood, appeared in the doorway making inarticulate sounds that seemed to stand for "Help!"

Benedict guessed what had happened. The doctor, less reserved towards him than towards the young girl, had told him what possibilities he feared, and evidently one of these possibilities had come to pass.

He rushed to Karl's room; the ligature of an artery had burst and blood was flowing in waves and in jets. Karl had fainted.

Benedict did not lose an instant; twisting his handkerchief into a rope he tied it round Karl's upper arm, broke the bar of a chair with a kick, slipped the bar into the knot of the handkerchief, and turning the stick upon its axis, made what is known in medical language as a *tourniquet*. The blood stopped instantly.

Helen flung herself distractedly upon the bed, she seemed to have gone mad. She did not hear Benedict calling to her: "The doctor! the doctor!"

With his free hand—the other was pressing upon Karl's arm—Benedict pulled the bell so violently that the servant, guessing something unusual to be the matter, arrived quite scared.

"Take the carriage and fetch the doctor," cried Benedict. In one glance the servant had seen all. He flung himself downstairs and into the carriage, calling out in his turn: "To the doctors'!"

As it was scarcely six o'clock in the morning, the doctor was at home, and within ten minutes walked into the room.

Seeing the blood streaming over the floor, Helen, half fainting, and, above all, Benedict compressing the wounded man's arm, he understood what had happened, the rather that he had dreaded this.

"Ah, I foresaw this!" he exclaimed, "a secondary hemorrhage; the artery has given way."

At his voice Helen sprang up and flung her arms about him.

"He will not die! he will not die!" she cried, "you will not let him die, will you?"

The doctor disengaged himself from her grasp, and approached the bed. Karl had not lost nearly so much blood as last time, but to judge from the pool that was spreading across the room he must have lost over twenty-eight ounces, which in his present state of weakness was exorbitant.

However, the doctor did not lose courage; the arm was still bare; he made a fresh incision and sought with his forceps for the artery, which, fortunately, having been compressed by Benedict, had moved only a few centimetres. In a second the artery was tied, but the wounded man was completely unconscious. Helen, who had watched the first operation with anxiety, followed this one with terror. She had then seen Karl lying mute, motionless, and cold, with all the appearance of death, but she had not seen him pass, as he had just done, from life to death. His lips were white, his eyes closed, his cheeks waxen; clearly Karl had gone nearer to the grave than even on the former occasion. Helen wrung her hands.

"Sir," she said to the doctor, "will he not reopen his eyes? Will he not speak again before he dies? I do not ask for his life—only a miracle could grant that. But, make him open his eyes, doctor. Doctor! make him speak to me! Let a priest join our hands! Let us be united in this world, so that we may not be separated in the next."

The doctor, despite his usual calm, could not remain cold in the presence of such sorrow; though he had done all that was in the power of his art and felt that he could do no more, he tried to reassure Helen with those commonplaces that physicians keep in reserve for the last extremities.

But Benedict, going up to him, and taking him by the hand, said:

"Doctor, you hear what she asks; she does not ask for her lover's life, she asks for a few moments' revival, long enough for the priest to utter a few words and place a ring upon her finger."

"Yes, yes!" cried Helen, "only that! Senseless that I was not to have yielded when he asked and sent at once for the priest. Let him open his eyes, let him say 'Yes,' so that his wish may be accomplished and I may keep my promise to him."

"Doctor," said Benedict, pressing the hand which he had retained in his, "how, if we asked from science the miracle that Heaven seems to deny? How if we were to try transfusion of blood?"

"What is that?" asked Helen.

The doctor considered for a second and looked at the patient: then he said:

"There is no hope; we risk nothing."

"I asked you," said Helen, "what is transfusion of blood?"

"It consists," replied the doctor, "in passing into the exhausted veins of a sick man enough warm, living blood to give him back, if only for a moment, life, speech, and consciousness. I have

never performed the operation, but have seen it once or twice in hospitals."

"So have I," said Benedict, "I have always been interested in strange things, so I attended Majendie's lectures, and I have always seen the experiment succeed when the blood infused belong to an animal of the same species."

"Well," said the doctor, "I will go and try to find a man willing to sell us some twenty or thirty ounces of his blood."

"Doctor," said Benedict, throwing off his coat, "I do not sell my blood to my friends, but I give it. Your man is here."

At these words Helen uttered a cry, flung herself violently between Benedict and the doctor, and proudly holding out her bare arm to the surgeon, said to Benedict:

"You have done enough for him already. If human blood is to pass from another into the veins of my beloved Karl it shall be mine; it is my right."

Benedict fell on his knees before her and kissed the hem of her skirt. The less impressionable doctor merely said:

"Very well! We will try. Give the patient a spoonful of some cordial. I will go home and get the instruments."

The doctor rushed from the room as rapidly as his professional dignity would allow.

During his absence Helen slipped a spoonful of a cordial between Karl's lips while Benedict rang the bell. Hans appeared.

"Go and fetch a priest," said Helen.

"Is it for extreme unction?" Hans ventured to ask.

"For a marriage," answered Helen.

Five minutes later the doctor returned with his apparatus, and asked Benedict to ring for a servant.

A maid came.

"Some warm water in a deep vessel," said the doctor, "and a thermometer if there is one in the house."

She came back with the required articles.

The doctor took a bandage from his pocket and rolled it round the wounded man's left arm, the right arm being injured. After a few moments the vein swelled, proving thereby that the blood was not all exhausted, and that circulation still continued, although feebly. The doctor then turned to Helen.

"Are you ready?" he enquired.

"Yes," said Helen, "but make haste. Oh, God, if he should die!"

The doctor compressed her arm with a bandage, placed the apparatus upon the bed so as to bring it close to the patient, and put it into water heated to 35 degrees centigrade, so that the blood should not have time to cool in passing from one arm to the other. He placed one end of the syringe against Karl's arm and almost simultaneously pricked Helen's so that her blood spurted into the vessel. When he judged that there were some 120 to 130 grammes signed to Benedict to staunch Helen's bleeding with his thumb, and making a longitudinal cut in the vein of Karl's arm he slipped in the point of the syringe, taking great care that no air-bubble should get in with the blood. While the operation, which lasted about ten minutes, was going on, a slight sound was heard at the door. It was the priest coming in, accompanied by Emma, Helen's sister, Madame von Beling, her grandmother, and all the servants. Helen turned, saw them at the door, and signed to them to come in. At the same moment Benedict pressed her arm; Karl had just quivered, a sort of shudder ran through his whole body.

"Ah!" sighed Helen, folding her hands, "thank God! It is my blood reaching his heart!"

Benedict had ready a piece of court-plaster, which he pressed upon the open vein and held it closed.

The priest approached; he was a Roman Catholic who had been Helen's director from her childhood up.

"You sent for me, my child?" he asked.

"Yes," answered Helen; "I desire, if my grandmother and elder sister will allow, to marry this gentleman, who, with God's help, will soon open his eyes and recover his senses. Only, there is no time to lose, for the swoon may return."

And, as though Karl had but waited this moment to revive, he opened his eyes, looked tenderly at Helen and said, in a weak, but intelligible voice:

"In the depth of my swoon, I heard everything; you are an angel, Helen, and I join with you in asking permission of your mother and sister that I may leave you my name."

Benedict and the doctor looked at each other amazed at the over-excitement which for the moment restored sight to the dying man's eyes and speech to his lips. The priest drew near to him.

"Louis Karl von Freyberg, do you declare, acknowledge, and swear, before God and in the face of the holy Church, that you now take as your wife and lawful spouse, Helen de Chandroz, here present?"

"Yes "

"You promise and vow to be true to

her in all things as a faithful husband should to his wife according to the commandments of God?"

Karl smiled sadly at this admonition of the Church meant for people who expect to live long and to have time for breaking their solemn vow.

"Yes," said he, "and in witness of it, here is my mother's wedding-ring, which, sacred already, will become the more sacred by passing through your hands."

"And you, Helen de Chandroz, do you consent, acknowledge, and swear, before God and the holy Church, that you take for your husband and lawful spouse, Louis Karl von Freyberg, here present?"

"Oh, yes, yes, father," exclaimed the girl.

In place of Karl, who was too weak to speak, the priest added:

"Take this token of the marriage vows exchanged between you."

As he spoke he placed upon Helen's finger the ring given him by Karl.

"I give you this ring as a sign of the marriage that you have contracted."

The priest made the sign of the cross upon the bride's hand, saying in a low voice:

"In the name of the Father, and of the Son, and of the Holy Ghost. Amen!"

Stretching out his right hand towards the pair, he added, aloud:

"May the God of Abraham, of Isaac, and of Jacob join you together and bestow His blessing upon you. I unite you in the name of the Father, and of the Son, and of the Holy Ghost. Amen!"

"Father," said Karl to the priest, "if you will now add to the prayers that you have just uttered for the husband the absolution for the dying, I shall have nothing more to ask of you."

The priest, raising his hand, pronounced the consecrated words, as if Karl's soul had delayed until this solemn moment to depart from the body. Helen, who had raised him in her arms, felt herself drawn to him by an irresistible power. Her lips clung to those of her lover, and between them escaped the words:

"Farewell, my darling wife; your blood is my blood. Farewell."

His body fell back upon the pillow. Karl had breathed his last breath upon Helen's mouth. One sob only was heard from the poor girl, and the complete prostration with which she fell back upon his body showed everybody that he was dead.

Lady Hamilton and Admiral Nelson

THE Court of Naples in the time of Queen Caroline was noted, as is often the case, not only for royal plots and intrigues, but for brilliant festivals attended by illustrious men and dazzling women.

Only those who were present at these intimate and intoxicating evenings of the Queen of Naples held at Caserta, evenings of which Emma Hamilton, wife of the English Ambassador, was both the great charm and principal ornament, have been able to relate to their contemporaries to what a point of enthusiasm and delirium the modern Armida brought her hearers and spectators. If her magical poses, if her voluptuous pantomime had had influence on cold Northern temperaments, how far more they were likely to electrify those violent Southern imaginations passionately fond of singing, music, and poetry, and knowing by heart Cimarosa and Metastasio!

We ourselves have known and questioned old men who were present at these magnetic evenings, and we have marked their expressions as, after the flight of fifty years, they spoke of their ardent remembrances.

Emma Hamilton was lovely, involuntarily. Let us try to grasp what she was upon this evening when she desired to be beautiful, both for the Queen and for Nelson, in the midst of all these elegant costumes of the end of the XVIIIth century which the Courts of Austria and of the Two Sicilies persisted in wearing as a protest against the French revolution. Instead of the powder still covering those ridiculously high coiffures erected on the top of the head, instead of those scanty dresses which would have stifled the grace of Terpsichore herself, instead of that violent rouge which turned women into bacchantes; Emma Hamilton, faithful to her traditions of liberty and art, was wearing a long tunic of pale blue cashmere, falling round her in folds to make an antique statue envious; her hair, waving in long curls on to her shoulders, displayed two rubies which shone like the fabulous carbuncles of the ancients; her girdle, a gift from the Queen, was a chain of valuable diamonds, which, knotted like a Franciscan Nun's, fell to her knees; her

arms were bare from the rise of the shoulder to her finger tips, and one of her arms was clasped at shoulder and wrist by two diamond serpents with ruby eyes. The hand of the arm without ornament was laden with rings, while the other, on the contrary, shone only by the brilliant fineness of the skin and tapering nails, transparently pink like rose leaves, while her feet, in flesh-coloured stockings, seemed bare as her hands in their blue sandals laced with gold.

This dazzling beauty, further increased by this strange costume, had something almost supernatural, and therefore terrible and dreadful in it; women turned aside from this resurrection of Greek paganism, from jealousy, men with fear. Possession or suicide were the only alternatives for whomsoever should have the misfortune to become enamoured of that Venus Astarté.

Under the stimulus of wealth, wine, and music, conversation became general; lips no longer let fall but let fly words; laughter displayed white teeth; men and women mingled; each to his taste sought wit or beauty; and in the midst of this gentle murmur, which seemed like the warbling of birds, one felt the atmosphere become warm and impregnated with youth, invisible, unseizable, intoxicating, composed of love, desires, and voluptuousness.

In this kind of gathering Caroline used to forget that she was Queen; her eyes glowed, her nostrils dilated, her bosom swelled. She came to Emma, and placing her hand on her shoulder, said: "Well, fair lady, have you forgotten that you do not belong to yourself this evening? You have promised us miracles, and we are in a hurry to applaud you."

Emma seemed as if in a languorous swoon; her head drooped now on this shoulder, now on that; her half-closed eyes were hidden beneath her long eyelashes; her black curls strikingly contrasted with the dead white of her bosom. She felt rather than saw the Queen's hand on her shoulder; and quivered from head to foot.

"What do you wish of me, dear Queen?" said she, with a supremely graceful motion of the head. "I am ready to obey you. Would you like the balcony scene? But there should be two for that, and I have no Romeo."

"No, no," said the Queen laughing, "no love scene; you would make them mad. No, something to terrify them. Juliet's monologue, that is all I permit you this evening."

"So be it; give me a large white shawl, my Queen, and clear a space for me."

The Queen took from a sofa a large shawl of white China, crape, which no doubt she had thrown down there purposely, gave it to Emma, and with a gesture in which she became Queen again, ordered everyone to stand aside.

In a moment Emma found herself alone in the midst of the room.

"Madame, I must ask you to be so kind as to explain the circumstances. That will distract attention from me for a moment, besides, and I need this little trick to produce my effect."

"You are all familiar with the play of Romeo and Juliet, are you not?" said the Queen. "It is desired to marry Juliet to Count Paris, whom she does not love, loving as she does poor banished Romeo. Friar Laurence. who has wedded her to her lover, has given her a sleeping draught to make her appear as if dead; she is to be laid in the tomb of the Capulets, and there Laurence will come to find her and to take her to Mantua, where Romeo is awaiting her. Her mother and her nurse have just left her room, leaving her alone, after having announced that at daybreak next day she will marry Count Paris."

Scarcely had the Queen finished this narrative, which had drawn all eyes to her, than a cry of pain made them turn again to Emma Hamilton. She had needed but a moment or two so to drape herself in the immense shawl as to leave nothing showing of her own dress; her head was hidden in her hands, which she let glide slowly down, gradually disclosing her pale face stamped with profound grief, and in which it was impossible to discover a trace of that sweet languor we have tried to depict; it displayed, on the contrary, a paroxysm of anguish; terror reaching its zenith.

She turned slowly about her as if to follow with her gaze her mother and her nurse, even out of sight, and in a voice whose every vibration pierced the hearts of the hearers, her arm extended as if to bid the world an eternal adieu:

"Farewell!" said she.

"God knows when we shall meet again.

"I have a faint cold fear thrills through my veins,

"That almost freezes up the heat of life:

"I'll call them again to comfort me;—

"Nurse!—What should she do here?

"My dismal scene I needs must act alone."——
And so continued to the end of the scene, when, carrying the phial containing the drug to her lips, she cried: "Romeo, I come! this do I drink to thee." And, making a gesture of swallowing it, she sank down and fell stretched on the carpet, where she remained lifeless and motionless.

One of the guests was the English Admiral Nelson who had defeated the French Republican fleet which with the Italian Republicans had warred against the Queen of Naples.

So great was the illusion of the actress that forgetting it was merely dramatic representation, Nelson, the rough sailor, more acquainted with ocean storms than with the deceits of art, uttered a cry, sprang towards Emma, and with his only arm raised her from the ground as if she had been a child.

He had his reward: on opening her eyes, Emma's first smile was for him. Only then did he comprehend his mistake and withdraw in confusion to a corner of the room.

To him succeeded the Queen, and everyone flocked round the sham Juliet.

Never did the magic of art, even if urged to this point, go beyond it. Although expressed in a foreign tongue, not a feeling agitating the heart of Juliet had escaped the spectators; she had rendered each with such magic and such truth that she had made them pass into the souls of the listeners for whom, thanks to her, fiction had become reality.

The emotions raised by this scene of which the noble company, completely a stranger to the mysteries of the poetry of the North, had not even any idea, were some time in calming down. To the silence of stupefaction succeeded enthusiastic applause; then the praise and charming flatteries so gently caressing to the artist's self-love.

Emma, born to shine on the scene of letters, but urged by her irresistible fortune into the scene of politics, on each occasion became once again the ardent and passionate actress.

But at this moment, when all eyes were on Emma, the Queen felt a hand grasp her wrist; she turned; it was Acton, Prime Minister.

"Come," said he, "I have important matters to discuss."

"Ladies," said she, "in my absence, for I am obliged to absent myself for some minutes; in my absence, Emma is Queen; I leave you, in place of power, genius and beauty."

Then, in Nelson's ear:
"Tell her to dance for you the shawl dance that she dances for me. She will do it." And she followed Acton, leaving Emma intoxicated with pride, and Nelson madly in love.

.   .   .   .   .

When the Queen returned to the drawing-room, Emma Hamilton, wrapped in purple cashmere with gold fringes, amid the frenzied applause of the spectators, was falling back on a sofa with all the abandon of a professional dancer who has just obtained her greatest success; and truly, never did a ballet dancer of San Carlo throw her public into such intoxication, so that the moment had come when, by an imperceptible attraction, the circle round her had contracted till she had scarcely room to breathe; but at sight of the Queen the crowd opened out to let her reach Emma; and the applause re-doubled. It was well known that to praise her favourite's grace, talent and magic was the surest way to pay court to Caroline.

"From what I see and hear," said the latter, "it appears to me that Emma has kept her word to you. She must now rest; besides it is one o'clock in the morning, and Caserta from Naples —my thanks that you have forgotten it—is distant several miles."

All understood this as a dismissal in due form; the Queen gave her hand to kiss to three or four of the more favoured, detained Nelson and two friends.

The Queen was then alone with Acton, Emma, two officers and Nelson.

"My dear lord," said she to the latter, "I have reason to think that to-morrow or the following day the King will receive from Vienna Court news relative to the war confirming your opinion; for you continue to hold, do you not, that never too soon one begins a campaign against the French and Italian Republicans.

"Not only do I think so, madame, but if this advice is taken, I am ready to lend you the support of the English fleet."

"We shall profit by it, milord; but it is not that which I have to ask of you for the instant."

"Whatever the Queen commands, I am ready to obey."

"I know, milord, how greatly the King confides in you; to-morrow, even though the reply from Vienna be fav-ourable to war, he will still hesitate; a letter from your lordship, in the same sense as that of the Emperor of Austria would remove all his irresolution."

"Should it be addressed to the King, madame?"

"No. My august consort has an in-vincible repugnance to follow advice given directly; I should therefore pre-fer it to come in a confidential letter written to Lady Hamilton. Write col-lectively to her and Sir William; to her as my best friend, to Sir William as the King's; coming by double re-bound, the advice will influence him more."

"As Your Majesty is aware," said Nelson, "I am neither diplomat nor politician; my letter will be that of a sailor who says frankly, roughly even, what he thinks, and not anything else."

"It is all I ask of you, milord. Be-sides, you are going away with the Captain-General, you will talk on the way; as no doubt something important will be decided in the morning, come and dine at the palace.

Nelson bowed.

"We shall be by ourselves," con-tinued the Queen. "Emma and Sir Wil-liam will be with us. We must urge and press the King; I should return to Naples myself this evening if my poor Emma were not so fatigued. You know, however," added the Queen, low-ering her voice, "that it is for you and for you only, my dear admiral, that she has said and done all the exquisite things you have seen and heard." Then still lower: "She obstinately declined, but I told her I was sure she would enrapture you; all her obstinacy gave way in that hope."

"Oh, madame, I entreat you! said Emma.

"There, don't blush, and give your beautiful hand to our hero: I would give him mine willingly, but I am sure he will prefer yours; mine will be therefore for these gentlemen." And, in fact, she held out her hands to the officers, who each kissed one, while Nelson, grasping Emma's with more passion perhaps than royal etiquette permitted, carried it to his lips.

"Is it true," he asked in a low voice, "that it was for me you consented to recite, sing and go through that dance which made me madly jealous?"

Emma gazed at him as she was accustomed when she wished to deprive her admirers of the little reason left to them; then with a tone still more intoxicating than her look: "Ungrateful being," said she; "he asks!"

No words were needed to reveal their future thoughts. An epoch not honorable in history was initiated.

The Honor of von Bulow

GENERAL STURM, head of the Prussian Brigade stationed at Frankfort, was a biggish, strongly made man of about two and fifty. He had a small head, with a high brow. His round face was red and when he was angry, which was often, it became crimson. His large eyes were almost always injected with blood, and he glared with fixed pupils when, as invariably was the case, he wished to be obeyed. All this, with his big mouth, thin lips, yellow teeth, menacing eyebrows, aquiline nose, and thick, short red neck, made him a formidable looking man. His voice was loud and penetrating, his gestures commanding, his movements brusque and rapid. He walked with long strides, he despised danger, but nevertheless seldom encountered any unless it was worth his while.

He had a passion for plumes, red, waving colours, the smell of powder, of gaming; he was as brusque in his words as in his movements; violent and full of pride he brooked contradictions ill and readily flew into a passion. Then his face grew a crimson-violet, his grey eyes became golden and seemed to emit sparks. At such times, he completely forgot all the decencies of life. he swore, he insulted, he struck. Nevertheless he had some common sense, for knowing that he must from time to time have duels to fight, he spent his spare time in sword exercise and pistol shooting with the *maître-d'armes* of the regiment. And it must be allowed that he was a first-rate performer with both weapons; and, not only so, he had what was called "an unfortunate hand," and where another would have wounded slightly he wounded badly, and frequently he killed his adversary. This had happened ten or twelve times. His real name was *Ruhig*, which means *peaceful*, so inappropriate to its owner that he received the surname of *Sturm*, meaning storm or tempest. By this name he was always known. He had made a reputation for ferocity in the war against the Bavarians in 1848–49.

Upon this occasion he had summoned his chief of staff, Frederick von Bulow.

When Frederic presented himself he was relatively calm. Sitting in a great chair, and it was rare for him to be seated, he almost smiled.

"Ah, it is you," he said. "I was asking for you. General Roeder was here. Where have you been?"

"Excuse me, general," Frederic answered. "I had gone to my mother-in-law for news of one of my friends, who was seriously wounded in the battle."

"Oh! yes," said the general, "I heard about him—an Austrian. It is too good of you to enquire about such imperial vermin. I should like to see twenty-five thousand of them lying on the battlefield, where I would let them rot from the first man to the last."

"But, your Excellency, he was a friend——"

"Oh, very well—the matter is not in question. I am satisfied with you, baron," said General Sturm, in the same voice in which another man would have said "I loathe you!" "and I wish to do something for you."

"I have a little service to ask."

Frederic bowed.

"It is about General Manteuffel's subsidy of twenty-five millions of florins. You know about it, don't you?"

"Yes," said Frederic, "and it is a heavy impost for a poor city with some 40,000 inhabitants."

"You mean 72,000," said Sturm.

"No, there are only about 40,000 Frankfortians, the remainder of the 72,000 counted as natives are strangers."

"What does that matter?" said Sturm, becoming impatient. "The statistics say 72,000 and General Manteuffel has made his calculation accordingly."

"But if he has made an error, it seems to me that those who are charged with the execution of his order should point it out."

"That is not our affair. We are told 72,000 inhabitants, and 72,000 there therefore are. We are told 25 million florins, and 25 million florins there are also. That is all! Justy fancy! the senators have declared that we can burn the town, but they will not pay the subsidy."

"I was present," said Frederic quietly, "and the sitting was admirably conducted, with much dignity, calm, and sorrow."

"Ta ta ta ta," said Sturm. "General Manteuffel before leaving gave General Roeder the order to get in these millions. Roeder has ordered the town to pay them. The Senate has chosen to deliberate; that is its own affair. Roeder came round to me about it, it is true; but I told him that it was nothing to worry about. I said: 'The chief of my staff married in Frankfort; he knows the town like his own land, everyone's fortune even to shillings and half-pence. He will indicate five and twenty millionaires.' There are twenty-five of them here, are there not?"

"More than that," answered Frederic.

"Good; we will commence with them, and if there is a balance the others shall supply it."

"And have you reckoned on me to give you the names?"

"Certainly. All I require is twenty-five names and five and twenty addresses. Sit down there, my dear fellow, and write them out."

Frederic sat down, took a pen and wrote:

"Honour obliging me to decline to denounce my fellow citizens, I beg the illustrious Generals von Roeder and

Sturm to obtain the desired information elsewhere than from myself.

"Frankfort, July 22nd, 1866.
"FREDERIC BARON VON BULOW."

Then, rising and bowing low, he put the paper in the general's hands.

"What is this?" he asked.

"Read it, general," said Frederic.

The general read it, and gave his chief of the staff a side glance.

"Ah! ah!" he said, "I see how I am answered when I ask a favour; let me see how I am answered when I command. Sit there and write——"

"Order me to charge a battery, and I will do it, but do not order me to become a tax collector."

"I have promised General Roeder to get him the names and addresses and have told him that you will supply them. He will send for the list directly. What am I to say to him?"

"You will tell him that I have refused to give it."

Sturm crossed his arms and approached Frederic.

"And do you think that I will allow a man under my orders to refuse me anything?"

"I think you will reflect that you gave me not only an unjust but a dishonouring order and you will appreciate the reason of my refusal. Let me go, general, and call a police officer: he will not refuse you, for it will be all in his work."

"Baron," replied Sturm, "I cannot reward a man of whom I have to complain." The general's face grew purple, livid marks appeared upon it, his eyes flamed.

"I will write to the king," he cried furiously, "and he will learn how his officers serve him."

"Write your account, sir, and I will write mine," answered Frederic, and he will see how his generals dishonour him."

Sturm rushed and seized his horse-whip.

"You have said dishonoured, sir! You will not repeat the word, I trust?"

"Dishonoured," said Frederic coldly.

Sturm gave a cry of rage and raised his whip to strike his young officer, but observing Frederic's complete calm he let it fall.

"Who threatens strikes, sir," Frederic answered, "and it is as if you had struck me."

He turned to the table and wrote a few lines. Then he opened the door of the ante-room and calling the officers who were there:

"Gentlemen," he said, "I confide this paper to your loyalty. Read what it says aloud."

"I tender my resignation as chief of General Sturm's staff and officer in the Prussian army.

"Dated at noon July 22nd, 1866.
"FREDERIC VON BULOW."

"Which means?" asked Sturm.

"Which means that I am no longer in His Majesty's service nor in yours, and that you have insulted me. Gentlemen, this man raised his horsewhip over me. And having insulted me, you owe me reparation. Keep my resignation, gentlemen, and bear witness that I am free from all military duty at the moment I tell this man that he is no longer my chief, and consequently that I am not his inferior. Sir, you have injured me mortally, and I will kill you, or you will kill me."

Sturm burst out laughing.

"You give your resignation," he said, "well, I do not accept it. Place yourself in confinement. Sir," said he, stamping his foot and walking towards Frederic, "to prison for fifteen days with you."

"You have no longer the right to give me an order," said Frederic, detaching his epaulettes.

Sturm, exasperated, livid, foaming at the mouth, again raised his whip upon the chief of his staff, but this time he slashed his cheek and shoulder with it. Frederic, who until now had held himself in, uttered a cry of rage, made a bound aside and drew his sword.

"Imbecile," shouted Sturm, with a burst of laughter, "you will be shot after a court martial."

At this Frederic lost his head completely and threw himself upon the general, but he found four officers in his path. One whispered to him: "Save yourself; we will calm him."

"And I," said Frederic, "I who have been struck; who will calm me?"

"We give you our word of honour that we have not seen the blow," said the officers.

"But *I* have *felt* it. And as I have given my word of honour that one of us must die, I must act accordingly. Adieu, gentlemen."

Two of the officers trying to follow him:

"Thunders and tempests! gentlemen," called the general after them. "Come back; no one leaves this room except this madman who will be arrested by the provost marshal."

The officers came back hanging their heads. Frederic burst out of the room. The first person he met on the stairs was the Baroness.

"Gracious heavens! what are you doing with a drawn sword?" she asked.

He put the sword in its scabbard. Then he ran to his wife and embraced her and the baby.

* * * * * *

Ten minutes later an explosion was heard in Frederic's room. The door was opened by his guard.

Frederic was lying on the floor dead, his forehead shattered by a bullet. He had left this note on the table:

"Struck in the face by General Sturm, who has refused to give me satisfaction, I could not live dishonoured. My last wish is that my wife in her widow's dress should leave this evening for Berlin, and there beg from Her Majesty the Queen the remission of the subsidy of twenty-five million florins, which the town as I testify is unable to pay.

"FREDERIC, BARON VON BULOW."

Gaetano the Gorger

WHEN the French Republic was warring upon Naples, one of the most savage Italian leaders was Gaetano Mammone, the executioner (beccaio) of King Ferdinand.

At a certain period he was staying at Capistrella, between Lake Fucina and the Liri, when he received what was to him joyful news.

He was told that an officer in French uniform, escorted by a guide, could be seen in the distance descending the source of the Liri.

"Bring them both to me," said Mammone.

Five minutes later they were before him. Instead of leading the officer to General Lemoine to whom he was charged to transmit an order from General Championnet, the guide had treacherously brought him to Gaetano Mammone. He was an aide-de-camp of the Commander-in-Chief, named Claie.

"You arrive opportunely," said Mammone to him. "I am thirsty." One knows with what kind of liquid Mammone used to quench his thirst.

He had the aide-de-camp stripped of his coat, waist-coat, cravat and shirt, and ordered that his hands should be bound and that he should be tied to a tree. Then he put his finger on the carotid artery to make sure of its position, and feeling it throb, plunged in his dagger. The aide-de-camp had neither spoken, pleaded nor uttered a groan; he knew into the hands of what cannibal he had fallen, and, like the gladiator of old, had thought of one thing only, to die well. Mortally wounded, he uttered no cry, and let no sigh escape. The blood spurted from the wound in jets, as it bursts from an artery.

Mammone set his lips to the aide-de-camp's neck, and gorged himself voluptuously.

After this, as spies informed him that a small party of republicans, numbering twenty or thirty, was advancing by the Tagliacozza road, he ordered that arms should be concealed, flowers and olive branches plucked; that women should take the former, boys and men the latter, and that they should go to meet the detachment, and invite the officer in command to come with his men and take part in a feast that the village of Capistrella, composed of patriots, was giving as a sign of rejoicing at their happy advent.

The messengers set out singing. Every house in the village opened its doors; a large table was set up on the square in front of the mayor's office; and wine, bread, meat, hams and cheese were brought out. Another table was arranged for the officers' in the mayor's parlour, the windows of which looked out on the square.

At a league's distance from the town, the messengers met the little detachment, commanded by Captain Tremeau. A guide, interpreter, and a traitor as usual, who was leading the detachment, explained to the republican captain what these men, children and women, coming with flowers and olive branches to meet him, wanted.

Full of courage and loyalty, the captain had not even an idea of treason. He kissed the pretty girls who were offering their flowers, he ordered the sutler to empty her barrel of brandy; all drank to the health of General Championnet, to the spread of the French republic, and made their way arm in arm towards the village singing the *Marseillaise*.

Gaetano Mammone, with all the rest of the inhabitants, was awaiting the French detachment at the gate into the village; it was welcomed by an immense ovation. Everyone fraternised once more, and amid cries of joy, proceeded to the mayor's.

There, as we have said, a table was set up; a plate was put for each soldier. The few officers dined, or rather were to have dined, with the magistrate, deputies and municipal body represented by Gaetano Mammone and the chief brigands enrolled under his orders. The soldiers, delighted with their reception, stacked their rifles at ten paces from the table prepared for them; the women took away their swords with which the children amused themselves playing at soldiers; then they sat down, bottles were uncorked and glasses filled.

Captain Tremeau, a lieutenant and two sergeants, at the same time sat down in the lower hall.

Mammone's men glided between the table and the rifles that the captain had had loaded for greater precaution, on setting out; the officers were separated at the table within in such a way as to have three or four brigands between each of them.

The signal for the massacre was to be given by Mammone; he would raise Claie's skull full of wine at one of the windows and drink to the health of King Ferdinand. Everything happened as arranged. Mammone went to the window unobserved, filled with wine the still bleeding skull of the unhappy officer, took it by the hair as one lifts a goblet by its stem, and, appearing at the middle window, raised it to the toast agreed upon.

The whole population immediately responded with the cry: "Death to the French!"

The brigands threw themselves upon the stacked rifles; those who, pretending to serve them had surrounded the French, stepped back; firing burst out point blank, and the republicans fell under shots from their own weapons. Those who had escaped or who were only wounded had their throats cut by the women and children who had seized their swords.

As to the officers inside the hall, wishing to rush to the aid of their men, they were each held in their places by five or six men.

Mammone, triumphant, approached them, his bleeding cup in his hand, and offered them their lives if they would drink to the health of King Ferdinand in their compatriot's skull.

All four refused in horror.

Then he had a hammer and nails brought, made the officers spread their hands on the table and nailed them to it. Then fagots and bundles of straw were thrown into the room, and, when they had been set alight, the doors and windows were shut.

However, the torture of the republicans was shorter and less cruel than their tormentor had hoped. One of the sergeants was courageous enough to tear his hands free of the nails, and with Captain Tremeau's sword he per-formed for his companions the terrible service of stabbing them, and he stabbed himself afterwards.

The four heroes died crying: "Long live the Republic!"

The Provisional Government

In the Hôtel de Ville, closely closeted, sat the Provisional Government of France. Over that stern old citadel, over the dismantled Palace of the Tuileries, from the tall summit of the Column of Vendôme, over the Hotêl des Invalides and in the Place de la Bastille is seen a blood-red banner, streaming out like a meteor on the keen northwestern blast. Eighty thousand armed men invest the Hôtel de Ville, and wave on wave, wave on wave, the living and stormy tide eddies and welters and dashes around that dark old pile. All its avenues are held; its courts are thronged; ordnance frowns from its black portals and against its gates; drums roll —banners stream—bayonets glitter; and from those tens of thousands of hoarse and stormy voices goes up but one shout of menace and command:

"Vive la République! Vive la République! No kings! No Bourbons! Down—down forever with the kings!"

And upward to that dark old pile of despotism, as to the temple of Liberty herself, are turned those tens of thousands of swarthy faces, dark with the smoke of battle, yet livid with excitement and exhaustion—and as they realize that within those walls the question of their fate and that of their country is then being settled—that from that night's counsels in that vast and ancient edifice are to flow peace and prosperity, and freedom and plenty, or else all the untold terrors of anarchy, civil war, bloodshed, violence and strife —what wonder that the sitting of the council seemed endless and their own impatience became intolerable—that all imaginable doubts and fears and absurd apprehensions took possession of their inflamed imaginations?—that at one time the rumor should fly, and win credence as it flew, that the Provisional Government were consulting with the friends of Henry V.—or again, that they were considering the question of a Regency—and that under such influences they should roar and yell, and thunder for admission at the gates, and burden the air with their shouts?

"No Bourbons! No kings! No Regency! Death—death to all kings! La République! La République! La République!"

At times, in terrific concert, would the thousands of uplifted throats roar forth the chorus of that startling canticle of '92:

"Vive la république! Vive la république! Debout, peuple Français! debout, peuple héroïque! Debout, peuple Français! Vive la république!"

Then the song would change and the mournful notes of the "Death Hymn of the Girondins,"—"Mourir Pour la Patrie"—would swell in wild yet solemn cadence on the wintry blast:

DEATH HYMN OF THE GIRONDINS.

By the voice of the signal cannon,
France calls her sons their aid to
    lend;
"Let us go," the soldier cries, "to
    battle!
'Tis our mother we defend!"
To die on Freedom's Altar—to die on
    Freedom's Altar!
'Tis the noblest of fates; who to meet
    it would falter!

We who fall afar from the battle,
Lone and unknown obscurely die,
But give at least our parting bless-
    ings
Unto France and Freedom high.
To die on Freedom's Altar—to die on
    Freedom's Altar!
'Tis the noblest of fates; who to meet
    it would falter!

And thus all that terrible night, even until the morning's dawn, thronged those men of the barricades around the Hôtel de Ville, and all the night, even until the morning's dawn, calmly continued those men of the Provisional Government of the French Republic, amid menace and mandate, uproar and confusion, in their noble, yet arduous work. At midnight a proclamation of the Provisional Government was read by torchlight to the excited masses by Louis Blanc, from the steps of the Hôtel de Ville, declaring for a government of the people by itself, with liberty,

equality and fraternity for its principles, while order was devised and maintained by the people—which served somewhat to allay their apprehensions and distrust. This proclamation appeared in all the morning journals, and was placarded all over the city the next day.

That day was Friday, the 25th of February. But still the Provisional Government remained in session, and still the armed masses of the barricades, in congregated thousands, rolled in tumultuous billows around the Hôtel de Ville. At length the populace, exasperated by impatience, hunger and sleeplessness, with brandished bayonets rushed into the very chamber of council, with furious cries, and with threats which were well nigh accomplished. Again and again, at the entreaty of his colleagues, did the brave, the eloquent, the wise Lamartine present himself upon the steps of the Hôtel de Ville to assuage and quiet the rising tempest. Again and again, throughout that fearful day, did he come forth, single handed, to wrestle with violence, turbulence, anarchy and strife; and again and again, beneath the magic of his eloquent tongue, the storm lulled, the tempest ceased. Again and again, throughout all that fearful day, were the acts of that noble Government matured and sent forth. Proclamation followed proclamation, and no branch of society seemed forgotten.

The names of the members of the Provisional Government were again published. Caussidiere and Sobrier were confirmed in the police department, and Etienne Arago in that of the post-office. Merchants of provisions were recommended to supply all who were in need; and the people were recommended to still retain their arms. The Chamber of Deputies was dissolved, the Peers were forbidden to meet, and the convocation of a National Assembly was promised. To all laborers labor was guaranteed and compensation for labor. At noon the garrison of the fort of Vincennes was announced to have acknowledged the Republic, just as the people were about to march upon it. To insure order and tranquillity, the Municipal Guard was disbanded, and the National Guard entrusted with the protection of Paris under M. Courtais, the commandant, who was ordered immediately to recruit twenty-four battalions for active service. All articles pledged at the Mont-de-Piété, from February 4th, not exceeding in value ten francs, were ordered to be returned, and the Tuileries was decreed the future asylum of invalid workmen. An attack on the machinery of the printing offices was checked by a proclamation.

General Bedeau was appointed Minister of War, General Cavaignac Governor of Algeria, and Admiral Baudin to the command of the Toulon fleet. On the part of the army Marshal Bugeaud and on the part of the clergy the venerable Archbishop of Paris gave in their adhesion to the Republic, while the entire press, Bourgeoise and the Provinces hesitated not an instant. Indeed, from all quarters came in adhesions to the Republic. The Bonapartes were among the first. Barrot and Thiers also came, but too late to save themselves from contempt. Mr. Rush, the American Minister, the first of foreign ambassadors acknowledged the Republic. The son of Mehemet Ali was next. The Papal Nuncio succeeded, together with the Ministers of the Argentine Republic and Uruguay. Next came the ambassador of England; but those of Austria, Prussia, Russia and Holland awaited instructions from home—little dreaming of the news they were about to receive! The city of Rouen sent three hundred of its citizens as a deputation, with abundant supplies of arms, by the morning cars of the railway.

At about noon, the Pont Louis Philippe was destroyed by fire. Henceforth it is to be "Le Pont de la Réforme." And so with all other names. Royal is to give place to République, and "Liberté, Egalité et Fraternité" is to be again inscribed on all public monuments.

The children of citizens killed in the Revolution were declared adopted by the country. The civil, judicial and administrative functionaries of the Royal Government were announced released from their oaths of office, the colonels of the twelve legions of National Guards were dismissed, and all political prisoners set free. Every citizen was declared an elector, and absolute freedom of thought, the liberty of the press, and the right of political and industrial associations secured to all were proclaimed.

A warrant for the arrest of the late Ministers was issued by the new Procureur-General, M. Portalis, based on an act of accusation presented to the Court of Appeals. But all of them had fled. Guizot is said to have escaped from the Foreign Office in a servant's livery. When the people broke into his hotel, they found only his daughter, and retired. The other members of the Ministry are said to have leaped from a low window of the Tuileries, and to have escaped at the moment of the King's abdication. M. de Cormenin was appointed Conseilleur d'Etat and M. Achille Marrast Procureur-General to the Court of Appeals in Paris, in place of the refugees.

Such were some of the acts of the seven men constituting the Provisional Government of the French Republic, during their first extraordinary session of sixty-four hours—from the hour of four o'clock in the afternoon of Thursday after the dissolution of the Chamber of Deputies to the hour of four o'clock in the morning of Sunday, the 27th of February, when the people of Paris consented to retire to their homes. But during all of this period, night and day without intermission, every moment was the Hôtel de Ville surrounded by tumultuous masses infuriated by suspicion, apprehension and distrust. For two whole days and two whole nights armed men incessantly inundated the square, the courts and halls of the Hôtel de Ville. They insisted on giving to the Republic the character, the attitude and the emblems of the first Revolution—they insisted on a Republican violent, sweeping, dictatorial and terrorist, in language, in gesture and in color, in place of that determined on, moderate, pacific, legal, unanimous and constitutional. At the peril of their lives the Provisional Government resisted this demand. Twenty times during those sixty-four hours was Lamartine taken up, dragged, carried to the door and windows or to the head of the grand staircase, into the courts and the square, to hurl down with his eloquence those emblems of terrorism, with which it was attempted to dishonor the Re-

public. But the vast and infuriated mass refused to listen, and drowned his voice in clamor and vociferation. At length, when well-nigh exhausted in defense of the emblem of a moderate Republic, he exclaimed: "The red flag has been nowhere except around the Champ-de-Mars, trailed in the blood of the people, while the tri-color has been around the world with our navy, our glory and our liberties!"

The furious and hitherto obdurate and blood-thirsty populace became softened —tears were shed, arms were lowered— flags were thrown away, and peaceably they departed to their homes. Never— never was there a more glorious triumph of eloquence—of patriotism!

It was on the morning of Sunday, the 27th day of February, that the Provisional Government deemed it prudent and proper for them to bring to a close their initiative labors, and once more, for the last time, Lamartine descended the steps of the great staircase of the Hôtel de Ville, and, presenting himself in front of the edifice surrounded by his colleagues, announced to the vast assembly the result of their protracted toil:

Royalty abolished——
A Republic proclaimed——
The people restored to their political rights——
National workshops opened——
The army and National Guard reorganized——
The abolition of death for political offences.

With louder and more prolonged acclamations than any other decree was this last received. And, instantly, in accordance with this proclamation, the director of criminal affairs, on the order of M. Crémieux, Minister of Justice, dispatched on the wings of the wind, all over France, the warrant to suspend all capital executions which were to have taken place, in virtue of Royal decrees, until the will of the National Assembly, at once to be convened, should be promulgated on the subject of the penalty of death. The effects of this decree, as it sped on the lightning's wings, like a saving angel, all over France, may be imagined perhaps, but portrayal is impossible! Who can imagine even the joy, the rapture it brought to many a dungeon-prisoner, who was counting the hours that yet remained to him of life and preceded his awful doom, or to those who sorrowed over his untimely—perchance his unjust fate!

Leaning on the arm of Louis Blanc, the youngest member of the Government, the venerable Dupont de l'Eure, the eldest, accompanied by the other members, now appeared on the balcony of the room formerly called the Chamber of the Throne, but now the Chamber of the Republic! Lamartine then advanced a step before his colleagues, and in a brief and eloquent address proclaimed to that immense throng the existence of the Republic.

The announcement was received with acclamations of joy, and shouts of "Vive le Gouvernement!"—"Vive Lamartine!" —"Vive Louis Blanc!" mingled with those of "Vive la République!" loudly rose.

From the Hôtel de Ville, the Provisional Government proceeded in a body, despite the rain which fell in torrents, accompanied by the people, to the Place de la Bastille, there officially to inaugurate the Republic, agreeably to announcement.

At the appointed hour, the Place de la Bastille was thronged. The National Guard, consisting of two battalions from each of the twelve legions of Paris, together with the Thirteenth Legion of cavalry and two battalions of the Banlieu, were drawn up from the Church of the Madeleine to the Column of July. And, there, at the base of that column erected in commemoration of the Revolution which had made Louis Philippe King of the French, his downfall was commemorated, and on the ruins of the throne then established was now inaugurated a Republic.

During the ceremony of the inauguration, the "Marseillaise" was sung by the National Guard and the people, and, at its conclusion, about the hour of three, the troops filed off before the Column of July to the thrilling strains of "Marseillaise" and the "Mourir Pour la Patrie" of the Girondins. The members of the Provisional Government preceded by a detachment of the National Guard and accompanied by the pupils of the Polytechnic School and the Military School of St. Cyr, then descended the boulevards, followed by the whole of the military and civic array, who chanted the national songs. The effect was stupendous. Hour after hour the immense procession moved on like a huge serpent through the streets of Paris; and, at length, when its head was at the Hôtel de Ville, its extremity had hardly left the Column of July.

It was night, on Sunday, the 27th of February, when members of the Provisional Government, for the first time during four days, returned to their homes. But their work was accomplished. A Republic was gained, proclaimed and inaugurated!

Cannibals

THE French army, unmoved as time, followed its triple road through the Abruzzi, the Terra di Lavoro, and part of the Campagna in its war against Naples.

All the movements of the Republicans being known at Naples, it had not escaped attention that the chief body, that commanded by Championnet in person, was advancing upon Capua by Nignano and Calvi.

The Prince of Maliterno and the Duke of Rocca Romana, each at the head of a regiment of volunteers recruited among the noble or wealthy youth of Naples and its neighbourhood, had come to take leave of the Queen, and had set out on their march to meet the Republicans. The nearer the danger approached, the more the King's party and the Queen's party separted into two camps.

The King's party was composed of all those who, clinging to the honour of the Neapolitan name, desired resistance at all price and the defence of Naples pushed to the last extremity.

The Queen's party, composed of the English Ambassador, Sir William, and Lady Hamilton, Nelson, General Acton, desired the abandonment of Naples, and a prompt flight.

Then, amid all this, the Queen was extremely agitated with the fear of the Minister Ferrari's return at any moment. He had been sent to the Court of Austria to seek help to hold Naples. The King, seeing himself insolently deceived knowing in short whom to blame for all the disasters overwhelming the kingdom, might, as weak natures do, have a moment's energy and escape for ever from the pressure put upon him for twenty years by a minister he had never liked and a spouse he no longer loved.

On the evening of the crisis there was a Council of State: the King announced himself openly and firmly for defense. The Council broke up at midnight. From midnight to one o'clock the Queen stayed in the dark room, and sent for Pasquale di Simone, who received secret instruction from Acton who was waiting for him there. Day commenced with one of those tempests which always last for three days at Naples, and which have given rise to this proverb: "*Nasce, pasce, mori*"— it is born, has its will, and dies.

In spite of the alternatives of rain falling in sheets, and of wind blowing in squalls, the people, who, full of emotion, had a vague feeling of a great catastrophe, were blocking up the streets, squares and cross-roads.

But what pointed to some extraordinary circumstance was that the people were not crowding the old parts of the town; and by the people we mean that multitude of sailors, fishers and lazzaroni who form the population at Naples. On the contrary, one noticed that the most animated groups, while surrounding the royal palace, seemed to be watching Toledo Street and the Strada del Piliero. Finally, three men, already conspicuous in the previous riots, were speaking loudly and agitating heatedly amid these groups. These three men were Pasquale di Simone,

49

Mammone, the public executioner and a compatriot.

The whole crowd, without knowing what it was waiting for, seemed to expect something or someone; and the King, who knew no more, but whom the concourse made uneasy, hidden behind the Venetian blind of a window on the ground floor, while mechanically petting Jupiter, was watching it as from time to time, like the rumbling of thunder or the roar of a waterfall, it emitted the double cry of "Long live the King!" and "Death to the Jacobins!"

The Queen, who had ascertained where the King was, kept within the room with Acton, ready to act according to circumstances, whilst Emma in the Queen's apartment with the Countess San Marco was packing up her royal friend's most secret papers and most precious jewels.

Towards eleven o'clock, a young man, exchanging signs with Pasquale di Simone and the butcher, galloped up on an English horse to the great gate in the palace courtyard, leaped down, threw the bridle to a groom, and as if he had known beforehand where to find the Queen, entered the room where she was waiting with Acton.

"Well?" they asked together.

"He is following me," said he.

"How soon will he be here?"

"In half-an-hour."

"Are those expecting him warned?"

"Yes."

"Well, go to my room and tell Lady Hamilton to inform Nelson."

While these orders were being received with respect, a courier arrived at the bridge of the Madeleine, and taking the route of the first, reached the Strada del Piliero.

There he began to find the crowd denser, and in spite of his dress, in which it was easy to recognise a special courier of the King's, he found a difficulty in continuing his way at the same pace. Besides, as if they had done it purposely, people got in the way of his horse, and, displeased at their hurts, began to abuse him. Ferrari, for he it was, accustomed to see his livery respected, at first responded with some strokes of his whip sturdily dealt to left and right. The lazzaroni scattered and kept quiet from habit. But, as he reached the corner of the Saint Charles theatre, a man wanted to get in front of the horse, and passed so clumsily that he was knocked down.

"Friends," cried as he fell, "this is not a King's courier as you might think from his dress. This is a Jacobin in disguise who is escaping! Death to the Jacobin! Death!"

Cries of "The Jacobin! The Jacobin! Death to the Jacobin!" were then heard in the crowd.

Pasquale di Simone flung his knife at the horse; it entered to the hilt. The butcher rushed to the beast's head, and, accustomed to bleed lambs and sheep, opened the artery in the neck. The horse reared, neighed with pain, beat the air with its fore feet, whilst a jet of blood spurted on the bystanders.

The sight of blood has a magical effect on southern peoples. No sooner did the lazzaroni feel themselves watered by the red and warm fluid, no sooner did they scent its acrid odour, than they rushed upon the man and the horse with ferocious cries.

Ferrari felt that if his horse fell he

was lost. He kept him up as well as he could with the bridle and with his legs, but the unfortunate animal was mortally wounded. He stumbled to left and right, then crossed his fore legs, rose through a desperate effort on his master's part, and made a bound forward. Ferrari felt the beast giving under him. He was at fifty paces only from the palace guard; he called for help; but the sound of his voice was lost in cries repeated a hundred-fold. "Death to the Jacobin!" He seized a pistol from his holsters, hoping that the report would be better heard than his cries. At that moment his horse fell. The shock made the pistol go off at random, and the bullet hit a boy of from eight to ten years old.

"He assassinates children!" a voice cried.

At that cry, another butcher rushed among the crowd, which he drove apart with elbows pointed and hard as oaken wedges. He reached the centre of the disturbance just as, fallen with his horse, the unhappy Ferrari was trying to get on his feet. Before he could succeed, the man's club came down on his head; he fell like an ox struck with a mallet!

But this was not what was wanted; it was under the King's own eyes that Ferrari had to die. The five or six police in the secret of the drama surrounded the body and defended it, whilst the butcher, dragging it by the feet, cried: "Room for the Jacobin!" They left the horse's corpse where it was, after having stripped it and followed the butcher. Twenty steps further on they were in front of the King's window. Anxious to know the cause of this frightful uproar, the King opened the blind. At the sight of him the cries changed. Hearing these yells, the King really thought that justice was being meted out to some Jacobin. He did not dislike this method of ridding him of his enemies. He saluted the people, a smile on his lips; the people, feeling encouraged, desired to show their King that they were worthy of him. They raised the unhappy Ferrari, bleeding, torn, multilated, but still alive, in their arms; the corpse had just recovered consciousness: he opened his eyes, recognised the King, and stretched out his arms toward him.

"Rescue! help! Sire, it is I! I, your Ferrari!"

At this unexpected, terrible, inexplicable sight the King sprang backwards, and going to the back of the room, fell half fainting into a chair—whilst, on the contrary, Jupiter, who, being neither man nor King, had no reason for ingratitude, uttered a howl of distress, and, with bloodshot eyes and foam at the mouth, leaping from the window, sprang to his friend's help.

At that moment the door opened: the Queen came in, seized the King's hand, forced him to rise, dragged him to the window, and showing him this cannibal people dividing up the remains of Ferrari:

"Sire," said she, "you see the men on whom you are relying for the defence of Naples and for ours; to-day they cut your servants' throats; to-morrow they will cut the throats of your children; the day after to-morrow they will cut our throats. Do you still persist in your wish to remain?"

"Have everything got ready!" cried the King; "this evening I set out . . ."

And, thinking he still saw the

slaughter of the unhappy Ferrari, still heard his dying voice appealing for help, he buried his head in his hands, closing his eyes, shutting his ears, and took refuge in the room in his apartments furthest from the street.

When he emerged, two hours later, the first sight he saw was Jupiter, the faithful dog, lying down all bleeding on a scrap of cloth, which seemed from the remains of fur and bits of braid to have belonged to the unfortunate courier.

The King knelt down by Jupiter, made sure that his favourite had no serious wound, and, wanting to ascertain on what the faithful and courageous animal was lying, he drew from under him, in spite of his howls, a part of Ferrari's jacket which the dog had wrested from his murderers.

By a providential chance, this piece was that in which was the leather pocket made for the despatches; the King unbuttoned it and found intact the imperial contents which the courier was bringing in answer to his letter.

The King restored to Jupiter the scrap of clothing, on which he lay down again, uttering a lugubrious howl: then he went back to his room, shut himself in, unsealed the imperial letter, and read:—

"To My Dear Brother and Beloved Cousin, Uncle, Father-in-Law, Ally and Confederate.

"I never wrote letter you sent me by your courier Ferrari, it is forged from one end to the other.

"The letter which I had the honour of writing was entirely in my own hand, and, instead of urging you to open a campaign, invited you to attempt nothing before the month of April next, the time when I myself count on the arrival of our good and faithful allies the Russians.

"If the guilty are those whom Your Majesty's justice can reach, I do not conceal that I should like to see them punished as they deserve.

"I have the honour to be, with respect, Your Majesty's very dear brother, beloved cousin, nephew, son-in-law, ally and confederate.

Francois of Austria, Emperor.

Queen Caroline and her Minister had been responsible for a useless crime.

Confession of the District Attorney

The sick-room of the ex-district attorney of Paris held one occupant. Monsieur de Villefort himself was alone.

With his head between his hands, he sat in his easy-chair. When the door opened he rose in his chair, and looking expectantly at the two physicians who entered, he said:

"Well, is the district attorney coming?"

"He will be here soon," replied d'Avigny, elder of the two, to quiet the old man.

"But I have no more time," exclaimed Villefort, passionately.

"Monsieur de Villefort," said the physician earnestly, "you know that the district attorney can only be informed in cases of the utmost importance, and——"

"And is it not an important case when a man who has himself filled the office of district attorney for years wishes to speak to his successor before he dies?" said Villefort, sharply. "What is the name of the new district attorney?"

"Monsieur de Flambois."

"Oh, my former assistant," muttered the sick man, with a bitter smile. "Doctor, it is a question of rehabilitation. Tell Monsieur de Flambois to hurry up."

"I will do so," said Fritz, after an interchange of looks with his father, and he immediately left the room.

The old physician also went away, and immediately afterward Morrel, merchant of Marseilles, conducted Valentine Villefort, daughter of the sick man, into the private office of the doctor.

Monsieur d'Avigny with deep emotion drew the young girl, who was attired in deep mourning, to his bosom, while the tears fell on Valentine's cheeks.

"My dearly beloved child," he said, with tenderness. "Thank God that my old eyes are permitted to see you once more."

"And my father?" asked Valentine, sobbing.

"You will see him, Valentine. Remain patient for a little while longer; he wants to see the district attorney, and, as far as I understand, it is about some former injustice which he wishes to repair. Confide in me, I shall call you when the time comes. In the meantime take some refreshments. as

you must be weak from the journey."

Valentine and Julie withdrew to an apartment which had been prepared for them, and d'Avigny and Morrel remained alone.

"If I could only understand," said the old man meditatively, "how Monsieur de Villefort ever could have such a daughter."

"Perhaps Valentine's mother, Mademoiselle de St. Meran, had a noble nature."

"I hardly think so. Of course I did not know Monsieur de Villefort's first wife, but, from what I have heard of her, she was very miserly, and a fit companion for her husband. Old Madame de St. Meran, too, was not exactly a tender-hearted woman."

"But she loved Valentine dearly," Morrel remarked.

"I admit that; although this love did not prevent her from trying to force Valentine into an obnoxious marriage. Monsieur d'Epinay was of an old aristocratic family, and that was why the old lady thought he would be a good match for her granddaughter. No, they were all selfish, and Valentine can congratulate herself for not being like them."

The entrance of the servant who announced the arrival of Monsieur de Flambois and Monsieur d'Avigny, put an end to the conversation. The old physician immediately conducted Monsieur de Flambois to the bedside of his patient, whose eyes lit up when he recognized the district attorney.

"Monsieur de Villefort," began the district attorney, bowing low, "you desired to speak to me to tell me something important. Do you wish our interview to be private?"

"No," said Villefort, solemnly. "I desire Monsieur d'Avigny to remain and act as a witness."

The physician seated himself on the bed, while Monsieur de Flambois took up a position at the writing desk.

"Monsieur de Villefort, we are ready."

"Gentlemen," said the sick man, in a clear, firm voice, "thanks to me and thanks to my wife, Heloise de Villefort, my family name has become infamous, and I am not surprised my father no longer wishes to bear it."

"But, Monsieur de Villefort," interrupted the official.

"Let me speak. What would you think of a man who, to save himself, condemns another in cold blood to imprisonment for life."

"I would call him a criminal," said Flambois solemnly.

"Well, I am such a criminal. In the year 1814, I condemned a young man to life imprisonment and the heavens did not fall; I rose step by step and for twenty-five years was looked upon as an honorable official whose reputation was above suspicion, although in my own heart I knew I was a rogue. But the man I thought had rotted away in jail, was alive and revenged himself upon me. The first wife who bore my name was my accomplice, the second was a poisoner. She murdered every one who stood in her way; my son and Valentine became her victims; my other son sprung from a criminal attachment. I tried to kill him by burying him alive; as a punishment for me, he was rescued to die on the gallows."

"No, Monsieur de Villefort, Benedetto's sentence was commuted to life imprisonment," said Monsieur de Flambois.

"That is worse than the gallows," stammered the sick man. "My first and my second wife, Benedetto and myself deserved to have our names looked upon with loathing, but Valentine, my poor innocent Valentine, did not deserve this shame, and on her account I speak to-day."

"I do not understand you," said the district attorney. "Your daughter Valentine——"

"Ah, what fools!" exclaimed Villefort. "How could you imagine that Valentine was my daughter? No, gentlemen, Valentine is not a Villefort! How could an angel be a member of such a sinful race!"

"I thought as much," muttered d'Avigny to himself, while Flambois looked at his former chief as if the latter were talking Sanscrit.

"When I married Renee de St. Meran," continued Monsieur de Villefort, after a short pause, "I was a young and ambitious official. My wife was also ambitious, and we were fitted in that respect for one another. Unfortunately for us both, there was a clause in the marriage contract, by which Monsieur and Madame de St. Meran pledged themselves to give our first child on its baptism a present of three hundred thousand francs. As soon as I was in possession of such a fortune, I could go to Paris, and once in the capital, I was sure to make my way. Renee was of the same mind as myself, she yearned to come to court and play a part in the world of society; Marseilles was too small for her. When Renee became *enceinte* we were both overjoyed. The birth of a child would smooth our path, and we only thought of the first smile of the little being, to arrange our plans. The event so anxiously awaited by us was to take place at the beginning of May, 1816. To have you understand what followed, I must go back to April, 1815. I was sitting at work on the evening of the 4th of April, when loud screams attracted my attention. I opened the window, it was ten o'clock, and in the moonlight, I observed that the street in front of our house was filled with a noisy and turbulent crowd of people. Collecting my thoughts, I blew out my lamp. I saw a man running rapidly along the street, followed by a great crowd shouting. 'Down with the Englishman.' The man ran so quickly that he distanced all his pursuers, and I already thought that he was saved, when I saw him stagger and fall. In a moment his pursuers were upon him, a loud cry was heard, and the next moment the unfortunate man was thrown into the river. Not long after all was still again. I lit my lamp again and was about to continue my work, when I heard a slight tap at the window. I became frightened. Who could want me at this hour? Grasping a pistol, I walked cautiously into the garden, from whence proceeded cries for help. I listened, and could now hear a soft voice with a foreign accent whisper:

" 'Help, my lord. For pity's sake help me.'

"I immediately thought of the cry, 'Down with the Englishman,' which I had heard before. This must be the man who had been thrown in the water. I grasped the man, who was shivering with cold and dripping with water, and led him into my library. By the light of the lamp I saw he was about thirty years old.

" 'You have rescued me, sir,' he said in a soft voice, with a peculiar accent, 'but you will not find me ungrateful.'

" 'Who are you, and what am I to do for you?' I asked him.

" 'I was thought to be an English spy in the service of the royalists,' he said, laughing sorrowfully, 'and the excited crowd threw me into the river. Fortunately, I did not lose my senses; I dived under, swam a short distance and then gained the bank.'

" 'Then you are not an Englishman?' I asked.

" 'I, an Englishman?' he repeated, with his eyes sparkling with rage, 'what are you thinking of?'

" 'But who then are you?' I exclaimed.

"He looked searchingly at me.

" 'You are young,' he then said, 'you do not know what betrayal is; I will confide in you! Besides, you are a Frenchman, and hate the English as I do. Tell me where is the Emperor Napoleon at present?'

" 'In Paris.'

" 'Are you sure?'

" 'Positive.'

" 'You love the emperor?'

" 'I am his faithful servant.'

" 'Thank Heaven. Would you assist me to reach Paris?'

" 'Paris?' I repeated in astonishment.

" 'Yes, I must reach the capital as soon as possible. I must rescue the emperor.'

" 'The roads are not safe,' I hesitatingly replied, 'and if you have no passport——'

" 'You are an official,' he interrupted me, 'perhaps a judge?'

" 'I am what is called in England attorney for the crown.'

" 'Ah, in England there are no judges,' he violently said. 'In England are only hangmen! Thank God I am in France; and my ancestors were French.'

" 'And your home?'

" 'Is the Orient, the land of the sun,' he said with emotion, as his eyes filled with tears. 'I am an Indian prince.'

" 'That is the reason you hate England!' I suddenly exclaimed, as a light dawned on me.

" 'Hate it! I curse it!' he said, in a choking voice. 'It is the home of traitors and murderers.'

" 'But did you not tell me a little while ago, that you were of French descent?'

" 'Yes, have you forgotten the names of those Frenchmen who fought so gloriously for India's independence? Dupleix, Labourdonnaye, and Lally came with an army to India; my father belonged to Lally's detachment, and fell on the 27th of October, 1803, in the battle of Laswari. During his stay in India, he married a Mahratta at Scindia's court. Two children resulted therefrom, a boy and a girl, and the son is the one you have rescued to-day.'

" 'Then you are really a Frenchman?'

" 'No; I call myself Mahratta; the blood of my mother betrays itself in my veins, for she was the daughter of a prince.'

" 'And her name?'

" 'I have almost forgotten it myself, as I was not permitted to pronounce it for such a long time. About five years ago Scindia began anew the strug-gle against English tyranny. We were defeated in the battle of Gwalior, and I and my sister Naya, a beautiful girl of fifteen, were taken prisoners by the English. For five years we suffered martyrdom; we were brought to England, and finally separated. About two months ago I managed to escape—I reached the coast, was taken on board a Spanish ship, and finally set foot on French ground. Paris is the place I desire to go to. Napoleon has promised us help if we assist him against the English. The whole of India will rise up and crush England, and Napoleon's throne will be secured forever.'

"The handsome youth stood before me like a prophet, and I enthusiasti-cally exclaimed:

" 'Whatever I can do to assist your plans shall be done. Tell me your name, and I will fill out your passport.'

" 'I am the Rajah Siwadji Daola,' he said.

" 'And your sister?' I asked; 'is she free, too?'

" 'No; but she will soon be so. A prince of the Mahratta's followed Naya to England; he loves her, and will soon bring her to France.'

" 'To France? Have they a place to go to here?' I eagerly asked.

" 'Let my sister and her husband find protection in your house,' he simply said, 'and the gods will reward you.'

"I hesitated for a moment, and then I cordially answered:

" 'Let it be as you say—my house shall be open to your sister!'

" 'A thousand thanks,' he joyfully cried. 'And so that you know my sister, look here.'

"He took out of his silk belt the half

of a peculiarly formed bracelet, and handed it to me with the words:

" 'Look at this bracelet! Whoever brings you the other half, receive in your house as a favor to me. I cannot leave the bracelet with you, but if you have a piece of wax I can make an impression which will answer the same purpose.'

"Wax was soon found, the broad gold plate, with its numerous hieroglyphics, was pressed in it, and after the impression had been secured, the rajah hid the bracelet in his belt.

" 'When can I get the pass?' he asked.

" 'To-morrow morning; what name shall I put in?'

" 'The name of my father—Jean d'Arras.'

"The rajah, upon my solicitation, threw himself on my bed and slept a few hours. As soon as the day dawned he left the house with me, enveloped in a wide mantle, and as we had no difficulty in getting the necessary passports from the prefecture, he was already that same morning on his way to Paris."

"Monsieur de Villefort," said d'Avigny, anxiously, "you are exerting yourself too much; postpone the continuation until to-morrow."

"No, no," replied Villefort, "I must speak to-day; to-morrow would be too late.

"Three months later Renee de St. Meran became my wife, the battle of Waterloo followed, and Napoleon was deposed forever. On the 6th of May, 1816, my wife gave birth to a child—a daughter. It was very sickly, though, and my mother-in-law feared it would not live until the next day. On the

night following the birth of the child I was sitting reading at my wife's wing side, when I heard my name being softly called from the direction of the garden. At first I thought I was mistaken, but the cry was repeated, and I quietly slipped out. Near the garden hedge lay a white form; the moon was shining brightly, and I saw a woman's face of extraordinary beauty. Giving vent to a low murmur of astonishment, I drew near to the figure; when I perceived the glistening eyes and the satiny dark curls, I no longer doubted but what the woman who lay before me was Naya, the sister of the Rajah Siwadji.

" 'You are Monsieur de Villefort?' she said, in a gentle voice.

" 'Yes, and you are Naya,' I said, to make sure.

" 'I am. My husband, the Rajah Duttjah, is dead. Save my child!'

"At these words the woman opened the white mantle which covered her, and I saw a new-born babe, which was wrapped up in a silk cloth. The poor mother looked anxiously at me. I took the child in my arms, and a happy smile passed over the pale face.

" 'Now I can die peacefully,' she whispered; 'my husband died as we were about to leave England—I felt myself a mother—I had to live. Night and day I have wandered. Barely two hours ago my child was born; I dragged myself up to the house, but my strength failed me—here—is—the—bracelet——'

"She paused suddenly—I bent over her—she was dead. From her cold hand I took the half of the gold bracelet, and ran into the house. My wife was fast asleep. I laid the child in the cradle near my little daughter, and just thinking whether I should call the nurse who slept in the next room, when I perceived that I had laid the living child next to a dead one. Our little daughter had breathed her last!

"I stood as if struck by lightning. All the proud hopes we had built on the child's birth were gone. Suddenly the strange child began to cry, and my plan was quickly made. With trembling hands I dressed the strange child —it was a girl, too—in the clothes of my own daughter, and gathering the silk cloth about the latter, I carried her to the garden and placed her in Naya's arms.

"One hour later my wife awoke, and when she asked for our child, I gave her Naya's daughter."

"Did not Madame de Villefort ever hear of the change which had been made?" asked the district attorney.

"Oh, yes; my wife had placed a small chain with a golden cross, around our child's neck, just after it was born; in my hurry I had forgotten to put this talisman on the strange child; I first denied, then confessed everything. Instead of heaping reproaches on me, she acquiesced in the fraud. The next day my father-in-law came; Naya's daughter was baptized under the name of Valentine de Villefort, and on the bed of the child, my happy parents-in-law laid my appointment as district attorney in Paris, and bonds to the value of three hundred thousand francs. Naya, with the dead child in her arms, was found the next day at our door. They were both buried in the potter's field. The papers Naya carried were written in the Indian language; they were given to me as a high official, and since then they, together with the wax impression

and the half of the bracelet, have lain in my private portfolio which always stands near my bed."

Upon a word from Villefort, Monsieur de Flambois opened the portfolio designated; everything was found there as he had said.

"Did you never hear again from Daola?" said d'Avigny after a pause.

"Yes; three years later the rajah wrote me from India. He had fought at Waterloo, was again a captive of the English, and only had an opportunity at the end of a year to escape. Together with the Rajah Scindia, who later went over to England, he had again begun the struggle for independence; he is now living in the interior of Hindoostan, waiting for a better opportunity. He asked me for news from Naya; I wrote him I knew nothing of her, and that ended our correspondence.

"This is my confession. Now use justice and erase from the headstone under which Naya's daughter rests the name of Valentine de Villefort."

"Suppose Valentine de Villefort is still alive?" asked d'Avigny solemnly.

Both Villefort and Monsieur de Flambois uttered a cry of astonishment, and while the latter stammered forth an "Impossible," the sick man whispered:

"To-day miracles do not occur any more!"

"Gentlemen," said the physician quietly, "you know I am a sensible man; why should I try to tell you a fable?"

"But I was at the funeral," stammered Flambois.

"I also, and yet I tell you the dead woman lives," persisted d'Avigny, "or if we want to call it by its proper name, Valentine de Villefort is dead and the daughter of Naya and the Rajah Duttjah lives."

"Then Valentine must have been buried alive," muttered Villefort, fixing his eyes upon the physician.

"And if that were the case?" said d'Avigny solemnly.

"Then I would say God has done a miracle to save the innocent," said Villefort, the tears starting in his eyes.

"Monsieur de Villefort," said the physician, earnestly, "do you know how Valentine died?"

"Too well—she was poisoned by my wife."

"What for?"

"Madame de Villefort wished to have Valentine's fortune go to her son."

"That is dastardly," said the district attorney.

"Do you remember, Monsieur de Villefort," continued d'Avigny, "to have seen a mysterious man in your house some time prior to Valentine's death, whose mission it appears is to reward the good and punish the guilty?"

"Yes, I remember; you mean the Count of Monte-Cristo," said Villefort, with emotion.

"The Count of Monte-Cristo," repeated the district attorney, contemptuously, "the adventurer?"

"Sir, do not blaspheme!" exclaimed Villefort, passionately, "if Valentine is saved she owes it to that God in the form of man—the Count of Monte-Cristo! He alone has the power to change the dead into the living; if Valentine lives, I will believe God has pardoned a portion of my sins."

"Gentlemen," said the district attorney, doubtingly, "I only believe what

I see; if Valentine de Villefort lives, let her show herself."

"Maximilian," called d'Avigny, opening the door, "tell Valentine to come in."

"Whom did you just call?" asked Villefort, when d'Avigny had closed the door again.

"Maximilian Morrel, Valentine's betrothed, the son of the shipping merchant Morrel, of Marseilles."

"Morrel — Marseilles — E d m o n d Dantès," murmured Villefort. "Ah, there is justice in Heaven!"

The door was now opened, and Valentine entered. She strode to Villefort's bed and sank on her knees beside it.

"Oh, father," she sobbed, embracing him tenderly. "Thank God, I see you again!"

Villefort gazed at Valentine as if she were a specter; but tears fell on the young girl's cheeks, and his lean hands were crossed as if in prayer.

"Father, dearly beloved father!" stammered Valentine, weepingly, "why do you not speak? Have you no word of welcome for your Valentine?"

"Monsieur de Flambois, do you still doubt?" asked d'Avigny, softly.

"Yes, not your statement, but my reason," said the district attorney, wiping the tears from his eyes.

"Valentine," whispered Villefort, in a broken voice, "kiss me. Now I can die easy."

"Oh, father, father, you must not die!" she weepingly cried.

"I must, darling, but I die happy since I know you will be well taken care of. Monsieur Morrel," he said, turning to the young man, "you know what unhappiness I once caused your father?"

"No, Monsieur de Villefort, I have forgotten everything, and only know that you are Valentine's father," said Maximilian, cordially. "Give us your blessing."

"No, no!" said Villefort, anxiously; "I dare not—I am not worthy of it! But one thing I can do; I can tell Valentine who she is, and Monsieur de Flambois and Monsieur d'Avigny will corroborate my words. Valentine, you, whom I have so often called daughter, look at me and listen to my words: you are the daughter of the Rajah Duttjah and his wife Naya. The marriage of your parents was celebrated at Epping Forest by a Brahmin, who was also a prisoner there; in the folio there you will find the paper relating to the marriage. Do not look at me so fearfully, my poor darling, I am speaking the truth, and these gentlemen will tell you later on all the details. Your parents are both dead. There is a letter in the portfolio from your mother's brother, the Rajah Siwadji Daola. It was written in 1818. If Daola still lives, he will find out that I deceived him; that I saw his sister die, and that Naya's child still lives."

"But, father," said Valentine, pas-sionately, "if my parents are both dead, and you brought me up, I am never-theless your daughter."

"Thanks, Valentine. But before my strength gives way, I must perform another duty. Doctor, a glass of wine, I have one more favor to ask of Valen-tine."

D'Avigny poured out a glass of red wine for Monsieur de Villefort, and Valentine put her arm around the dy-ing man's neck, and rested his head against her bosom.

"I want you to look after my son, Valentine," whispered Villefort. "Oh, what would I not give if I could wear the chains instead of him—what is death to the life led by a galley-slave? If it is in your power to do anything for Benedetto, do not fail to do it. He is a scoundrel, but I was the cause of his downfall. Have mercy on him, and I die peacefully!"

"Father," said Valentine, solemnly, "your wish shall be sacred to me. I shall go in search of Benedetto, and bring him your last wishes."

"You are—an—angel," stammered Villefort. "Farewell, Ah — this — is death!"

A shiver ran through Villefort's bones —a deep groan—a long breath—he was dead.

Vindication

IN THE same year were successively produced at the Théâtre-Historique the Queen Margot, Intrigue et Amour, Les Girondins, and Monte-Cristo in two nights' performances. The reader will recall, no doubt, the famous song of the Girondists—Mourir pour la patrie; the day it was rehearsed for the first time, I observed to the leader of the orchestra—

"And to think, my dear Varney, that the next Revolution will be made to that tune!"

As a matter of fact the Revolution

of 1848 *was* made to the air I had foretold.

While rejoiced to see the principles I have upheld all my life triumphing, while taking a personal part in the Revolution of 1848 almost as active as I had in that of 1830, I was yet sore and grieved at heart.

The political cataclysm, while bringing in new men who were my friends, yet removed others who likewise held a place in my affections. I had a brief and momentary hope that a Regency might be thrown as a connecting bridge between the Monarchy and the Republic. But the revolutionary avalanche was precipitated with irresistible violence; it swept away with it, not only the old King, not only the four Princes, his stay and support, but even the mourning mother and the weakly child, who knew neither what this tempestuous blast was, nor whence it came, nor whither it was carrying him.

There came a moment in the history of France when nothing stood where once it had, when the place where for seven centuries had risen the throne of the Capets, the Valois, the Bourbons, was mowed as smooth as in September is the plain where a week before the harvest was still waving.

Then France gave a great cry, half of amazement, half of distress; she knew no longer where she was, searching vainly with startled eyes for what she was used to see. She called to her help the most intelligent of her sons, and told them: "See what my people have done in a fit of passion; perhaps they have gone too far, but at any rate what is done is done. In this empty place, which terrifies me by its emptiness, build me up something on which

may rest the foundations of society, public wealth, morality, and religion."

I had been one of the first to hear this appeal of my Country, and I held I had a right to count myself in the number of the men of intelligence she was summoning to her aid.

It only remained to decide to what Department I should go and offer myself for election.

It seemed simple enough to address myself to my native Department, that of the Aisne. But I had ceased to reside in it in 1823. I had scarcely ever returned there since, while one of the few occasions I had done so was to carry out that famous expedition of Soissons which the reader knows of, if he has ever read my Memoirs, in which I came very near being shot.

But, although it was for the same cause I was fighting, whether in 1830 or in 1848, I feared I might be looked upon as too ardent a Republican for the Republic such as the majority of the electors wished to see it, and I gave up all thoughts of standing for the Department of the Aisne.

Then right before my eyes was the Department of the Seine-et-Oise, where I had been living for the last four or five years. I had even held in it the eminent position of Chief of Battalion of the National Guard of Saint-Germain. But, inasmuch as, during the three days of the Revolution of 1848, I had had the drums beaten and an appeal made to the seven hundred and thirty men of my command to follow me to Paris and intervene forcibly in the struggle, the wives, children, fathers, and mothers of my seven hundred and thirty National Guards, making a grand total of perhaps three thousand individuals, had all protested with one voice against the recklessness with which I was for endangering the lives of my men. So at the mere suspicion that I might possibly offer myself for election in their town, the good folk of Saint-Germain had uttered a universal cry of alarm and indignation. More than that, they had assembled in general committee and resolved that I should be invited to give in my resignation as Commander of the National Guard for having compromised myself so unjustifiably during the three days of revolutionary disturbance.

You see they understood the question of national representation and the oath of fidelity to the Republic in pretty much the same sense in the Department of the Seine-et-Oise as in that of the Aisne.

Things were in this state when a young man, to whose family I had rendered some services and who had connections, he told me, in Lower Burgundy, assured me that, were I to offer myself in the Department of the Yonne, I could not fail to be elected. Now I am bursting with a genial simplicity which ill-natured people call self-conceit. Call it simplicity or self-conceit, whichever you please, the result was the same. I imagined myself well enough known even in the Department of the Yonne to out-distance any competitors that might be set up against me. Poor simpleton that I was! I quite forgot the fact that every Department makes a point of having *local* men to represent it, and, alas! my *locality* was the Department of the Aisne. Accordingly, hardly had I set foot in the Department of the Yonne before the journals of all the *localities* rose

up in arms against me. What business had I in the Department of the Yonne? Was I a Burgundian? Was I in the wine trade? Had I any vineyards? Had I ever studied the question of vine-growing? Was I a member of the *Société Œnophile?* So I had no Department, it seemed, of my own; I was a sort of political bastard. Or rather no, I was none of these things; I was an agent of the Orléanists, and was offering myself, simultaneously with M. Gaillardet, my collaborator on the *Tour de Nesle,* as a candidate of the Regency party.

Needless to say, the men who had invented and disseminated this fine story did not believe one single word of it themselves.

True, I had been injudicious enough, it must be owned, to give some excuse for these statements on the occasion of the Orléans Princes leaving the country. Instead of abusing, insulting, and black-guarding them like the men who, a week before, were dancing attendance in their anterooms, *I,* on March 4, 1848,—that is to say, seven days after the revolution of February, in the midst of the popular excitement which filled the streets of Paris with noise and clamour,—I had written the following letter in the columns of *La Presse,* one of the most generally read newspapers of that day:—

"To Monseigneur le Duc de Montpensier

"PRINCE,—If I knew where to find your Highness, it would be with my own lips, it would be face to face, that I should offer you the expression of my sorrow at the catastrophe that overwhelms you as well as others.

"I can never forget how, for three

years, in defiance of all political ties, and contrary to the King's wishes, who was aware of the opinions I held, you were pleased to receive me and treat me almost as a personal friend.

"This title of *friend*, Monseigneur, when you lived at the Tuileries, I was proud of; to-day, when you have left the country, I claim it still.

"However, Monseigneur, your Highness, I am convinced, had no need of this letter of mine to be assured that my heart was of those that are his for all time.

"God forbid I should fail to preserve in all its purity the religion of the tomb and the worship and respect of fallen greatness.

"I have the honour to be, with deep respect, your Royal Highness's most obedient and most humble servant,

"ALEX. DUMAS."

Nor was this all; indeed, I must surely have been bitten by that devil of contradiction which lives in me, and is even more powerful than that other devil of pride. The celebrated Colonel Desmoulins, Commandant of the Louvre, having deemed it proper to throw down the equestrian statue of the Duc d'Orléans which stood in the courtyard of the Louvre, I returned home in a furious passion, and wrote to M. de Girardin the letter given below. The individual for whom it was really intended was plain enough, and it could hardly fail—at least, so I firmly believed—to procure me the pleasure of cutting throats with the Colonel first thing next morning. It ran as follows:—

"MY DEAR GIRARDIN,—Yesterday, as I crossed the courtyard of the Louvre,

I saw with astonishment that the statue of the Duc d'Orléans was no longer on its pedestal.

"I asked if it was the people of Paris that had thrown it down; I was informed it was the Governor of the Louvre who had ordered its removal.

"Why is this? Whence this proscription that violates the tombs of the dead?

"When the Duke was alive, whatever constituted in France the advanced section of the Nation had based its hopes on him.

"And it was but justice; for, as every one knows, the Duc d'Orléans was in constant opposition to the King, and he was the victim of a veritable disgrace in consequence of his pronouncement in open council: 'Sire, I had rather be slain on the banks of the Rhine than in a gutter of the Rue Saint-Denis!'

"The people, the French people, that is always just and intelligent, knew and understood this as well as we. Go to the Tuileries and see for yourself which are the only apartments respected by the people: they are those once occupied by the Duc d'Orléans. Why, then, be more severe than the people have been towards this poor Prince, who has the good fortune to belong henceforth only to History?

"The future—the future is the block of marble that events may hew at their pleasure and caprice; the past is the statue of bronze cast into the mould of eternity.

"You cannot annihilate the past. You cannot abolish the fact that the Duc d'Orléans, at the head of the French columns, carried the Col de Mouzaïa. You cannot abolish the fact that for ten years he has given the third part of his civil list to the poor. You cannot abolish the fact that he has repeatedly asked mercy for men condemned to death, and by dint of urgent prayers has won their pardon in several instances. If we can to-day clasp the hand of Barbès, to whom do we owe that bliss? To the Duc d'Orléans!

"Ask the artists who followed his coffin to the grave; summon the chiefest among them—Ingres, Delacroix, Scheffer, Gudin, Barye, Marochetti, Calamatta, Boulanger.

"Call to witness the poets and historians: Hugo, Thierry, Lamartine, de Vigny, Michelet, myself, any others you please—ask them, ask us, if we deem it well his statue should be replaced where once it stood. And with one voice we shall tell you: 'Yes; for it was raised at once to a Prince, a soldier, an artist, to the great and enlightened soul that has gone to the skies, to the noble and kindly heart that has been laid in the earth.'

"The Republic of 1848 is strong enough, believe me, to consecrate this sublime anomaly of a Prince left standing on his pedestal, in face of a Royalty falling from his throne.

"ALEX. DUMAS."

The journals which accused me of being a *Regentist* candidate may well have done so in all good faith, for I had indeed done all I could to make the exiled family, now that it was in power no longer, believe I was a *Regentist*, as I had done, when it was in power, whatever I could to persuade its members I was a Republican.

Let me try to explain the contradiction to any who will waste their time in reading what I write.

Compounded of two elements, aristocratic and popular,—the former on my father's side, the latter on my mother's, —no one unites to a higher degree than myself in a single heart at once a respectful admiration of all that is great and noble and a tender and profound sympathy with all that is unfortunate. I have never spoken so much of the Napoleon family as under the younger branch of the Royal Family; I have never spoken so much of the Prince of the younger branch as under the Republic and the Empire. I am a faithful worshipper of those whom I have known and loved in adversity, and I only forget them if they become powerful and prosperous. So no fallen greatness passes before me but I salute it, no merit stretches forth its hand to me but I clasp it. It is when all the rest of the world seems to have forgotten those who are no more in place and power that, like an obstinate echo of the past, I proclaim their name aloud. Why? I cannot say. It is the voice of my heart that awakes suddenly and impulsively, apart altogether from my mind and will. I have written a thousand volumes, composed sixty plays. Open them at random,—at the first page, in the middle, at the end,— you will see I have always advocated clemency, whether peoples were the slaves of kings or whether kings were the prisoners of peoples.

Thus, it is a noble and lowly family I have gathered round me, such as no one has but myself. The moment a man falls, I go to him, I hold out my hand to him, let him be called the Comte de Chambord or the Prince de Joinville, Louis Napoléon or Louis Blanc. Through whom did I learn the death of the Duc d'Orléans? Through

Prince Jérôme Napoléon. Instead of paying my court at the Tuileries to those in power, I was at Florence offering my sympathy to the exile. True, I instantly left the exile to seek the dead, and started on a journey of five hundred leagues, to meet, in spite of my very sincere tears of mourning, a Royal rebuff at Dreux—fit pendant to that which awaited me at Claremont, when, after having followed out of affection the funeral of the son, I thought propriety demanded I should attend the father to the grave.

On the eve of July 13 I was the declared enemy of M. Ledru-Rollin, whom I was in the habit of attacking daily in my journal Le Mois; on July 14 M. Ledru-Rollin sent me word to have no further anxiety—that he was in safety.

This is why I am more often a visitor to prisons than to palaces; this is why I have been thrice to Ham, once only to the Elysée, never to the Tuileries.

Naturally, I had not vouchsafed all these explanations to the electors of the Yonne; so, when I entered the great hall of the Club, where three thousand persons awaited me, I was received with sounds that betokened anything but friendliness.

At that critical moment a coarse insult was launched at me. Unluckily for the individual who took this liberty, he was within reach of my hand. The gesture with which I answered him was striking enough to leave no one present in doubt as to its nature. Groans changed to yells, and it was amid a perfect hurricane of protest I mounted the tribune to speak.

The first question asked me was a demand for explanations of my fanati-cal attitude with regard to the Duc d'Orléans. This was taking the bull by the horns indeed. But for once the bull proved the stronger. I made them all feel shame—some for their forgetfulness, the rest for their ingratitude. I reminded them of the cry of universal sorrow that rose, on July 13, 1842, from the heart of thirty million Frenchmen, and brought me, five hundred leagues away, the fatal news. I pictured the poor Prince, young, handsome, gallant, graceful, artistic, a Frenchman to the finger-tips, a patriot if ever there was one. I spoke of Antwerp, the Col de Mouzaïa, the Portes-de-Fer, the respite of Bruyant the huzzar, granted at my instance, the pardon of Barbès, accorded to Victor Hugo's prayers. I repeated some of his sayings, so full of wit they might have fallen from the lips of Henri IV; others so replete with genial kindliness they could only have come from his own heart. The end was that in a quarter of an hour half my audience were in tears—and I with them; in twenty minutes, the whole room was clapping hands; and from that evening forth I possessed not merely three thousand votes but three thousand friends.

What has become of these three thousand friends whose names I never knew? God knows! They are scattered, each carrying away in his heart the precious bit of gold we call a kindly memory. Two or three only have survived from this great shipwreck of time, which will end by engulfing these likewise, and me with them; but these not only have remained friends, but have become brothers—brothers in friendship, brothers in St. Hubert's mysteries.

Madame Dubarry

In the suite of rooms at Versailles which Madame Adelaide, daughter of Louis XV., had once occupied, his majesty had installed his mistress, the Countess Dubarry, not without keenly studying beforehand the effect which this piece of policy would produce on his court. The favourite, with her merry whims and her careless, joyous humour, had transformed that wing of the palace, formerly so quiet, into a scene of perpetual merriment and tumult; and every hour she issued thence her commands for a banquet or a party of pleasure.

But what happened still more unusual on these magnificent staircases was the never-ceasing stream of visitors ascending them, and crowding an antechamber filled with curiosities from all parts of the globe,—certainly containing nothing so curious as the idol worshipped by this crowd.

At her accustomed hour, nine in the morning, Jeanne de Vaubernier, dressed in a muslin embroidered robe which disclosed through its gauzy texture her rounded limbs and alabaster arms,—Jeanne de Vaubernier, afterwards Mademoiselle Lange and then Countess Dubarry by the grace of Jean Dubarry, her former protector, rose from her bed, we will not say like to Venus, but surely more beautiful than Venus to the eyes of a man who prefers the real to the ideal.

Her blond hair, artistically dressed, a skin of white satin with blue veins, eyes in turn languishing and spiritual, a small mouth pencilled with purest carmine, and which when opened disclosed to view a double row of pearls, dimpled cheeks, chin and fingers and a throat like that of the Venus de Milo, the suppleness of an adder, and perfectly developed breasts,—thus behold Madame Dubarry about to disclose these charms to the chosen one at her little levee.

Thus behold what his Majesty Louis XV., the chosen one for the night longed for. For some time the favourite had been awake. At eight o'clock she had allowed the sunlight, her first courtier, to enter the chamber little by little.

There was no sign of drowsiness in the eyes, bright as carbuncles, which laughingly questioned a small handglass with a gold rim studded with pearls.

The supple body which we have tried to describe glided from the bed where it had reposed, lulled by sweet dreams, to the ermine rug, where feet of which Cinderella would not have been ashamed touched hands holding two slippers, one of which would have made a woodman in Jeanne's native forest rich for life.

As the seductive form arose, becoming more and more alive, an attendant threw over it a superb wrap of Malines lace, while upon the rounded feet, taken from the slippers for a moment, were placed silk stockings of a texture so fine that it would have been hard to distinguish it from the skin they covered. Her day was a day of calm waiting. The king's was one of vexatious killing of time.

Louis XV. had left the palace and sought something to please the eye. He seated himself on a mossy bank, from which the view before him was charming.

There lay the little lake, with its velvet slopes of turf; beyond it a village nestled between two hills; further off, the towers of Saint Germain, with their wooded terraces, and further still the blue declivities of Saunois and Cormeilles; whilst, above all this, the grey and rose-tinged sky hung like a magnificent cupola. The weather had been stormy, and the foliage of the trees looked dark and heavy against the pale green of the meadows; the waters of the lake, glassy and immovable as a vast surface of oil, were disturbed from time to time by some silvery flashing fish springing up to seize the unwary fly, and chequering it with widespreading circles of alternate black and white. At the margin might be perceived the enormous snouts of a number of fish, which, fearless of hook or net, sucked the leaves of pendent plants, and with their huge fixed eyes, which semed incapable of sight, stared at the grey lizards and green frogs sporting among the bulrushes.

When the king, like a man profoundly skilled in the art of killing time, had looked at the landscape on all sides, when he had counted the houses in the village and the villages in the distance, he took a plate with the loaf, placed it beside him, and began to cut off large pieces of the bread.

The carp heard the sound of the knife in the crust, and accustomed to that noise, which announced their dinner hour, they immediately flocked as close as possible to the bank, to show themselves to his Majesty and solicit their daily meal. They would have done the same for any footman in his service, but the king naturally thought that all this trouble was for him alone.

He threw in one after another the pieces of bread, which first disappearing for an instant, and then returning to the surface, were contended for some time, then, gradually crumbling away by the action of the water, were seized and seen no more. It was indeed a curious and amusing enough sight to see all these crusts pushed thither by the invisible snouts, and tossed on the surface of the water, until the moment when they were swallowed.

At the end of about half an hour, his Majesty, having in that time patiently cut one hundred bits of crust, had the satisfaction of seeing that not one remained floating. He began now, however, to feel rather tired of the sport, and he remembered that Monsieur Boucher might amuse him a little; he would not certainly be as good a resource as the carp, but in the country we must take what we can get.

Louis, therefore, turned towards the summer-house. Boucher had heard that he was at Luciennes, and though he went on painting, or seeming to paint, he followed the king with his eyes, saw him turn in the direction of the summer-house, and radiant with joy, he adjusted his ruffles and mounted on his ladder; for he had been warned not to appear to know that the king was there. He heard a step on the floor of the room, and began to daub a fat Cupid stealing a rose from a shepherdess in a blue satin gown and straw hat. His hand trembled, his heart beat. The king stopped on the threshold.

"Ah, Boucher," cried he; "how you smell of turpentine!" and he walked on

Poor Boucher, although he knew the king had no taste for the fine arts, did expect some other kind of compliment, and was nearly falling from his ladder. He came down and went away with the tears in his eyes, without scraping his pallet or washing his brushes, which, in general, he was so careful to do.

His Majesty pulled out his watch; it was seven o'clock.

Louis returned to the house, teased the monkey, made the parrot speak, pulled out all the drawers of the cabinets, one after the other, and ransacked their contents.

Evening drew on. The king was not fond of darkness, and the apartments were lighted up. But he did not like solitude either.

"My horses in a quarter of an hour!" said he. "*Ma foi!*" added he, "I shall just give her one quarter of an hour; not a minute longer."

As he said this, he stretched himself on a sofa opposite the fireplace, to watch the course of the fifteen minutes, that is, of nine hundred seconds. At the four hundredth beat of the timepiece, which represented a blue elephant carrying a pink sultana, he was asleep.

As may be supposed, the footman who came to announce his Majesty's carriage took care not to awake him. The result of this attention to his august slumber was that when he awoke of his own accord, he found himself face to face with the Countess Dubarry, who was looking at him with her eyes wide open. Zamore, the little negro slave, stood in a corner waiting for orders.

"Ah! you are here at last, countess," said the king, sitting up on the sofa.

"Yes, sire, here I am," said the coun-

tess; "and here I have been a pretty long time."

"Oh! a pretty long time?"

"An hour and a half at least. But how your Majesty does sleep!"

"Faith, countess, you were not here, and I was getting shockingly tired; and then I sleep so badly at night. Do you know, I was on the point of going away!"

"Yes, I saw your Majesty's carriage at the door."

The king looked at his watch.

"Half-past ten; then I have slept nearly three hours!"

"After that, sire, say that you cannot sleep well at Luciennes!"

"Oh, faith, very well; but what the devil do I see there?" said he, looking at Zamore.

"You see the governor of Luciennes, sire."

"Not yet, not yet," said the king, laughing. "The little wretch has put on his uniform before having been appointed; he reckons on my word, then!"

"Sire, your word is sacred, and he is right in reckoning on it. But Zamore has something more than your word, or rather something less,—he has his commission; the vice-chancellor sent it to me. The oath is now the only formality which is wanting; make him swear quickly, and then betake himself to his post."

"Approach, governor," said the king. Zamore came forward. He was dressed in a uniform, with an embroidered collar and a captain's epaulets, with short breeches, silk stockings, and a sword like a spit. He walked with a stiff, measured step, an enormous three-cornered hat under his arm.

"Can he swear?" asked the king.

"Oh, yes, sire; try him."

"Advance," cried he, looking curiously at the black puppet.

"On your knees!" said the countess.

"Swear!" said the king.

The child placed one hand on his heart, the other in the king's hand, and said, "I swear fealty and homage to my master and mistress; I swear to defend to the death the castle in my keeping, and to eat the last pot of sweetmeats rather than surrender, should I be attacked."

The king laughed as much at the form of the oath as at the gravity with which Zamore pronounced it.

"In return for this oath," he replied, with suitable gravity, "I confer on you the sovereign rights of justice on high and low, on all inhabiting air, earth, fire, and water, in this castle."

"Thank you, master," said Zamore, rising.

"And now," said the king, "go and show off your fine clothes in the kitchens, and leave us alone; go!"

As Zamore went out at one door, Chon, sister of Mme. Dubarry, entered by another.

"Ah, and you there, too, my little Chon! Come, I shall hear the truth from you."

"Take care, sire, that you are not disappointed in your expectations!" said Chon; "the truth is, it would be for the first time in my life. If you wish to learn the truth, apply to my sister; she is incapable of speaking falsely."

"Is that true, countess?"

"Sire, Chon has too flattering an opinion of me. Bad example has ruined me; and from this evening forth I am determined to lie like a real countess, if the truth will not serve me."

"Oh, ho!" said the king; "I suspect Chon has something to conceal from me. I must get from the police a report of what has occurred to-day."

"From which police, sire,—Sartines' or mine?"

"Oh, from Sartines', the Minister."

"What will you pay him for it?"

"If he tell me anything worth hearing, I shall not be niggardly."

"Well, then, give my police the preference, and take my report. I shall serve you—royally."

"You will even sell your own secrets?"

"Why not, if I am well paid?"

"Come, then, let me hear the report,—but no fibs, remember!"

"Sire, you insult me."

"I mean, no equivocations."

"Well, sire, get your funds ready; I am about to begin my report."

"They are ready," said the king, jingling some money in his pocket.

"In the first place, the Countess Dubarry was seen in Paris, in the Rue de Valois, about two o'clock in the afternoon."

"Well, I know that; go on!"

"About six o'clock Zamore proceeded to join her there."

"Very possibly; but what did Madame Dubarry go to Paris for?"

"Sire, to meet the lady who is to present her."

"Pooh!" said the king, with a grimace which he could not altogether conceal; "she is very well as she is, without being presented."

"You know the proverb, sire: 'Nothing is so dear to us as that which we have not.'"

"So she is absolutely determined to find this lady to present her?"

"We have found her, sire."

The king started, and shrugged his shoulders.

"I like that movement, sire; it shows that your Majesty would be annoyed at the defeat of the Grammonts, the Guéménées, and all the hypocrites of the court," said the countess.

"I beg your pardon; did you speak?"

"Yes, I am sure you are in league with those persons."

"In league? Countess, learn one thing, that the king only leagues with kings."

"True, but all your kings are friends of the Duke de Choiseul."

"Let us return to your chaperon, countess."

"With all my heart, sire."

"You have succeeded in manufacturing a lady, then?"

"I found one ready made, and very well made,—a Countess de Béarn; a family who have numbered princes in their ranks. She will not dishonour the relative of the relatives of the Stuarts, I hope!"

"The Countess de Béarn!" exclaimed the king, with surprise. "I know only of one, who lives somewhere near Verdun."

"It is the very same; she has come to Paris on purpose to present me."

"Ha! and when is the affair to take place?"

"To-morrow, at eleven o'clock in the morning, I am to give her a private audience, and at the same time, if it be not too presumptuous, she will request the king to name a day; and you will name the earliest, will you not, dear France?"

The king burst into a forced laugh.

"Certainly, certainly," said he, kissing the countess's hand. Then, all at once, "To-morrow, at eleven?" added he.

"Yes, at breakfast."

"Impossible, my dear countess."

"Impossible!—why?"

"I shall not breakfast here; I must return this evening."

"What!" said the countess, who felt an icy pang shoot through her heart at these words; "you are going to leave us, sire?"

"I am forced to do so, dear countess; I have to meet Sartines on very important business."

"As you please, sire; but you will at least sup here, I hope?"

"Oh, yes, I shall sup, I think; yes, I am rather hungry,—I shall sup."

"Order supper, Chon," said the countess, making at the same time a private signal to her, which no doubt referred to some previous arrangements. Chon left the room. The king had seen the signal in a mirror, and although he could not comprehend its meaning, he suspected some snare.

"Ah!" said he, "on second thoughts I think it will be impossible to stay even for supper. I must not lose a moment; I have some papers to sign,—to-day is Saturday."

"As you please, sire; shall I order the horses?"

"Yes, fairest."

"Chon!"

Chon re-appeared.

"His Majesty's horses!" said the countess.

"Very well," said Chon with a smile, and she left the room again.

A moment afterwards her voice was heard in the ante-room, ordering the king's carriage.

The king, delighted at this exercise of his authority, which punished the countess for leaving him alone so long, at the same time that it freed him from the trouble of settling the affair of her presentation, walked towards the door of the salon.

Chon, sister of Mme. Dubarry, entered.

"Well, are my attendants there?"

"No, sire, there is not one of them in the ante-room."

The king advanced into the ante-room himself. "My attendants!" cried he. No one answered; there seemed not to be even an echo in the silent château.

"Who the devil would believe," said the king, returning to the salon, "that I am the grandson of the man who once said, 'I was very near having to wait'?" and he went to a window, opened it, and looked out.

The space in front of the château was as deserted as the ante-rooms; no horses, no attendants, no guards. Night alone displayed to the eyes and to the soul all its calmness and all its majesty. The lovely moon shone brightly on the woods of Chatou, whose lofty summits rustled gently like the waves of the sea rippled by a breeze. The Seine, on whose bosom glittered a long line of light, looked like a gigantic serpent trailing its slow slength along, its windings being visible from Bougival to Maisons, that is, for four or five leagues; and then, in the midst of this heavenly scene, a nightingale burst forth with such a sweet and varied song as she only gives in the month of May, as if she felt that nature was worthy of her music in the early days of spring alone,

—days which are scarcely come ere they are gone.

All this beauty and harmony were lost on Louis XV.,—a king not much of a dreamer, a poet, or an artist, but, on the contrary, a good deal of a sensualist.

"Come, countess!" said he, considerably annoyed, "give the necessary orders, I entreat; what the deuce!—this jest must have an end."

"Sire," replied the countess, with that charming pouting air which became her so well, "I do not command here."

"Nor do I," replied the king, "for you see how I am obeyed."

"It is neither you nor I who command."

"Who is it, then? Is it you, Chon?"

"I?" said the young lady, who was seated on a couch on the other side of the apartment exactly opposite the countess, who occupied a similar one on the near side; "I find the task of obeying so difficult that I have no inclination for that of commanding."

"But who is the master, then?"

"The governor, sire, certainly."

"Monsieur Zamore?"

"Yes."

"Ah, very true! Well, let some one ring for him."

The countess stretched out her arm with a most graceful air of nonchalance to a silken cord ending in a tassel of beads. A footman, who had no doubt received his lesson beforehand, was ready in the ante-room and appeared.

"The governor," said the king.

"The governor," replied the valet, respectfully, "is on guard, watching over his Majesty's precious life."

"Where is he?"

"Going his rounds, sire."

"Going his rounds?" repeated the king.

"Yes, with four officers, sire."

The king could not help smiling.

"That is droll enough," said he; "but it need not prevent my horses from being harnessed immediately."

"Sire, the governor ordered the stables to be closed, lest some marauder might enter them."

"And where are my grooms?"

"Gone to bed, sire."

"Gone to bed!—by whose orders?"

"The governor's, sire."

"And the gates of the castle?"

"Are locked, sire."

"Very well; then you must get the keys."

"The governor has them at his belt, sire."

"A well-guarded castle indeed! *Peste!* what order is kept!"

The footman, seeing that the king ceased to question him, retired. The countess reclining gracefully on a couch, continued to bite off the leaves of a beautiful rose, beside which her lips seemed like coral. "Come, sire," said she at length, with a fascinating smile, "I must take compassion on your Majesty; give me your arm and let us set out in search of some one to help you. Chon, light the way."

Chon went before, ready to apprise them of any dangers which they might encounter. At the very first turn in the corridor the king's nose was saluted by an odour quite sufficient to awaken the appetite of the most fastidious epicure.

"Ah, ha! what is that, countess?" said he, stopping.

"Oh, only supper, sire! I thought your Majesty intended doing me the honour of supping at Luciennes, and I made arrangements accordingly."

The king inhaled the gastronomic perfume two or three times, whilst he called to mind that his stomach had already given him certain tokens of its existence; then he thought what a fuss there must be before his grooms could be awakened; that would take half an hour at least; a quarter more to harness the horses; ten minutes to reach Marly, and when at Marly, where he was not expected, he should only get a put-off of a supper. All these things passed through his mind as he stood at the dining-room door, inhaling the seductive steam of the viands. Two covers were placed on the table, which was splendidly lighted and sumptuously laid out.

"*Peste!*" said Louis, "you have a good cook, countess."

"Oh, sire, this is merely his first effort; the poor devil has been doing wonders to deserve your Majesty's approbation. Indeed, he is so sensitive that he might, perhaps, in his disappointment, cut his throat, as poor Vatel did."

"Really, do you think so?"

"There was to be an omelet of pheasants' eggs, on which he especially prided himself."

"An omelet of pheasants' eggs? I adore omelets of pheasants' eggs."

"What a pity you must go!"

"Well countess, we must not vex your cook," said the king, laughing; "and perhaps, whilst we are supping, Master Zamore may return from his rounds."

"Ah! sire, a capital idea," said the countess, unable to conceal her delight at having gained this first step. "Come, sire, come!"

"But who will wait on us?" said the king, looking round in vain for an attendant.

"Ah! sire," said Madame Dubarry, "is your coffee less grateful when presented to you by me?"

"No, countess; and still more when you make it for me."

"Well, come then, sire."

"Two covers only! Has Chon supped, then?"

"Sire, I did not venture, without your Majesty's express command—"

"Come, come," said the king, taking a plate and cover from a sideboard himself, "come, my little Chon; sit there opposite us."

"Oh, sire!" said Chon.

"Yes, yes! play the very humble and very obedient subject, you little hypocrite. Sit here, countess, near me—beside me. What a beautiful profile you have!"

"Is this the first time you have observed it, dear France?"

"How should I observe it, when I am so happy in looking at your full countenance? Decidedly, countess, your cook is first-rate. What soup!"

"Then I was right in sending away the other?"

"Quite right, quite right."

"Sire, follow my example; you see it will be to your advantage."

"I do not understand you."

"I have turned off my Choiseul; turn off yours."

"Countess, no politics. Give me some madeira."

The king held out his glass: the countess took up a decanter to help him, and as she raised it up, her white fingers and rosy nails were seen to advantage.

"Pour gently and slowly," said the king.

"Not to shake the wine, sire?"

"No, to give me more time to admire your hand."

"Assuredly, sire," said the countess, laughing; "your Majesty is in the vein of making discoveries!"

"Faith, yes," said the king, now in perfect good-humour again, "and think I am in the fair way of discovering—"

"A new world?"

"No, I am not so ambitious; besides, I find a kingdom as much as I can manage. No, only an isle,—a little nook, an enchanted mountain, a palace of which a certain fair lady will be the Armida, and the entrance to which will be defended by all kinds of monsters."

"Sire," said the countess, presenting the king with a glass of iced champagne, a luxury quite new at that period, "here is some water just drawn from the river Lethe."

"The river Lethe, countess? Are you sure?"

"Yes, sire; it was poor Jean who brought it from the shades below, from which you know he has just narrowly escaped."

"Countess, I drink to his happy resurrection. But no politics, I beg."

"Then I don't know what to talk about, sire. If you would relate something,—you, who have such a happy gift of telling a story."

"No, but I shall repeat you some verses."

"Verses?"

"Yes, verses. Is there anything surprising in that word?"

"I thought your Majesty detested them."

"*Parbleu!* out of each hundred thousand manufactured, ninety thousand are against myself!"

"And those which your Majesty is going to give me belong to the ten thousand which cannot even make you look favourably on the ninety thousand."

"No, countess; these are addressed to you."

"To me? By whom?"

"By Monsieur de Voltaire."

"He charged your Majesty to deliver them?"

"Not at all; he sent them direct to your Highness."

"How?—without a cover?"

"No, enclosed in a charming letter."

"Ah, I understand; your majesty has been at work this morning with the postmaster. But read the verses, sire; read Monsieur de Voltaire's verses."

Louis XV opened the paper and read:—

Goddess of pleasure, soft queen of the graces,
Why blend, with the fêtes which make Paphos to ring,
Foul threat'ning suspicions and hideous disgraces—
The fate of a hero, oh! why should'st thou bring?
Still dear our Ulysses his country shall hold,
The State's mighty bulwark, the monarch's delight;
None wiser in council, in battle more bold,
And Ilion can tell how resistless his might!

Fair Venus, thy throne all the gods shall surround,
Thy beauty celestial all tongues shall declare,
The roses of joy in thy path shall abound;
Then calm the rough waters and smile on our prayer,
Ah, why should thy anger burn fiercely and high
'Gainst the hero whom foremen still tremble to meet;
For how can he draw from such beauty a sigh,
Save in breathing his vows as he kneels at her feet?

"Decidedly, sire," said the countess, more piqued than gratified by this poetical offering, "Monsieur de Voltaire wishes to recommend himself to your favour."

"He loses his pains, then," said the king. "He is a fire-brand who would burn Paris if he returned to it. Let him stay with his friend, my cousin Frederick II.; we can do very well with Monsieur Rousseau. But take the verses, countess, and study them."

She took the paper, made a match of it, and laid it beside her plate.

"Some tokay, sire," said Chon.

"From the vaults which supply his Majesty the Emperor of Austria," said the countess.

"From the emperor's vaults?" said the king. "*Pardieu!* no one is supplied from them but myself."

"Very true, sire," said the countess; "so I had it from your butler."

"Ah!" said the king, "and you have seduced—"

"No, sire, I have *ordered.*"

"Well answered, countess! I was a fool."

"Will the king take coffee?" asked Chon.

"Oh, certainly."

"And will his Majesty burn it as usual?" asked the countess.

"If the lady of the castle permit." The countess rose. "But what are you doing?"

"I am going to wait on you myself."

"Well," said the king, leaning back in his chair like a man who had made an excellent supper, and whose humours were, therefore, in a happy state of equilibrium. "Well, I see that my best plan is to let you do as you like, countess."

The countess brought a silver stand, with a little coffee-pot containing the boiling mocha; she then placed before the king a plate on which was a silver cup and a carafe of Bohemian glass, and beside the plate she laid the taper which she had just folded.

The king, with that profound attention which he always bestowed on this operation, calculated his sugar, measured his coffee, and, having gently poured on it the brandy, so that it swam on the surface, he took the little roll of paper, lighted it at a candle, and communicated the flame to the liquor. Five minutes afterward he enjoyed his coffee with all the delight of a finished epicure.

The countess looked on till he had finished the last drop; then she exclaimed, "Oh, sire, you have burned your coffee with M. de Voltaire's verses. That is a bad omen for the Choiseuls!"

"I was wrong," said he, laughing; "you are not a fairy, you are a demon."

The countess rose.

"Does your Majesty wish to know whether the governor has returned?"

"Zamore? Bah! for what purpose?"

"To allow you to go to Marly, sire."

"True," said the king, making a great effort to rouse himself from that state of comfort in which he found himself. "Well, countess, let us see; let us see."

The countess made a sign to Chon, who vanished.

The king began his search for Zamore again; but, it must be confessed, with very different feelings from those which had before influenced him. Philosophers say that we behold things either dark or bright, according to the state of our stomachs, and, as kings have stomachs like other men,—in general, indeed, not so good as other men, but still communicating the sensation of comfort or discomfort to the rest of the body in the same manner,— our king appeared in the most charming humour which it was possible for a king to be in. Just inside the corridor a new perfume greeted the king's nostrils. A door leading into a delightful chamber, hung in blue satin, embroidered with natural flowers, opened, disclosing, illumined by a mysterious light, the recess toward which for the past two hours the steps of the enchantress had been pointed. "Sire," said she, "it seems that Zamore has not returned, and we are still confined, unless we leave the chateau through the windows."

"By the aid of the bedclothes?" asked the king.

"Sire," said the countess, with a charming smile, "let us use, not abuse."

The king, laughing, opened his arms, and the countess let fall the pretty rose, which scattered its petals on the carpet.

Storming the Bastile

This inner yard of the Bastile in Paris was the prisoners' exercise ground. Eight giant towers guarded it: no window opened into it. The sun never penetrated its well-like circuit where the pavement was damp, almost muddy.

Here, a clock, the face upheld by chained captives in carving, dropped the seconds like water oozing through a ceiling on the dungeon slabs. At the bottom of this pit, the prisoner, lost in the stony gulf, would glance up at the inexorable nakedness and sue to be led back into his cell.

Governor Launay, Commander, was about fifty years of age: he wore a grey linseywoolsey suit this day; it was crossed by a red sash of the Order of St. Louis, and he carried a swordcane. He was a bad man: Linguet's Memoirs had just shown him up in a sad light and he was hated almost as much as the jail. His father had been governor before him.

The officers here were on the purchase system, so that the officials tried to make all the money they could squeeze out of the prisoners and their friends. The governor, chief warder, doubled his 60,000 francs appointments by extortion.

In the way of meanness Launay outdid his foregoers: he may have had to pay more highly for the post than his father and so had to put on the screw to retrieve his outlay. He fed his household out of the prisoners' rations; he reduced the firing allowance and doubled the hire of furniture. Maybe he foresaw that he was not to enjoy the berth long.

He had the right to pass a hundred casks of wine into Paris free of duty He sold it to a wine-shopkeeper who got in the best vintage and supplied him for the prisoners with vinegar.

The latter had one relief, one pleasure—a little garden made on a bastion where they got a whiff of sweet air and saw flowers and grass and sunshine. He let this ut to a truck-gardener, robbing the prisoners for fifty livres a-year.

On the other hand he was yielding to rich captives: he let one furnish his room in his own style and have any visitors he liked.

For all this Launay was brave.

He might be pale, but he was calm, although the storm had raged against him from the previous evening. He felt aware of the riot becoming a revolt for the waves broke at the foot of his castle wall.

It is true that he had four cannon and a garrison of old soldiers and Swiss —with only one unarmed man now confronting him. That unarmed man was Billet, farmer and leader of revolutionists. When entering the stronghold he understood that a weapon might get him into trouble beyond the barrier.

With a glance he remarked everything; the governor's calm and menacing attitude; the Swiss ranked in the guard-houses; the Veterans on the platforms, and the silent bustle of the artillerists loading up their caissons with ammunition.

The sentinels had their muskets on their shoulders and their officers carried drawn swords.

As the commander stood still, Billet was obliged to go to him. The grating cosed behind the people's parliamentarian with an ugly grinding of metal on metal which made him shudder to the marrow, brave though he was.

"What do you want?" challenged Launay.

"I come on behalf of the people," rejoined the visitor proudly.

"That is all very well," sneered Launay, smiling; "but you must have shown some other warrant, for otherwise you would not have passed the first dead-line of sentries."

"True, I have a pass from your friend Flesselles, Lord Provost."

"Flesselles? why do you dub him my friend?" exclaimed the prison warden, looking at the speaker to read to the bottom of his mind. "How do you conclude that he is a friend of mine?"

"I supposed as much."

"Is that all? never mind. Let us see your safe-conduct."

Billet presented the paper which Launay read more than once in order to catch a hidden meaning or concealed lines; he even held it up to the light to see if there was secret writing.

"Is that all? are you perfectly sure? nothing by word of mouth in addition?"

"Not a bit."

"Strange!" said Launay, plunging his glance by a loophole on Bastile Square. "Then tell me your want and be quick."

"The people want you to give up the Bastile.

"What do you say?" cried Launay, turning quickly as if he must be mistaken in his hearing.

"I summon you in the people's name to give up the Bastile."

"Queer animals the people," sneered Launay, snapping his fingers. "What do they want with the Bastile?"

"To demolish it."

"Why, what the mischief is the Bastile to the people? is any common man ever shut up herein? why, the people ought to bless every stone of the Bastile. Who are locked up here? philosophers, learned men, aristocrats, statesmen, princes—all the enemies of the dregs."

"This only proves that the people are not selfish and want to do good to others."

"It is plain that you are not a soldier, my friend," said the other with a kind of pity.

"It is true and come fresh from the country."

"For you do not know what the Bastile is: come with me and I will show you."

"He is going to pull the spring of some trap which will open beneath my feet," thought the adventurer, "and then good-bye, Old Billet!"

But he was intrepid and did not wince as he prepared to accede to the invitation.

"In the first place," continued Launay, "it is well to know that I have enough powder in the store to blow up the castle and lay half the suburbs in ashes."

"I knew that," was the tranquil reply.

"Do you see these cannon? They rake this gallery, which is defended by a guardhouse, and by two ditches only to be crossed by draw-bridges; lastly, there is a portcullis."

"Oh, I am not saying that the Bastile will be badly defended, but that it will be well attacked."

"To proceed: here is a postern opening on the moats: observe the thickness of the walls. Forty feet here and fifteen above. You see that though the people have nails they will break against such walls."

"I am not saying that the people will demolish the Bastile to master it but that, having mastered it, they will demolish it," said the leader of the revolutionists.

"Let us go upstairs," said the governor, leading up thirty steps, where he paused to say: "This embrasure opens on the passage by which you would be bound to come. It is defended by one rampart gun, but it enjoys a fair reputation. You know the song:

"'Oh, my sweet-voiced Sackbut, I love your dear song?'"

"Certainly, I have heard it, but I do not think this a time to sing it, or anything else."

"Stay; Marshal Saxe called this gun his Sackbut, because it sang the only music he cared anything for. This is a historical fact. But let us go on."

"Oh," said Billet when upon the tower top, "you have not dismounted the cannon, but merely drawn them in. I shall have to tell the people so."

"The cannon were mounted here by the King's command and by that alone can they be dismounted."

"Governor Launay," returned Billet, feeling himself rise to the level of the emergency, "the true sovereign is yonder and I counsel you to obey it."

He pointed to the grey-looking masses, spotted with blood from the battling, and reflecting the dying sunlight on their weapons up to the very moats.

"Friend, a man cannot know two masters," replied the royalist, holding his head up haughtily: "I, the Governor of the Bastile, know but one: the Sixteenth Louis, who put his signmanual at the foot of the patent which made me the commander over men and material here."

"Are you not a French citizen?" demanded Billet warmly."

"I am a French nobleman," said the Count of Launay.

"True, you are a soldier, and speak like one."

"You are right," said the gentleman bowing. "I am a soldier and carry out my orders."

"Well, I am a citizen," went on Billet, "and as my duty as such is opposed to yours as the King's soldier, one of us must die. He who fulfills his orders or his duties."

"That is likely, sir."

"So you are determined to fire on the people?"

"Not unless I am fired at. I pledged myself to that effect to Lord Provost Flesselles' deputation. You see the guns have been retired, but at the first shot, I will roll one—say this one—forward out of the embrasure with my own hands, train it and point it, and fire with the slow-match you see there."

"If I believed that," said Billet, "before you could commit such a crime——"

"I have told you that I am a soldier and know nothing outside my orders."

"Then, look!" said Billet, drawing Launay to the gap in the battlements and pointing alternately in two different directions—the main street from the town and the street through the suburbs, "behold those who will henceforth give you orders."

Launay saw two black, dense, roaring bodies, undulating like snakes, with head and bodies in sight but the rearmost coils still waving onwards till lost in the hollows of the ground. All the bodies of these immense reptiles glittered with the scales. These were the two armies to which Billet had given the Bastile as the meeting-place, Marat's men and Gonchon's Paris beggars. As they surged forward they brandished their weapons and yelled blood-curdling cries.

At the sight Launay lost color and said as he raised his cane.

"To your guns!" Then, threatening Billet, he added: "You scoundrel, to come here and gain time under pretence of a parley, do you know that you deserve death?"

Billet saw the attempt to draw the sword from the cane and pierce him; he seized the speaker by the collar and waistband as swift as lightning, and raising him clear off the ground, he replied:

"And you deserve to be hurled down to the bottom of the ditch to be smashed in the mud. But, never mind, thank God I can fight you in another manner."

At this instant, an immense howl, a universal one, rose in the air like a whirlwind, as Major Losme, Commander of Military, appeared on the platform.

"Oh, sir, for mercy's sake," he said to Billet: "Show yourself for the people there believe something has happened you and they call for you."

Indeed, the name of Billet, set afloat by Pitou, leader of the peasants, ascended on the clamor.

The farmer let go Launay who replaced the blade in the stick. The three men hesitated for a moment while the innumerable cries of vengeance and menace arose.

"Show yourself, sir," said Launay, "not because the noise frightens me but to prove that I have acted fairly."

The farmer thrust his head out of the porthole, waving his hand.

At this sight the populace burst with cheering: it was in a measure Revolution standing up in Billet's stead as this man of the lowest ranks trod the Bastile turret like a master.

"That is well, sir," went on Launay. "Now all is ended between us; you have no further business here. They ask for you below; go down."

Billet appreciated this moderation on the part of a man who had him in his power: he went down by the same stairs, the governor following. The major remained up there as the governor had whispered some orders to him.

It was evident that Count Launay had but one wish, that the bearer of the flag of truce should be his active enemy as soon as possible.

Without speaking a word the envoy crossed the yard, where he saw the cannoniers were at their pieces and the lintstocks were lighted and smoking. He stopped before them.

"Friends," he cried, "remember that I came to your commander to stay the shedding of blood, but that he refused me."

"In the King's name, be off from here!" said Launay, stamping his foot.

"Have a care," retorted the farmer:

"I am ordered out in the King's name but I shall return in that of the People. Speak out," he added, turning to the Swiss, "who are you for?"

The foreign soldiers were silent. Launay pointed to the iron door. But Billet attempted a final effort.

"Governor, in the name of the nation, in the name of your brothers!"

"Brothers? is that what you call them who are bellowing 'Down the Bastile,' and 'Death to the Governor?' they may be brothers of yours, but surely they are none of mine."

"In humanity's, then!"

"Humanity—which urges you to come a hundred thousand strong against one hundred hapless soldiers immured in these walls and cut their throats?"

"But by giving up the Bastile you save their lives."

"And I lose my honor."

Billet was hushed, for the soldierly argument crushed him; but again he addressed the soldiers, saying:

"Surrender, friends, while it is yet time; in another ten minutes it will be too late."

"I will have you shot unless you are out of this instantly," thundered Launay, "as true as I am noble."

Billet stopped an instant, folded his arms in token of defiance and, crossing glances for the last time with the exasperated governor, walked forth.

Under the burning July sun the crowds awaited, shuddering with fever. Gonchon's men had joined in with Marat's, the suburbs hailing each other as brothers. Gonchon was at the head of his patriots but Marat had disappeared.

The scene on the open place was terrifying.

On seeing Billet the cheering was tremendous.

"He is a brave man," said Billet to Gonchon, "or rather I should say he is stubborn. He will not surrender the Bastile but will sustain the siege."

"Do you think he will hold out long?"

"To death."

"All right, he shall have that."

"But how many men will be killed by us?' said the farmer, no doubt fearing that he had not the right usurped by generals, kings, and emperors, those who take out licenses to kill and maim.

"Rubbish," said Gonchon; "there are too many, since we have not enough for half the population. Is not that about the size of it, boys?" he asked of the bystanders.

"Yes, yes," was the reply in sublime abnegation.

"But the moat?" queried Billet.

"It need be filled up in only one place," responded the beggar's leader: "and I calculate that we could choke it up altogether, eh, lads?"

The friends answered unanimously in the affirmative.

"Have it so," said Billet, overpowered.

At this moment, Launay appeared on a terrace, followed by Major Losme and two or three other officers.

"Commence," shouted Gonchon.

The governor turned his back on him.

Gonchon might have put up with a threat but he would not bear contempt: he lifted his gun and fired at him. A man near him fell. Instantly a hundred, nay, a thousand gunshots sounded, as if it were awaited as a signal, and the grey towers were striped with white.

A few seconds' silence succeeded this discharge, as if the assailants were frightened at what they had done.

Then a gush of flame lost in a cloud of smoke crowned the crest of one tower. A detonation thundered. Shrieks of pain were heard in the throngs closely pressed. The first cannonshot had been fired by the royalists, the first blood shed.

The battle between people and Bastile was begun.

An instant previously menacing, the multitudes felt something like terror. By defending itself with so little of its weapons the Bastile seemed impregnable. In this period of concession the majority had no doubt supposed that they would always have their way.

That was a mistake: this cannonshot fired into them gave the measure of the Titanic work they had undertaken.

A firing of muskets, well aimed, from the platform, immediately followed.

The fresh silence was broken by renewed screams, groans and a few complaints. But nobody thought to flee, and had the thought struck any one, he must have been ashamed seeing the numbers.

Indeed all the thoroughfares were streams of human beings: the square an immense sea, with each billow a human head: the eyes flamed and the mouths hurled curses.

In a trice all the windows on the square were filled with sharpshooters who fired, though out of range. If a soldier appeared at a loophole or an embrasure, a hundred barrels were leveled at him, and the hail of bullets chipped away the edge of the stone angle shielding him.

But soon they were tired of firing at insensible stone: they wanted the flesh to aim at, and to see the blood spurt.

Everybody shouted ideas of an assault. Billet, weary of listening, caught up an ax from a carpenter's hand, and rushed forward, in the midst of a shower of missiles, striking down the men around him like a scythe lays the grain, till he reached a small guardhouse before the first drawbridge. While the grapeshot was hurling and whistling about him, he hacked at the chains till down came the bridge.

During the quarter of an hour that this insane enterprise went on, the lookers-on held their breath. At each volley they expected to see their champion laid low. Forgetting their own danger, they thought solely of that the audacious worker ran. When the drop came down, they uttered a loud whoop and dashed into the first yard.

The rush was so unexpected, rapid and impetuous that no resistance was made.

The frenziedly joyful cheers announced the first advantage to Launay. Nobody noticed that a man had been mangled under the bridge.

Then, as if at the depth of a cavern, the four guns, pointed out to Billet by the governor, were shot off with a dreadful crash and all the outer yard was swept clear. The iron hurricane cleft a long swath of blood through the mass; on the path lay ten or twelve dead and double as many wounded.

Billet had stood on the guardhouse roof to reach the chain well up; he slid down where he found Pitou, who had reached the spot he knew not how. The young man had a quick eye, a poacher's habit. He had seen the gunners step up to the touchhole with the lighted matches, and seizing his patron by the coat, he had pulled him back behind a corner of the wall which sheltered both from the cannonade.

From this period on, the war was real. The tumult was alarming; the onslaught murderous; ten thousand gunshots poured upon the fort at risk of slaying the assaulters with the garrison. To cap all, a field-piece brought up by the French Guardsmen, added its boom to the cracking of small arms.

The frightful uproar intoxicated the amateur fighters and began to daunt the besieged who felt that they could never raise a commotion equal to this deafening them. The officers saw that their soldiers were weakening: they had to snatch their muskets from them and fire themselves.

At this juncture, amid the roar of great guns and smaller ones, and the shouting, as the mob were rushing forward to carry away the injured and dead on litters, a little body of citizens appeared calm and unarmed at the yard entrance. It was a deputation of electors from the City Hall. They were sacrificing life under protection merely of the white flag before and after them to indicate they came to parley.

Wishing to stop the effusion of blood, after hearing that the attack had commenced, they forced Flesselles to renew negotiations with the governor. In the name of the city, they summoned the governor of the citadel to cease firing, and to receive in the place a hundred of the town guards to guarantee his safety, the garrison's and the inhabitants.

The deputies called this out as they marched along. Frightened by the magnitude of the task they had set themselves, the people were ready to accept the proposal, seeing, too, the dead and wounded carried by. If Launay accepted the partial defeat they would be content with a half-victory.

At sight of them, the inner-yard firing ceased; they were beckoned to approach and they scrambled over the corpses, slipped in gore and held their hands out to the maimed. Under their shelter the others grouped. The injured and lifeless were borne out, streaking the marble flags with broad purple stains.

Firing ceasing on the fort side, Billet went out to get his party to refrain. At the doors he met Gonchon, without arms, exposing his naked breast like a man inspired, calm as though invulnerable.

"What has become of the deputation?" he inquired.

"It has got in," replied Billet. "Cease firing."

"It is useless; he will not give in," said the beggar leader, with the same certainty as if he had been gifted with reading the future.

"No matter; respect the usages of war, since we have become soldiers."

"I do not mind," said Gonchon; "Elie, Hullin, go," he said to two men who seemed to rule the crowd together with him: "Do not let a shot be fired till I say so."

At the voice the two darted away, cleaving the throng, and soon the sound of the musketry dying away, stopped entirely.

During the short rest the wounded were attended to; they were upwards of forty. Two o'clock struck: they had been hammering away two hours, from noon. Billet had returned to the front where Gonchon found him. His impatience was visible as he watched the iron grating.

"What is wrong?" asked the farmer.

"All is lost if the Bastile is not taken in two hours," was the beggar's reply.

"How so?"

"Because the royal court will learn what we are at. It will send us Bezenval's Switzers and Lambesq's heavies, who will help catch us between three fires."

Billet was forced to confess the truth in the prospect. At length the deputies appeared: by their woe-begone aspect it was clear their errand had failed.

"What did I tell you?" cried the popular orator, gladly; "What was foretold by Balsamo and Cagliostro will come to pass. The accursed fortress is doomed. To arms, boys, to arms," he yelled without waiting for the deputies to relate their doings, "the commandant refuses."

In fact, scarcely had the governor read Flesselles' letter introducing the party than he brightened up in the face and exclaimed, instead of yielding to the proposition:

"You Parisian gentlemen wanted the fight and it is too late to draw back."

The citizens had protested and persisted in picturing the horrors which the defense would entail. But he would heed nothing and finishing by saying to them what he had told Billet a couple of hours anteriorly:

"Begone or I will have you shot."

The citizens were glad to get out of it.

Launay took the offensive this time. He was wild with impatience. Before the deputation crossed the threshold, the Sackbut of Marshal Saxe played its tune: three men fell—one dead and two wounded, the latter being a French guardsman and the other one of the flag-of-truce bearers. At sight of this victim, whose errand made him sacred, carried away smothered in blood, the fury of the numbers was exalted once more.

Gonchon's aide-de-camps had returned to take their places by his side; but each had run home to change his dress. Elie had been the Marquis Conflans' running-footman and his livery resembled a Hungarian officer's uniform. Elie put on the uniform he had worn when an officer of the Queen's own Regiment, and this gave more confidence to the masses with the thought that the army was on their side.

The firing recommenced more fiercely than before.

At this Major Losme approached his superior. He was a brave and honorable soldier, but he had some manhood left him and he saw with pain what had happened and foresaw with more pain what would occur.

"You know we have no food," he said.

"I know that," answered Launay.

"And we have no order to hold out."

"I ask your pardon, Military Governor of the Bastile, but I am the governor of it in all respects; my order is to shut the doors and I hold the keys."

"My lord, keys are to open locks as well as fasten them. Have a care that you do not get the garrison massacred without saving the castle. That will be two triumphs for the revolters in one day. Look at the men we kill—they spring up again from the pavement. This morning only three thousand were there: three hours ago, there were six. Now they are over sixty thousand and to-morrow they will number a hundred thousand. When our cannon are silenced, and that will be the upshot, they will be strong enough to pull down the Bastile with their bare hands."

"You do not speak like the military governor of the Bastile, Major Losme."

"I speak like a Frenchman, my lord. I say that his Majesty having given us no special order—and the Provost of the Traders having made us a very acceptable proposition, to introduce a hundred Civil Guards into the castle—you might avoid the misery I foresee by acceding to Provost Flesselles' proposition."

"In your opinion, the City of Paris is a power we ought to obey?"

"Yes, in the absence of special royal order."

"Then, read, Major Losme," said the prison chief, leading his lieutenant aside into a corner.

On the small sheet of paper which he let him read, was written:

"Hold out firmly: I will amuse the Parisians with Cockades and promises. Before day is done, Bezenval will send you reinforcements.

"FLESSELLES."

"How did this advice reach you?" inquired the major.

"In the letter the deputies carried. They thought they were bearing a desire for the Bastile to be surrendered, and it was the order to defend it that they handed me."

The major bent his head.

"Go to your post and do not quit it till I command you, sir," continued Launay. Losme obeying, he coldly folded up the paper, replaced it in his pocket, and went over to the cannoniers to advise them to aim true and fire low. They obeyed like the major.

But the fortalice's fate was settled. No human power could delay the accomplishment.

To every cannon shot the reply was: "We mean to have the Bastile!"

While the voices claimed it, arms were not idle.

Pitou's and Billet's arms and voices peasant's and farmers were among those asking most energetically and working most efficaciously.

Each worked according to his character. Courageous and confident as the bulldog, Billet, the farmer, had run at the enemy, heedless of shot and steel. Pitou, the peasant, prudent and circumspect as the fox, endowed to the highest degree with self-preservation, utilized all his faculties to watch danger and anticipate it. His sight knew the most deadly embrasures, and distinguished the least move of the bronze tube to enter it. He could guess the exact moment when the rampart-gun was about to fire through the portcullis. His eyes having done their office, he made his limbs work for their owner.

Down went his shoulders and in went his chest, so that his frame offered no more surface than a board seen edgewise.

In these moments, of the filling-out Pitou, thin only in the legs, nothing remained but the geometrical expression of a straight line.

He chose a spot where the masonry shaped out cavities and projections so that his head was shielded by a stone, his heart by another and his knees by still another slab. Nowhere could a mortal wound be got in on him.

He fired a shot now and then, to relieve his feelings and because Billet told him to "blaze away." But he had nothing but wood and stone before him.

For his part he kept begging his friend not to expose himself to the firing. "There goes the Sackbut," or "I hear a hammer coming down."

Despite these injunctions the farmer executed prodigies of daring and energy, all in pure waste, till the idea struck him to go along the woodwork of the bridge and chop the chains of the second one, as he had done with the first.

Ange howled for him to stay and seeing that howls were useless, he followed him, from cover saying:

"Dear Master Billet, your wife will be a widow if you get killed."

The Swiss thrust their guns through the loopholes by which the Sackbut was fired to try to pick off the daring fellow who was making the chips fly off their bridge.

Billet called on his single gun to answer the Sackbut, but when the latter fired, the other artillerists retreated and the farmer was left alone to serve the cannon. This again drew Pitou out of his refuge.

"Master," he sued, "in the name of Catherine! think if you are done for, that Catherine will be an orphan."

Billet yielded to his plea, and because he had a new idea.

He ran out on the square, holloaing. "A cart!"

"Two carts," added Pitou, thinking you cannot have too much of a good thing."

Ten carts were immediately trundled through the multitude.

"Dry hay and straw!" shouted Billet.

"Straw and hay," repeated Pitou.

Like a flash, two hundred men brought each a truss of straw or half a bale of hay. Others brought dry fodder on litters. They were obliged to call out that they had ten times more than was wanted. In an hour they would have smothered the Bastile.

Billet put himself in the rails of a cart, laden with hay, and pushed it before him instead of dragging it.

Pitou did the same with another, without knowing why, but thinking the farmer's example was worthy of imitation.

Elie and Hullin guessed what the farmer proposed; they supplied themselves with carts and pushed them into the prison yard.

Scarcely did they enter than small shot and canister received them but the hay and straw deadened the bullets and slugs and only a few rattled on the wheels and shafts. None of the assailants were touched.

As soon as this discharge was fired, two or three hundred musketmen dashed on behind the cart-pushers and lodged under the sloping shed of the bridge itself, under cover of the moving breastwork.

There Billet pulled out a scrap of

paper, and flint and steel; he wrapped up a pinch of gunpowder in the paper, struck a light and ignited it and shoved the flaring piece into the heap of hay. Others took lighted wisps and scattered the flames. It caught the pentroof and the four blazing carts set fire to beams high up and sneaked along the bridge supports.

To put out the fire the garrison would have to come out and to show oneself was to court death.

The glad cheer, started in the yard, was caught up on the square where the smoke was seen above the towers. Something fatal to the besieged was surmised to be going on.

Indeed the redhot chains drew out and snapped from the ringbolts. The half-broken bridge fell, smoking and sending up sparks.

The firemen came up with their engines, but the governor ordered them to be fired upon though the prison might be thus burned over the garrison's heads.

The old French soldiers refused. The Swiss were willing, but as they were not artillerists they could not work the carriage-guns. These had to be abandoned.

On the other side, seeing that the cannonade ceased, the French Guards resumed their field piece work and with the third ball sent the portcullis flying.

The governor had gone upon the tower to see if the promised succor was arriving when he suddenly found himself enwrapped in smoke. He ran downstairs and ordered the gunners to keep up the firing. The refusal of the French Veterans exasperated him.

On hearing the portcullis smashed in, he recognized that all was lost.

He was fully aware that he was hated. He guessed that there was no safety for him. During the whole of the action, he had cherished the thought of burying himself under the ruins of his castle.

As soon as he acknowledged that all resistance was useless, he snatched a lintstock from an artillerist and precipitated himself towards the powder magazine.

"The powder, the powder!" shrieked twenty terrified voices.

On seeing the governor with the burning match they divined his intention. Two soldiers crossed their bayonets before his breast at the very instant when he opened the ammunition-storeroom door.

"You may kill me," he said, "but you cannot do that so quickly that I shall not have had time to toss this brand into one of the open kegs. Then, all of us, besieged and besiegers, go up!"

The soldiers stopped with the steel at his breast, but he was still their commander and commanded, for he held the lives of all in his hands. His movement riveted everybody to their place.

The assailants perceived that something extraordinary was going on. They peered into the yard and saw the governor threatening and being threatened.

"Hark to me," said he, "as true as I have death in my grasp for all of you, I will fire the powder if one of you dare step within this yard."

The hearers might fancy the earth quaked beneath their feet.

"What do you want?" several voices gasped with the accent of a panic.

"An honorable capitulation."

As the assailants could not fully comprehend the extent of Launay's despair and did not believe his speech, they began to enter, Billet at the head. It little mattered to the farmer whether the Bastile was torn down or blown up.

"Stop," shouted Billet, "for the sake of the prisoners!"

Elie and Hullin, and their men, who had not shrank from death on their own behalf, recoiled, white and trembling like he had.

"What do you want?" they demanded of the governor, renewing the question his garrison had put to him.

"Everybody must retire," replied Count Launay. "I will listen to no proposition while there is an intruder inside the Bastile walls."

"But you will take advantage of our withdrawal to repair damages," remonstrated Billet.

"If the capitulation be refused, you will find things in the same condition; you there, I at this door, on the faith of a nobleman!"

Some shook their heads.

"Is there any here who doubt a nobleman?" questioned the count.

"No, no, nobody," rejoined five hundred voices.

"Bring me pen, ink and paper," continued the governor. "That is well," he went on as his orders were executed. "Now, retire!" he said to the assaulters.

Billet, Elie and Hullin set the example, and all followed them.

Launay laid the match by his side and began to write the terms of surrender on his knee. The French Veterans and the Swiss, aware that their safety was at stake, silently looked at him in superstitious terror. When he turned, before writing the document out fair, all the yards were clear.

In a twinkling all the concourse outside had learnt what was proceeding. As Losme had said, it was the population which issued from beneath the flagstones and pavement. Not only workmen and beggars, the homeless and the imperfectly clad, but citizens of the better classes. Not only men but women and children. Each had a weapon and uttered a warcry.

From spot to spot, amid groups, was seen a woman, disheveled, wringing her hands and waving her arms, howling curses at the giant of stone: it was a mother, a wife or a sweetheart whose dearest one had been incarcerated in its flanks.

But since a short space the giant had ceased to vomit flame and scowl in the smoke; the fire was extinct and the whole mute as a tomb. On the blackened walls the bullet grazes stood out white and were above count; everybody had wanted to leave his mark on the granite brow of his personification of tyranny.

They could hardly believe that the Bastile was about to be turned over to them; that its governor would surrender.

In the midst of this general doubt, as none ventured to congratulate another, and all waited in silence, a letter stuck on a spearpoint was seen thrust through a loophole.

Between the despatch and the besiegers was the great moat deep and wide and full of water.

Billet called for a plank, but three were too short, and the fourth, while long enough, was ill adjusted. Still he balanced himself as well as he could and unhesitatingly risked himself on the bending bridge.

All in dumbness fixed their eyes on the man who seemed suspended over the stagnant water, while Pitou, quivering, sat on the brink and hid his face.

All of a sudden, when Billet was two-thirds over, the plank shifted, and throwing up his arms he fell in the moat, where he sank out of sight.

Pitou uttered a roar and dived after his master like a Newfoundland dog.

A man went right out on the plank, without hesitation, choosing the same road as Billet: it was Stanislas Maillard, the prison clerk. On reaching the point beneath which he saw two men struggling, he looked, but seeing that they could swim ashore, he continued his way.

In half a minute he was across and took the letter off the pike.

With the same tranquil nerve and steadiness of gait, he passed back over the plank.

But at the very second when all crowded round him to read the message, a hail of bullets rained down from the battlements at the same time as a tremendous report was heard.

From all breasts a cry arose, one announcing that the people meant to have revenge.

"Trust the tyrants again," said Gonchon.

Nobody cared any more about capitulations, the powder, the prisoners or himself—nothing was wanted but retaliation and the besiegers strewed into the yards not by hundreds but by thousands. The only thing preventing them entering still faster was not the muskets but the narrowness of the doorways.

On hearing the firing, the two soldiers who had not gone away from their commander, jumped at him and a third set his foot on the slowmatch, and crushed it out. Launay drew the sword hidden in his cane and tried to stab with it but it was wrenched off from him and broken, while in his grip.

He was convinced that he could do no more, and he waited for his doom.

The mobs rushing in met the soldiers, holding out their hands to them —and so the Bastile was not taken under a surrender but by assault.

This came from the royal castle having ceased to enclose inert matter; latterly the King had shut up human brain there and the spirit had burst the vessel.

The people entered at the breach.

As for the treacherous volley fired in the midst of silence during the suspension of hostilities, and unforseen, impolitic and deadly aggression, it will never be known who gave the order, inspired it and accomplished it.

There are moments when the future of a nation is exactly poised in the scales of Fate. One of the plates bears up the other, even while each party thinks his side will make the other kick the beam. An invisible hand has flung into the dish a dagger or a pistol and all changes. The only cry heard is:

"Woe to the vanquished!"

While the multitude poured, roaring with delight and anger same time, into the yards of the prison, two men were floundering in the ditch: Billet and Pitou. The latter was keeping up the other whom no bullet or blow had struck, but the fall had a trifle stunned him. Ropes were thrown to them and poles thrust down.

In five minutes they were rescued, and were hugged and carried in triumph, muddy though they were.

One gave Billet a drink of brandy, another crammed the younger peasant with bread and sausage. A third dried them off and led them into the sunshine.

Suddenly an idea or rather a memory crossed the good farmer's mind: he tore himself from the friendly arms and ran towards the fort.

"The prisoners, help the prisoners!" he shouted.

"Yes, the prisoners," repeated Pitou, darting into the tower after his leader.

Only thinking of the jailers, the mob now shuddered on remembering the captives. The cries were reiterated. A fresh flood of assailants burst any remaining barriers and seemed to enlarge the flanks of the prison to expand it with liberty.

A frightful scene was presented to Billet and his friend. The mob had crowded into the court, enraged, drunken and furious. The first soldier falling under hand was torn to pieces.

Gonchon looked on quietly, no doubt thinking that popular wrath is like a great river, doing more mischief if one tries to dam it than if letting it make its course. On the contrary, Elie and Hullin leaped in between defenders and attackers; they prayed and supplicated, vociferating the holy lie that the soldiers were promised their lives.

Billet and Pitou's arrival was reinforcement to them.

Billet, whom they were revenging, was alive; not even hurt; the plank had swerved underfoot and he was clear with a mud bath, that was all.

The Swiss were most detested: but they were not to be found. They had time to put on overalls and smockfrocks of dull linen, and they passed off as servants.

With sledges the invaders broke the captive images on the clock face. They raced up to the turret tops to kick the cannon which had belched death on them. They laid hands on the stones and endeavored to dislodge them.

When the first of the conquerors were seen on the battlements, all without, below, a hundred thousand or so, cast up an immense clamor.

It spread over Paris, and flew over France like a swift-winged eagle:

"The Bastile is taken!"

At this news, hearts melted, eyes were moist with tears of gladness, and hands clasped; no longer were there opposition parties or inimical castes, for all Parisians understood that they were brothers and all men that they were free.

Millions of men mutually embraced.

Aurora

In ALL truth, Henrietta de Hautfort was exceedingly lovely. She was of rosy complexion and ruddy hair, well-earning the title of Aurora, as Lady Fargis, maid of honor to the queen, Anne of Austria, had said. Vaultier, agent of King Louis XIII., had discovered her in a trip of his into Perigord, and, having conceived the possibility of corrupting the girl, he had the idea of making the phantom of a king seriously enamored.

He had arranged everything beforehand, making sure that no relation, no lover or even friend was there to oppose the devotion; but, upon Marie de Medici's hint, mother of Louis XIII., he had delayed until the return of Lady Fargis, under the impression that she was the only person who could hopefully present the wormwood to her majesty with a honeyed air.

When the fair young creature threw herself at her majesty's feet, held out her hands and cried:

"Oh, all, all for you, my queen!" she saw clearly that so unblemished a beauty, with a voice so fresh, could not lie, and she lifted her up with pleasure.

That same evening, all was arranged. Henrietta was to endeavor to charm the king, and, as soon as she should have enchained him fast, she should lead him over to the queen, and make him dismiss Richelieu, the minister, her enemy.

The only puzzle was to make the temptress appear in the most favorable position before the monarch.

The queen gave out that, as the king was only at Fontainebleau, they would go and spend the Easter with him. On Palm Sunday eve they arrived.

On the next day, the king went to hear mass in the castle chapel, where everybody of the court was summoned. Only a few feet from the sovereign, in the light of a sunbeam variegated by streaming through the gold and purple stained glass, was a girl kneeling on the pavement.

She had nothing intervening between her dress and the marble.

The king knelt on a golden-tasselled cushion.

He felt ashamed of having a carpet under him while so lovely a girl had none. He called a page and bade him take his cushion to her.

But Henrietta, as if not deeming herself worthy of using the royal cushion, she arose, curtseyed to the offerer and respectfully placed the boon on a chair, with virginal freedom and boldness.

Such gracefulness attracted the king. He had hardly returned to the castle before he began to inquire who was the ravishing enchantress whom he had seen at church. He learnt that she was the grand-daughter of one Mistress Flotte, who had only the evening before entered the services of Queen Marie de Medici as governess of her maids of honor.

From that day forward, to the high astonishment of everybody and the great satisfaction of those interested, there was a complete change in the king's habits.

Instead of locking himself up in the

90

darkest room as he was wont to do at the Louvre and had done for a week at Fontainbleau.

In fact, the king was completely enthralled.

But the designs of the Queen and Fargis were frustrated by the appearance of the Count of Moret, Antoine de Bourbon, son of Henry of Navarre. He had been sent by Richelieu to convey important despatches to the king. The instant Aurora's glance fell on the Count's handsome face, she exclaimed: "I cannot fulfil my pledge to the queen!"

The Count of Moret's appearance at Court awakened feelings of love in Anne of Austria's breast such as she had never experienced since her interview with the splendid Buckingham. Aurora was no less impressed by his noble appearance.

It chanced that Fargis had so managed Aurora that the latter agreed to meet the King in secret. The queen meanwhile dispatched an invitation to the Count of Moret for the same evening. Neither of the messages contained names. The waiting-maids had passed the notes to the pages of the Count and the King. But a slight mistake took place in the delivery.

As time wore on the hopes of the antecardinalistic party rose. For once the minister seemed to have had a mind but for one thing. Busy with the army, Richelieu, while despatching the usual couriers to inquire of the king's health, no longer entreated the sovereign to the battle-fields.

*   *   *   *   *   *

It was about five o'clock one morning that a great rattle of wheels and a great clatter of hoofs resounded on the main road from the south, and there appeared, coming straight to the chateau, a coach surrounded by a number of guards, who wore the cardinal's uniform.

The guards on duty and the servants who were up so early hastened to collect at the foot of the grand staircase, and shout:

"Long live the cardinal!"

From the coach, Richelieu himself alighted!

"Long live the cardinal!" thought to have been so far away.

From end to end, from foundation to roof the cry echoed and re-echoed. All were aroused. They had heard Richelieu had accomplished a truce with the Spanish forces.

In one chamber, a sleeping-apartment, the gorgeous form of Anne of Austria started up from the embrace of one, at view of whom in the dawning light she uttered an exclamation, in the height of surprise:

"Louis, my king!"

The king lifted his head languidly. But the memories of the joys of night, of the pleasures, of the caresses which Anne had treasured up to pour upon the not-come Count of Moret, inspirited the monarch, and as the queen was about to cover her bosom with the lace, he tore it away and kissed her again and again. And, exhausted herself by a vigor which she had never expected to find in him, she sank back on the pillow and returned his fondlings.

In a room not far from this, the exclamation over the cardinal's arrival, awakened another slumberer.

Aurora de Hautfort opened her eyes

to see—not the sullen, dark face of the monarch next her own, but the healthful brown and ruddy countenance of the Count of Moret.

He pretended to be asleep, but he kept his arms clasped, and, as no man could have unloosed his grip, little could she do towards undoing the embrace.

And bursting into tears, she wound her slender arms around his neck and nestling her head down on his breast amid her dishevelled tresses and his curly beard, she lay panting as if about to die till he pretended to wake up and began to quiet her child-like vexation at the deception so advantageous to her.

Branded

CRONE was the most delighted of Chiefs of Police known in the history of Paris.

The fruit of a criminal magistrate is the conviction as the blossom is the arrest. Arrest after arrest succeeded that of the Prince of Rohan.

Finally the apprehensions led to Lady Lamotte, last of the Valois.

She was to be branded, whipped, and kept in a Magdalen Asylum forever.

First his men captured Reteau, who led to the apprehension of Lady Lamotte.

In the Justice Court, a scaffold was erected eight feet high in full sight of the three thousand sightseers. On it stood a post, having iron rings set in it, with a placard on the top which was not legible.

The way up to the platform was by a ladder in the lack of steps. The bayonets of the archers formed a railing with spikes around it.

The door in the wall opened and out came the doomed countess, while shouts of "down with the thief, the forger!" sounded.

Jeanne was at the end of her forces, for she had been fighting with the exe-cutioners, but not of her rage. She ceased to shriek because the clamor of the mob overcame her: but she called out some shrill metallic words which hushed the murmurs as by enchantment.

"Do you know whom I am? I come of the blood of your kings. In me is struck, not a culprit, but a rival. More than that, an accomplice."

She was interrupted by the police hirelings.

"Yes, an accomplice who knews the secrets of——"

"Look out!" whispered the turnkey.

She looked up—the executioner was flourishing a scourge!

At this she forgot all and screamed for mercy.

Hooting drowned her yell, while she giddily clung to the flagellator's knees and tried to seize the whip which he used but feebly. At the first lash she sprang up and began to struggle for the weapon.

Suddenly she relaxed her violence, for his aid was holding up a redhot iron for him. The heat it sent forth made her bound back with a savage howl.

"Branded? brand me?" she screamed.

"Yes, yes," roared a thousand voices.

"Help, help," said Jeanne, bewildered, trying to get the rope off from round her hands.

As the executioner could not open her dress, he tore it off her shoulder; but Jeanne rushed upon him and made him retreat so that he dared not touch her: the mob hooted him for his clumsiness and piqued him in his conceit. The crowd admired the courage of the little, frail woman holding the burly headsman at bay: impatience rose: the jailer had got off the platform: the soldiers looked on in disorder.

"Have done!" called out an imperious voice which the executioner no doubt recognized, for he pushed Jeanne down with a vigorous repulse and held her head with his left hand. But she rose, hotter than the iron threatening her, and yelled in a voice superior to the uproar:

"Cowards, will you see me tortured? will you not defend me?"

"Be quiet," said the judge's clerk.

"Yes, what good will that do me? the more fool I, for if I spoke all that I know about the Queen, I might be slain but not dishonored!"

She said no more, for the King's Commissioner rushed upon the scaffold with help, and they held the woman while the executioner impressed her shoulder with the royal brand. She uttered a howl, with no equivalent in human cries.

Shame and pain vanquished her. The executioner carried her, bent double, down the ladder of ignominy.

She did not work out the rest of her sentence; by some means she made her escape from France and, going to London, the Last of the Valois lost her life by jumping out of a window to avoid arrest for debt. Beginning life as a beggar, thus she perished in poverty.

The hushed crowd broke up and went away. Two of the spectators accosted each other.

"Do you think, Maximilian, that it is really Countess Lamotte whom the fellow branded?"

"They say so," replied the taller of the two young men.

"Like the rest, you will go away believing this was not some trick. They have paid some wretch who was to be branded anyway to play the fine lady's part. The only person really branded was the Queen."

The hearer laughed loudly and clapped hands for the jest, and looking round him, said:

"Good-bye, Robespierre!"

"Good-bye, Marat," and they parted.

The Tragedy of Nantes

AT THE time of which we write there had been a serious revolution against the regent of France, Philippe le Debonnaire. Gaston de Chanlay had been pardoned, though the real leader, because Helene, the regent's beautiful daughter, had fallen in love with his noble character and fearless sway.

Gaston was soon posting along the road to Nantes, seat of judgment, leaving behind all postilions in his mad haste, whose place then as now was to hold the horses instead of urging them on.

He had already passed Sevres and Versailles, and on arriving at Rambouillet just at daybreak, he saw the innkeeper and some postilions gathered round a horse which had just been bled. The horse was lying stretched on its side, in the middle of the street, breathing with difficulty.

Gaston at first paid no attention to all this; but as he was mounting himself, he heard one of the bystanders say, "If he goes at that pace he will kill more than one between this and Nantes."

Gaston was on the point of starting, but struck by a sudden and terrible idea, he stopped and signed to the innkeeper to come to him.

The innkeeper approached.

"Who has passed by here?" asked Gaston, "going at such a pace as to have put that poor animal in such a state?"

"A courier of the minister's," answered the innkeeper.

"A courier of the minister's!" exclaimed Gaston, "and coming from Paris?"

"From Paris."

"How long has he passed, more or less?"

"About two hours."

Gaston uttered a low cry which was like a groan. He knew Dubois, the wily minister—Dubois, who had tricked him under a disguise. The good will of the minister recurred to his mind and frightened him. Why this courier despatched post haste just two hours before himself?

"Oh! I was too happy," thought the young man, "and Helene was right

when she told me she had a presentiment of some great misfortune. Oh, I will overtake this courier, and learn the message that he bears, or perish in the attempt." And he shot off like an arrow.

But with all these doubts and interrogations he had lost ten minutes more, so that on arriving at the first post station he was still two hours behind. This time the courier's horse had held out, and it was Gaston's which was ready to drop. The innkeeper tried to make some remarks, but Gaston dropped two or three louis and set off again at a gallop.

At the next posting-house he had gained a few minutes, and that was all. The courier who was before him had not slackened his pace. Gaston increased his own; but this frightful rapidity redoubled the young man's fever and mistrust.

"Oh!" said he, "I *will* arrive at the same time that he does, if I am unable to precede him." And he doubled his speed, and spurred on his horse, which, at every station, stopped dripping with blood and sweat, or tumbled down exhausted. At every station he learnt that the courier had passed almost as swiftly as himself, but he always gained some few minutes, and that sustained his strength.

Those whom he passed upon the way, leaving them far behind, pitied, in spite of themselves, the beautiful young man, pale-faced and haggard, who flew on thus, and took neither rest, nor food, dripping with sweat, despite the bitter cold, and whose parched lips could only frame the words:—"A horse! a horse! quick, there, a horse!"

And, in fact, exhausted, with no strength but that supplied him by his heart, and maddened more and more by the rapidity of his course and the feeling of danger, Gaston felt his head turn, his temples throb, and the perspiration of his limbs was tinged with blood.

Choked by the thirst and dryness of his throat, at Ancenis he drank a glass of water: it was the first moment he had lost during sixteen hours, and yet the accursed courier was still an hour and a half in advance. In eighty leagues Gaston had only gained some forty or fifty minutes.

The night was drawing in rapidly, and Gaston, ever expecting to see some object appear on the horizon, tried to pierce the obscurity with his bloodshot glances; on he went, as in a dream, thinking he heard the ringing of bells, the roar of cannon, and the roll of drums. His brain was full of mourning strains and inauspicious sounds; he lived no longer as a man, but his fever kept him up, he flew as it were in the air.

On, and still on. About eight o'clock at night he perceived Nantes at length upon the horizon, like a dark mass from out the midst of which some scattered lights were shining starlike in the gloom.

He tried to breathe, and, thinking his cravat was choking him, he tore it off and threw it on the road.

Thus, mounted on his black horse, wrapped in his black cloak, and long ago bareheaded (his hat had fallen off), Gaston was like some fiendish cavalier bound to the witches' Sabbath.

On reaching the gates of Nantes his horse stumbled, but Gaston did not lose his stirrups, pulled him up sharply, and driving the spurs into his sides, he made him recover himself.

The night was dark, no one appeared upon the ramparts, the very sentinels were hidden in the gloom; it seemed like a deserted city. But as he passed the gate a sentinel said something which Gaston did not even hear. He held on his way. At the Rue du Château his horse stumbled and fell, this time to rise no more. What mattered it to Gaston now?—he had arrived. On he went on foot; his limbs were strained and deadened, yet he felt no fatigue, he held the paper crumbled in his hand.

One thing, however, astonished him, and that was meeting no one in so populous a quarter.

As he advanced, however, he heard a sullen murmur coming from the Place de Bouffay, as he passed before a long street which led into that Place.

There was a sea of heads, lit up by flaring lights; but Gaston passed on— his business was at the castle—and the sight disappeared.

At last he saw the castle—he saw the door gaping wide before him. The sentinel on guard upon the drawbridge tried to stop him; but Gaston, his order in his hand, pushed him roughly aside and entered the inner door.

Men were talking, and one of them was wiping his tears off as he talked.

Gaston understood it all.

"A reprieve!" he cried, "A re—"

The word died upon his lips; but the men had done better than hear, they had seen his despairing gesture.

"Go, go!" they cried, showing him the way, "go and perhaps you may yet arrive in time."

And they themselves dispersed in all directions. Gaston pursued his way; he traversed a corridor, then some empty rooms, then the great chamber, and then another corridor.

Far off, through the bars, by the torchlight, he perceived the great crowd of which he had caught a glimpse before.

He had passed right through the castle, and issued on a terrace; thence he perceived the esplanade, a scaffold, men, and all around the crowd.

Gaston tried to cry, but no one heard him, he waved his handkerchief, but no one saw him; another man mounts on the scaffold, and Gaston uttered a cry and threw himself down below.

He had leaped from the top of the rampart to the bottom. A sentinel tried to stop him, but he threw him down, and descended a sort of staircase which led down to the square, and at the bottom was a sort of barricade of wagons. Gaston bent down and glided between the wheels.

Beyond the barricade were all St. Simon's grenadiers,—a living hedge; Gaston, with a desperate effort, broke through the line, and found himself inside the ring.

The soldiers, seeing a man, pale and breathless, with a paper in his hand, allowed him to pass.

All of a sudden he stopped, as if struck by lightning. Talhouet!—he saw him!—Talhouet kneeling on the scaffold!

"Stop! stop!" cried Gaston, with all the energy of despair.

But even as he spoke the sword of the executioner flashed like lightning, a dull and heavy blow followed, and a terrible shudder ran through all the crowd.

The young man's shriek was lost in the general cry arising from twenty thousand palpitating breasts at once.

He had arrived a moment too late,— Talhouet was dead: and, as he lifted his eyes, he saw in the hand of the headsman the bleeding head of his friend,— and then, in the nobility of his heart, he felt that, one being dead, they all should die; that not one of them would accept a pardon which arrived a head too late. He looked around him; Du Couëdic mounted in his turn, clothed with his black mantle, bare-headed and bare-necked.

Gaston remembered that he also had a black mantle, and that his head and neck were bare, and he laughed convulsively.

He saw what remained for him to do, as one sees some wild landscape by the lightning's livid gleam,—'tis awful, but grand.

Du Couëdic bends down; but, as he bends, he cries: "See how they recompense the services of faithful soldiers! —see how you keep your promises, oh ye cowards of Bretagne!"

Two assistants force him on his knees; the sword of the executioner whirls round and gleams again, and Du Couëdic lies beside Talhouet.

The executioner takes up the head; shows it to the people; and then places it at one corner of the scaffold, opposite that of Talhouet.

"Who next?" asks the headsman.

"It matters little," answers a voice, "provided that Monsieur de Pontcalec be the last, according to his sentence."

"I, then," says Montlouis, "I." And he springs upon the scaffold. But there he stops, his hair bristling; at a window before him he has seen his wife and his children.

"Montlouis! Montlouis!" cried his wife, with the despairing accent of a breaking heart, "Montlouis! look at us!"

At the same moment all eyes were turned towards that window. Soldiers, citizens, priests, and executioners look the same way. Gaston profits by the deathlike silence which reigns around him, springs to the scaffold, and grasps the staircase and mounts the first steps.

"My wife! my children!" cried Montlouis, wringing his hands in despair; "oh! go, have pity upon me!"

"Montlouis!" cries his wife, holding up afar the youngest of his sons, "Montlouis, bless your children, and one day, perhaps, one of them will avenge you."

"Adieu! my children, my blessing on you!" cries Montlouis, stretching his hands towards the window.

These mournful adieus pierce the night, and reverberate like a terrible echo in the hearts of the spectators.

"Enough," says the executioner, "enough." Then, turning to his assistants,—

"Be quick!" says he, "or the people will not allow us to finish."

"Be easy," says Montlouis; "if the people should rescue me, I would not survive them."

And he pointed with his finger to the heads of his companions.

"Ah, I had estimated them rightly, then," cried Gaston, who heard these words. "Montlouis, martyr, pray for me."

Montlouis turned round, he seemed to have heard a well-known voice; but at the very moment the executioner seized him, and almost instantly a loud cry told Gaston that Montlouis was like the others, and that *his* turn was come.

He leapt up; in a moment he was on the top of the ladder, and he in his turn looked down from the abominable platform upon all that crowd. At three corners of the scaffold were the heads of Talhouet, Du Couëdic, and Montlouis.

But there arose then a strange emotion in the people. The execution of Montlouis, attended by the circumstances we have narrated, had upset the crowd. All the square, heaving and uttering murmurs and imprecations, seemed to Gaston some vast sea with life in every wave. At this moment the idea flashed across him that he might be recognised, and that his name uttered by a single mouth might prevent his carrying out his intention. He fell on his knees, and laid his head himself upon the block.

"Adieu!" he murmured, "adieu my friends, my tender, dear Helene; thy nuptial kiss has cost me my life indeed, but not mine honour. Alas! those fifteen minutes wasted in thine arms will have struck down five heads. Adieu! Helene, adieu!"

The sword of the executioner gleamed.

"And you, my friends, pardon me," added the young man.

The steel fell; the head rolled one way, and the body fell the other.

Then the executioner raised the head and showed it to the people.

But then a mighty murmur rose from the crowd; no one had recognised Pontcalec.

The executioner mistook the meaning of this murmur; he placed Gaston's head at the empty corner, and with his foot pushing the body into the tumbril where those of his three companions awaited, he leant upon his sword, and cried aloud,—

"Justice is done."

"And I, then," cried a voice of thunder, "am I to be forgotten?"

And Pontcalec, in his turn, leapt upon the scaffold.

"You!" cried he, recoiling as if he had seen a ghost. "You! who are you?"

"I," said Pontcalec; "come, I am ready."

"But," said the executioner, trembling, and looking one after the other at the four corners of the scaffold—"but there are four heads already."

"I am the Baron de Pontcalec, do you hear? I am to die the last,—and here I am."

"Count," said he, as pale as the baron, pointing with his sword to the four corners.

"Four heads!" exclaimed Pontcalec; "impossible." At this moment he recognised in one of the heads the pale and noble face of Gaston, which seemed to smile upon him even in death.

And he in his turn started back in terror.

"Oh, kill me then quickly!" he cried, groaning with impatience; "would you make me die a thousand times?"

During this interval, one of the commissioners had mounted the ladder, called by the chief executioner. He cast a glance upon Pontcalec.

"It is indeed the Baron de Pontcalec," said the commissioner; "perform your office."

"But," cried the executioner, "there are four heads there already."

"Well, then, his will make five; better too many than too few."

And the commissioner descended the steps, signing to the drums to beat.

The headsman reeled upon the boards of his scaffold. The tumult increased. The horror was more than the crowd could bear. A long murmur ran along the square; the lights were put out; the soldiers, driven back, cried, "To arms!" there was a moment of noise and confusion, and several voices exclaimed,—

"Death to the commissioners! death to the executioners!" Then the guns of the fort, loaded with grape, were pointed towards the people.

"What shall I do?" asked he.

"Strike," answered the same voice which had always spoken.

Pontcalec threw himself on his knees; the assistants placed his head upon the block. Then the priests fled in horror, the soldiers trembled in the gloom, and the headsman, as he struck, turned away his head lest he should see his victim. Ten minutes afterwards the square was empty,—the windows closed and dark. The artillery and the fusiliers encamped around the demolished scaffold looked in silence on the spots of blood that incarnadined the pavement.

The priests to whom the bodies were delivered recognised that there were indeed, as had been said, five bodies instead of four. One of the corpses still held a crumpled paper in his hand.

This paper was the pardon of the other four. Then only was all explained,—and the devotion of Gaston, which he had confided to no one, was divined.

The priests wished to perform a mass, but the president, Châteauneuf, fearing some disturbance at Nantes, ordered it to be performed without pomp or ceremony.

The bodies were buried on the Wednesday before Easter. The people were not permitted to enter the chapel where the mutilated bodies reposed, the greater part of which, report says, the quicklime refused to destroy.

Not long after this tragedy a queer carriage went out from Paris and proceeded along the road to Nantes. A young woman, pale and almost dying, was seated in it by the side of an Augustine nun, who uttered a sigh and wiped away a tear every time she looked at her companion.

A man on horseback of royal mien was watching for the carriage a little beyond Rambouillet. He was wrapped in a large cloak which left nothing visible but his eyes.

Near him was another man also enveloped in a cloak.

When the carriage passed, he heaved a deep sigh, and two silent tears fell from his eyes.

"Adieu!" he murmured, "adieu all my joy, adieu my happiness! adieu Helene, my child, adieu!"

"Monseigneur," said the man beside him, "you must pay for being a great prince; and he who would govern others must first conquer himself. Be strong to the end, monseigneur, and posterity will say that you were great."

"Oh, I shall never forgive you," said the regent, Philippe d'Orleans, with a sigh so deep it sounded like a groan; "for you have killed my happiness."

"Ah, yes!—work for kings," said the companion of this sorrowful man, shrugging his shoulders. "'Noli fidere principibus terræ nec filiis eorum.'"

The two men remained there till the carriage had disappeared, and then returned to Paris.

Eight days afterwards the carriage entered the porch of the Augustines at Clisson. On its arrival, all the convent pressed round the suffering traveller,— poor floweret! broken by the rough winds of the world.

"Come, my child; come and live with us again," said the superior.

"Not live, my mother," said the young girl, "but die."

"Think only of the Lord, my child," said the good abbess.

"Yes, my mother! Our Lord, who died for the sins of men."

Helene returned to her little cell, from which she had been absent scarcely a month. Everything was still in its place, and exactly as she had left it. She went to the window: the lake was sleeping tranquil and sad, but the ice which had covered it had disappeared beneath the rain, and with it the snow, where, before departing, the young girl had seen the impression of Gaston's footsteps.

Spring came, and everything but Helene began to live once more. The trees around the little lake grew green, the large leaves of the water-lilies floated once more upon the surface, the reeds raised up their heads, and all the families of warbling birds came back to people them again. Even the barred gate opened to let the sturdy gardener in.

Helene survived the summer, but in September she faded with the waning of the year, and died.

The very morning of her death, the superior received a letter from Paris by a courier. She carried it to the dying girl. It contained only these words:—

"My mother, obtain from your daughter her pardon for the regent."

Helene, implored by the superior, grew paler at that name, but she answered,—

"Yes, my mother, I forgive him. But it is because I go to rejoin him whom he killed."

At four o'clock in the afternoon she breathed her last.

She asked to be buried at the spot where Gaston, her lover, used to untie the boat with which he came to visit her; and her last wishes were complied with.

And there she sleeps beneath the sod, pure as the flowers that blossom over her grave; and, like them, broken by the cruel gusts that sweep the delicate blossoms so mercilessly down, and wither them with a breath.

Cripple and Giant

GENERAL TRAVOT was sent to La Vendée to quell the peasant uprising. We all know the result of his operations; the Vendéan army defeated, Jolly killed, Couëtu enticed into an ambush and taken by a traitor whose name has never been known, Charette made prisoner in the woods of La Chabotière and shot in the market-place of Nantes.

The guard-house, which had been occupied for the last few days by a detachment of troops of the line, was a vast building, with a front toward the courtyard, while its rear looked out upon the country road that leads from Saint-Colombin to Saint-Philbert-de-Grand-Lieu, about a kilometre from the first of these two villages and a stone's throw from the high-road between Nantes and the Sables-d'Olonne.

This building, constructed on the ruins and with the fragments of an old feudal fortress, occupied an eminence that commanded the whole neighborhood. It answered the purpose of a block-house, where expeditionary columns could find, on occasion, a resting-place or a refuge, and at the same time it might be made a sort of station for prisoners, where they could be collected until a sufficiently imposing force was mustered to escort them to Nantes, without danger of rescue.

The accommodations of the guard-house consisted solely of a somewhat vast hall and a barn. The hall served as the guard-room. It was reached by a flight of steps, made with the old stones of the fortress, placed parallel with the wall.

The barn was used as barracks for the men; they slept there on straw. The post was guarded with all military precautions. A sentry stood before the gate of the courtyard which opened to the road, and a lookout was stationed in an ivy-covered tower, the sole remains left standing of the old feudal castle.

Now, about six o'clock one evening, the soldiers who formed the little garrison were seated on some heavy rollers which had been left at the foot of the outside wall of the house. It was a favorite spot for their siesta; there they enjoyed the gentle warmth of the setting sun and a splendid view of the lake of Grand-Lieu in the distance, the surface of which, tinted by the beams of the star of day, resembled at that hour an immense sheet of scarlet tin. At their feet ran the road to Nantes, like a broad ribbon through the midst of the verdure which at that season covered the plain; and we must admit that our heroes in red trousers were more interested in what happened on that road than in all the beauties which Nature spread before them.

On the evening of which we write, the laborers leaving the fields, the flocks returning to their stables made the road a somewhat lively and varied panorama. Each heavy hay-cart, each group returning from the Nantes market, and, above all, every peasant-woman in her short skirt was a text for remark and jocularity, which, it must be owned, were not restrained.

"Goodness!" cried one of the men, suddenly, "what's that I see down there?"

"A fellow with bagpipes," said another.

"Bagpipes, indeed! Do you think you are still in Britany? Down here they don't groan bagpipes they only whine complaints."

"What has he got on his back, then, if it isn't his instrument?"

"That's an instrument, sure enough,"

said a fourth soldier; "it must be an organ."

"Queer organ!" said a fifth. "I tell you that's a sack; the man's a Beggar. You can tell him by his clothes."

"Then his sack has eyes and a nose, like the rest of us. Why, look at him, Limousin!"

"Limousin's arm is long, but his sight is short," said another; "you can't have everything."

"Pooh!" said the corporal; "I see what it is. It is one man carrying another on his shoulders."

"The corporal is right!" chorused the soldiers.

"I am always right," said he of the woollen stripes, "first as your corporal, next as your superior; and if there are any of you who doubt after I have once said a thing, he is going to be convinced now, for here come the men straight toward us."

And coming indeed was a personage whom, with a very slight stretch of fancy, one might have taken for some uncanny or impish being. This personage advanced slowly, looking cautiously about him,—a matter which seemed to be the more easy because, at first sight, he appeared to have two heads, with which to keep a double watch over his safety.

He was clothed in the sordid rags of an old jacket and the semblance of a pair of breeches, the original cloth of which had completely disappeared beneath the multifarious patches of many colors with which its decay had been remedied; and he appeared, as we have said, to belong to the class of bicephalous monsters who occupy a distinguished place among the choice exceptions which Nature delights to create in her fantastic moments.

The two heads were entirely distinct the one from the other, and though they apparently came from the same trunk there was no family resemblance between them. Beside a broad and brick-dust colored face, seamed with small-pox and covered with unkempt beard, appeared a second face, less repulsive, very astute, and rather malign in its ugliness, whereas the other countenance expressed only a sort of idiocy which might at times amount to ferocity.

These two distinct countenances did, in truth, belong to two men, namely, to Aubin Courte-Joie Short-Joy, a cripple and tavern keeper, and—if the reader will pardon an almost too expressive name, but one we think we have no right to change—to Trigaud the Vermin, the beggar, whose herculean strength played a noted part in a riot at Montaigu by lifting the general's leg from the stirrup and throwing him out of his saddle.

By a judicious arrangement, Aubin Courte-Joie had supplemented, or recompleted, his own personality by the help of this species of beast of burden whom he had, by good luck, encountered on his path through life. In exchange for the two legs he had lost, the truncated cripple had obtained a pair of steel limbs, which resisted all fatigue, feared no task, and served him as his own original legs never did and never could have done,—legs, in short, which did his will with passive obedience, and had reached, after a certain period of association, such adaptability that they instinctively guessed the very thoughts of Aubin Courte-Joie, if conveyed by a mere word, a single sign,

or even a slight touch of a hand on the shoulder or a knee on the flank.

The strangest part of this affair was that the least satisfied partner in the firm was not Trigaud-Vermin; quite the contrary. His thick brain knew that Aubin Courte-Joie was a real leader of Chouans and was directing his physical strength in the direction of his sympathies. The words "White" and "Blue," which dropped into his large ears, always pricked up and listening, proved to him that he supported, in his quality of locomotive to the tavern-keeper, a cause whose worship was the one glimmer of light which had survived the collapse of his brain. He made it his glory. His confidence in Aubin Courte-Joie was boundless; he was proud of being linked body and soul to a mind whose superiority he recognized, and he was now attached to the man who might indeed be called his master, with the self-abnegation that characterizes all attachments which instinct governs.

"As we are all here together they come and beg," said a soldier.

"I'll be shot if I give 'em a penny," said the soldier who had spoken first.

"See here!" said another, picking up a stone; "I'll put something into his hat."

"I forbid you," said the corporal.

"Why so?"

"Because he hasn't any hat."

The soldiers burst out laughing at the joke, which was recognized at once as very choice.

"Let's have a look," said a soldier, "at what the fellow is really carrying; don't discourage him. For my part, I don't find such delight in this beggarly guard-house that I despise any sort of fun that comes along."

"Fun?"

"Yes, any kind,—music perhaps. Every tramp in this region is a sort of troubadour. We'll make him sing what he knows, and a good deal he doesn't know; it will help pass the evening."

By this time the mendicant, now no longer an enigma to the soldiers, was close beside them, holding out his hand.

"You were right, corporal; he has got another man perched on his shoulders."

"I was wrong," responded the corporal.

"How so?"

"That isn't a man,—only a section of humanity."

The soldiers laughed at the second joke as heartily as they laughed at the first.

"He can't spend much on trousers," said one.

"And less for boots," added the facetious corporal.

"Aren't they hideous?" said the Limousin. "Upon my word, you might think 'em a monkey mounted on a bear."

While these poor waggeries were flying about and reaching Trigaud's ear, he stood immovable, holding out his hand and giving a most pitiable expression to his face, while Aubin Courte-Joie, in his capacity as orator of the association, repeated, in his nasal voice, the unvarying formula:—

"Charity, if you please, my good gentlemen!—charity for a poor cartman with both legs taken off by his cart, coming down the hill at Ancenis."

"What ignorant savages they must be to expect alms of soldiers in gar-rison. Scamps! I'll bet if we searched their pockets we'd find double what we have got in our own."

Hearing which suggestion, Aubin Courte-Joie modified the formula, and came down to a precise request:—

"A bit of bread, just a bit of bread, if you please, my good gentlemen," he said. "If you haven't any money you have surely a bit of bread."

"Bread!" said the corporal. "Yes, you shall have bread, my good man; and with the bread, soup, and with the soup a bit of meat. We'll do that for you; but I should like to know what you'll do for us."

"My good gentlemen, I'll pray God for you," replied Courte-Joie, in his nasal whine, which formed the treble to his partner's bass.

"That will do no harm," said the corporal,—"no, certainly, there's no harm in that; but it isn't enough. Come, haven't you anything funny in your sack?"

"How do you mean?" asked Courte-Joie, assuming ignorance.

"I mean, villainous old black-birds that you are, you must be able to whistle an air or two; in which case, let's have the music first. That will pay for the soup and the bread and the meat."

"Ah, yes, yes; I understand. Well. we don't refuse. On the contrary, officer," said Aubin, flattering the corporal, "it is fair enough that if you give us the charity of the good God we should try to amuse you and your company as best we can."

"Good; the more the better. You can't go too far, for we are dying of dullness in your devilish land."

"All right," said Courte-Joie; "we'll

begin by showing you something you never saw before."

Although the promise was nothing more than the usual exordium of clowns at a circus, it roused the curiosity of the soldiers, who clustered round the mendicants in silence, with an eagerness that was almost respectful. Courte-Joie, who until then had kept his seat on Trigaud's shoulders, made a movement of his body, indicating that he wished to be deposited on the ground, and Trigaud, with that passive obedience which he practised to the will of his master, seated him on a fragment of the old battlement half-buried in nettles, which lay near the rollers on which the men were seated.

"Hey! how neatly that was done!" cried the corporal. "I'd like to recruit that fellow and turn him over to the fat major, who can't find a cob fit to carry him."

During this time Courte-Joie had picked up a stone, which he gave to Trigaud. The latter, without further directions, closed and then opened his hand, showing the stone reduced to fragments.

"Good Lord! he's a Hercules! You must tackle him, Pinguet," said the corporal, addressing the soldier we have hitherto called the Limousin.

"All right," said the latter, jumping up; "we'll see about it."

Trigaud, taking no notice of the words or actions of Pinguet, continued his exercises. He seized two soldiers by the straps of their knapsacks, gently raised and held them aloft at arm's-length for a few seconds, and then as gently put them down, with perfect ease.

The soldiers cheered him loudly.

"Pinguet! Pinguet!" they cried, "where are you? Here's some one who can knock you into a cocked-hat."

Trigaud continued his performances as if these experiments on his strength were a pre-arranged matter. He invited two other soldiers to seat themselves astride of the shoulders of the first two, and he carried all four with almost as much ease as if there were but two. As he put them down, Pinguet arrived with a gun on each shoulder.

"Bravo, Limousin! bravo!" cried the soldiers.

Encouraged by the acclamations of his comrades, Pinguet cried out:—

"All that is mountebank business. Here, you braggart, let me see you do what I am going to do."

Putting a finger of each hand into the muzzle of a gun, he held the weapons out before him, at arm's-length.

"Pooh!" said Courte-Joie, while Trigaud looked on with a movement of the lips that might pass for a smile at Pinguet's feat,—"pooh! bring two more guns."

When the guns were brought Trigaud put all four muzzles on the fingers of one hand and raised them to the level of his eye, without any contraction of the muscles that betrayed an effort. Pinguet was distanced forever in the struggle.

Then rummaging in his pocket, Trigaud brought out a horse-shoe, which he folded in two as easily as an ordinary man would fold a leather strap. After each of his experiments he turned his eyes to Courte-Joie, asking for a smile; then Courte-Joie would signify by a nod that he was satisfied.

"Come," said Aubin, "you've only

earned our suppers so far; now you must get us a night's lodging. Isn't that so, my good gentlemen? If my comrade does something more wonderful still, won't you give us a little hay and a corner in the stable to lie on?"

"As for that, it is impossible," said the sergeant of the company, who, being attracted by the shouts and plaudits of the soldiers, had come to share the sight; "the orders are strict."

This answer seemed to discourage Courte-Joie greatly; his weasel-face grew serious.

"Never mind," said one of the men; "we'll club together, and get you ten sous, which will pay for a bed at the nearest tavern, and that will be softer than buckwheat hay."

"If the ox you ride has legs as solid as his arms," said another, "a mile or two farther won't trouble you."

"First, let's see the performance!" cried the soldiers. "Show us his best thing."

There was no repelling this enthusiasm, and Courte-Joie yielded with an alacrity which showed his confidence in his comrade's biceps.

"Have you a grindstone here, or anything that weighs about twelve or fifteen hundred pounds?" he asked.

"There's the block of stone you are sitting on," said a soldier.

Courte-Joie shrugged his shoulders. "If that stone had a handle Trigaud would pick it up for you with one hand."

"There's that millstone we tipped up before the grating of the dungeon," said a soldier.

"Why not tell him to lift the whole building at once?" said the corporal. "It took six of you men to put it

where it is, and with levers, too. I was furious that my rank forbade me from lending a hand to what I called a pack of idlers."

"Besides, you must not touch that millstone," interposed the sergeant; "that's also against orders. There's a prisoner in the cellar."

Courte-Joie gave Trigaud a glance, and the latter, paying no attention to the sergeant's remark, went straight to the millstone.

"Don't you hear me?" said the sergeant, raising his voice, and catching Trigaud by the arm; "you are not to touch it."

"Why not?" said Courte-Joie. "If he moves it he'll replace it; don't be afraid."

"Besides," said a soldier, "if you look at the mouse they have got in the trap you'll see it would never run away if it could,—a poor little monsieur who might be taken for a woman in disguise. I thought at first he was the Duchesse de Berry herself."

"Yes, and he's too busy crying to think of escape," said the corporal, who was evidently burning with the desire to see the feat. "When we took him his food, Pinguet and I,—that is, I and Pinguet,—he burst into tears; I declare if his eyes weren't two faucets!"

"Well, well," said the sergeant, who was no less curious than the rest to see how the tramp would accomplish his Titanic task, "I will take the responsibility of allowing it."

Trigaud profited by the permission. He seized the millstone between his arms at its base, leaned his shoulder on its centre, and with a powerful effort tried to raise it. But the weight of this enormous mass of stone had sunk it into the ground on which it rested to the depth of some four or five inches, and the adherence of this earth socket, thus hollowed, neutralized Trigaud's efforts.

Courte-Joie, who had entered the circle of soldiers by creeping on his hands and knees, like a huge scarabœus, called attention to the nature of the difficulty; then with a large flat stone which he picked up, and partly also with his hands, he grubbed out the earth which hindered the success of Trigaud's feat. The giant then applied himself once more to the work. Soon he raised the huge block and held it up for a few seconds, resting against his shoulder and also against the wall, about a foot from the ground.

The enthusiasm of the soldiers knew no bounds. They pressed around Trigaud and overwhelmed him with congratulations to which he seemed perfectly insensible; they shouted in frantic admiration, which was shared by the corporal, and then, through the natural hierarchy of rank, by the sergeant himself. They talked of carrying Trigaud in triumph to the sutler's, where the reward of his vigor awaited him, swearing by every oath known to the sons of Mars that Trigaud deserved not only the bread and soup and meat promised by the corporal, but the rations of a general, or indeed of the king of France, which would be none too much to maintain the strength required for such prowess.

As we have said, Trigaud seemed in no way puffed-up by his triumph; his countenance remained as impassible as that of an ox allowed to breathe after some powerful exertion. His eyes, however, sought those of Aubin Courte-Joie, as if to ask "Master, are you satisfied?"

Courte-Joie, on the other hand, looked radiant, possibly because of the impression made upon the spectators by a strength he considered his own, though it far exceeded that which Nature had originally bestowed upon him. Perhaps, however, his satisfaction was really caused by the success of a little manœuvre he had cleverly performed while the attention of all was concentrated on his companion,—a manœuvre which consisted in slipping under the millstone the large flat stone he held in his hand, placing it in such a way that the enormous mass which closed the grating of the cellar was so poised upon its smooth surface that the strength of a child would suffice to displace it.

The two beggars were taken to the sutler's, and there Trigaud furnished still another text of admiration to the soldiers. After he had swallowed an enormous canful of soup, four rations of beef and two loaves of bread were placed before him. Trigaud ate the first loaf with the first two rations; then, as if by changing his method of deglutition he changed and improved the taste of the objects swallowed, he took his second loaf, split it in two, scooped out and ate, by way of pastime, the crumb within it, placed the meat in the cavity, put the two halves of the crust together, and proceeded to bite through the whole with a coolness and force of jaw which brought down thunders of applause from the delighted audience.

After about five minutes of this exercise nothing remained of either bread or meat but a few crumbs of the loaf.

which Trigaud, apparently ready to begin all over again, carefully collected. His admirers hastened to bring him a third loaf, which, though stale and dry, Trigaud treated like the first two.

The soldiers were not yet satisfied; they would have liked to push their investigations still further, but the sergeant thought it more prudent to bring their scientific curiosity to an end. Courte-Joie had now become thoughtful, and his expression was noticed by the soldiers.

"Ah, ça!" said the corporal; "here you are, eating and drinking on the earnings of your comrade. That's not fair; it seems to me you might give us a song, if only to pay your scot."

"Unquestionably," said the sergeant.

"Yes, yes, a song!" cried the soldiers, "and then the affair will be complete."

"Hum!" muttered Courte-Joie. "I know some songs, of course I do."

"All right then, sing away!"

"But my songs mayn't be to your liking."

"Never mind,—so long as it isn't a fugue for the devil's funeral, anything will be fun to us; we are not hard to please at Saint-Colombin."

"Yes," said Courte-Joie, "I can see that; you are horribly bored."

"Monstrously," said the sergeant.

"We don't expect you to sing like Monsieur Nourrit," observed a Parisian.

"Make it a bit quizzical," said another man, "and the more the better."

"As I have eaten your bread and drunk your wine," said Courte-Joie, "I have no right to refuse you anything; but, I repeat it, my songs will probably not be to your taste."

And thereupon, he trolled out the following stanza:—

"Look! look my gars, down there! down there!
Don't you see the infernal band?
Spread out, spread out, surprise them there,
Behind the gorse, across the land.
Spread out! I say, my gars! my gars!
Await the Blues with steady hand."

Courte-Joie got no farther. After a moment of surprised silence at his first words a roar of indignation arose; ten soldiers sprang upon him and the sergeant, seizing him by the collar, threw him on the ground.

"Villain!" he cried, "I'll teach you to come here in our midst and sing praises to your brigands."

But before the words were well out of his mouth (words to which he added a variety of adverbs that were customary with him) Trigaud, his eyes flashing with anger, made his way through to Courte-Joie, pushed back the sergeant and stood before his comrade in so threatening an attitude that the soldiers remained for some moments silent and uncertain.

But soon, mortified at being held at bay by an unarmed man, they drew their sabres, and rushed upon the beggars.

"Kill them! kill them!" they cried; "they are Chouans!"

"You asked me for a song; I warned you that the songs I knew were not to your taste," cried Courte-Joie, in a voice that rose high above the tumult. "You ought not to have insisted. Why do you complain?"

"If you only knew such songs as you have just sung you are a rebel, and I arrest you peremptorily."

"I know such songs as please the people of the towns and villages whose alms are my living. A poor cripple like me and an idiot like my comrade can't be dangerous. Arrest us if you choose; but such captures won't do you any honor."

"That may be," replied the sergeant, "but meantime you'll sleep in the lock-up. You were puzzled where to go for a night's lodging, my fine fellow; well, I'll give you one. Come, men, seize and search them, and let us lock them up incontinently."

But, as Trigaud still maintained a threatening attitude, no one hastened to execute the sergeant's order.

"If you don't go with a good grace," said the latter, "I'll send for some loaded muskets, and we'll see if your skin is bullet-proof."

"Come, Trigaud, my lad," said Courte-Joie, "if we must resign ourselves, we must; besides, it can't matter, they won't detain us long. Their fine prisons are not built for poor devils like us."

"That's right," said the sergeant, much pleased at the pacific turn the affair was taking. "You will be searched, and if nothing suspicious is found upon you, and you behave properly during the night, we'll see about letting you out to-morrow morning."

The two beggars were searched, but nothing was found upon them except a few copper coins; which confirmed the sergeant in his ideas of clemency.

"After all," he said, pointing to Trigaud, "that great ox is not guilty;

I see no reason why I should lock him up."

"If you do," said the Limousin, "he might take it into his head, like his forefather Samson, to shake the walls and bring them down about our ears."

"You are right, Pinguet," said the sergeant, "because that's my opinion, too. We should only embarrass ourselves by holding the pair. Come, off with you, friend, and quick too!"

"Oh! my good monsieur, don't separate us," cried Courte-Joie, in a tearful voice. "We can't do without each other; he walks for me, and I think for him."

"Upon my word," said a soldier, "they are worse than lovers."

"No," said the sergeant to Courte-Joie. "I shall make you pass the night in the dungeon to punish you, and to-morrow the officer of the day will decide what is to be done with your carcass. Come, to the cellar!"

Two soldiers approached Courte-Joie; but he with an agility not to be expected in so helpless a body, sprang upon Trigaud's shoulders, and the giant walked peacefully along toward the door of the dungeon, under escort of the soldiers.

On the way Aubin put his lips close to the ear of his comrade and said some words in a low voice concerning the flat stone under the millstone. Trigaud deposited his master at the cellar-door, through which the sergeant thrust the cripple, who made his entrance by rolling forward like an enormous ball.

The soldiers then took Trigaud outside the courtyard gate, which they closed behind him. The giant stood for a few moments motionless and bewildered, as if he did not know what course to decide upon. He tried at first to sit down on the rollers, where, as we have seen, the soldiers took their siesta. But the sentry made him understand that that was impossible, and the beggar departed in the direction of the village of Saint-Colombin.

About two hours after Aubin Courte-Joie's incarceration the sentry of the post heard a cart coming up the road which led past the guard-house. "Qui vive?" he cried; and when the cart was only a short distance from him he ordered it to halt. The cart, or rather the cartman, obeyed.

The corporal and four soldiers came out of the guard-room to inspect both man and vehicle. The cart was a harmless one, loaded with hay, and was like all the others that were plodding along the road to and from Nantes during the evening. Only one man was with it; he explained that he was going to Saint-Philbert with hay for his landlord,—adding that he went by night to economize time, which was precious at this season of the year. The corporal gave orders to let him pass.

But this permission was wasted on the poor fellow. His cart, drawn by a single horse, had stopped at the steepest part of the rising ground about the guard-house, and in spite of the efforts made by horse and cartman it was impossible to start the heavy vehicle again.

"There isn't any sense," said the corporal, "in overburdening a beast like that! Don't you see that your horse has double the load he can draw?"

"What a pity," remarked one of the soldiers, "that the sergeant let that big ox of a fellow we had here go. We might have harnessed him to the horse

and I'll warrant he'd have pulled to the collar."

"That's supposing he would have let himself be harnessed."

If the man who spoke last had looked behind the cart, he would have seen good reason why Trigaud should not allow himself to be harnessed to the front of the cart to pull it forward; he would also have understood the difficulty the horse found in starting the cart. For this difficulty was chiefly owing to Trigaud himself. The giant, completely hidden in the darkness and behind the hay, was dragging at the rear bar of the cart and opposing his strength to that of the horse, with as much success as he had won when exhibiting his prowess in the evening.

"Shall we lend you a hand?" said the corporal.

"Wait till I try again," said the driver, who had turned his cart obliquely, to lessen the sharpness of the acclivity, and now, grasping the horse by the bridle, prepared for a final effort to disprove the blame the corporal laid upon him.

He whipped his beast vigorously, exciting him by voice and pulling on the bridle, while the soldiers joined their cries to his. The horse stiffened all four legs for the effort, making the sparks fly from his heels among the stones of the road; then, he suddenly fell down, and at the same moment, as if the wheels had encountered some obstacle which disturbed their equilibrium, the cart swayed over to left and upset against the building.

The soldiers ran forward and helped to release the horse from the harness and get him on his legs. The result of their friendly eagerness was that none of them saw Trigaud, who, satisfied no doubt with a result to which he had powerfully contributed by slipping under the cart and hoisting it on his Herculean shoulders, until it lost its centre of gravity, now retired composedly behind a hedge to await events.

"Shall we help you to set your cart back on its pin?" said the corporal to the driver. "If so, you must get an additional horse."

"Faith, no!" cried the cartman. "To-morrow I'll see about it. It is evident the good God doesn't mean me to keep on,—mustn't go against His will."

So saying, the peasant threw the reins on the crupper of his horse, pushed up the collar, mounted the animal, and departed, after wishing good-night to the soldiers, and saying he should be back in the morning to remove the hay. Two hundred yards from the guard-house Trigaud joined him.

"Well," said the peasant, "was that done to your liking? Are you satisfied?"

"Yes," replied Trigaud, "that was just as *gars* Aubin Courte-Joie ordered."

"Good luck to you, then! As for me, I'll put the horse back where I found it. But when the cartman wakes up to-morrow and looks for his cart and his hay he'll be rather surprised to find it up there."

"Well, tell him it is for the good of the cause, and he won't mind," replied Trigaud.

The two men parted.

Trigaud, however, did not leave the place; he roamed about its neighborhood till he heard the stroke of twelve from the steeple of Saint-Colombin. Then he returned to the guard-house, *sabots* in hand, and without making the slightest noise, or rousing the attention of the sentry, who was pacing up and down, he crept to the grating of the dungeon. Once there he softly drew the hay into a thick heap beside the millstone, which he then, as softly, turned over upon it. Then he leaned behind it to the grating, wrenched off the boards that closed it, drew out Courte-Joie, after which, putting him on his shoulders, Trigaud, still bare-footed, walked rapidly away from the neighborhood of the guard-house, making, in spite of his immense size and the weight he carried, no more noise than a cat on a carpet.

They traveled thus for a long time and finally rested to suit Aubin at the Bouaimé moor.

The Bouaimé moor lies about three miles from the village of Saint-Hilaire; the river Maine must be crossed to reach it. It extends on the north as far as Rémouillé and Montbert; the lay of the land is very uneven, and it is strewn with granite rocks, some evidently placed there by the hand of man. Druidic stones and dolmens lift their brown heads crowned with moss amid tufts of heather and the yellow flowers of the gorse and broom. It was to one of the most remarkable of these stones that they went. This stone was flat, and rested on four enormous corner-stones of granite. Ten or a dozen persons could easily have lain in its shadow.

Trigaud was stationed as sentinel on the dolmen; aboriginal statue on an aboriginal pedestal, he called to mind by his mighty outline the giants of two thousand years ago, who raised that altar. Courte-Joie, unstrapped, lay down to sleep.

For about two hours Trigaud's eyes had roved over the broad expanse of the savanna before and around him. Not a sound had reached his ear, attentively listening, except the monotonous hum of bees and wasps pilfering sweetness from the broom and the wild thyme. The mists which the sun was drawing from the earth began to assume to Trigaud's eyes a variety of rainbow tints, the shimmerings of which, added to the rays of the sun, which were now falling plumb on his tufts of red hair, benumbed his brain; various somniferous combinations were about to plunge him into a siesta, not induced, unfortunately for him, by any meal, when the sudden report of a firearm roused him from his torpor.

He looked in the direction of Saint Hilaire and saw the white vapor produced by the shot. With one bound Trigaud was off his pedestal, and immediately waked up Courte-Joie.

Trigaud took the cripple in his arms and hoisted him above his head till he was fully ten feet off the ground, saying but two words, which, however, needed no commentary:—

"The enemy."

Whenever intelligence was needed instead of senses, Courte-Joie no longer trusted to Trigaud. He had himself hoisted to the top of the dolmen, although, small as his truncated body was, he thought best not to display it too openly on that pedestal. He therefore lay down flat on his stomach with his face turned in the direction of the hill.

Soon he saw a soldier, then another, then a third; he counted them up to twenty. The hill ended in a sharp point of rocks, at the foot of which was a bog. It was on that spot that Courte-Joie's attention was now fixed.

"Hum!" said Trigaud, suddenly.

"What is it?" asked Courte-Joie.

"Red-breeches," replied the other, pointing to the bog.

Courte-Joie followed the direction of Trigaud's finger and saw the barrel of a gun in the midst of the reeds; then a form. It was that of a soldier, and he, like the one first seen on the heath, was followed by twenty others. Courte-Joie saw them crouching among the reeds like sportsmen on the watch.

Courte-Joie glanced about him, apparently studying each point of the horizon; he wet a finger and lifted it to discover the direction of the wind, and felt the heather anxiously, to be sure that the sun, which was hot, and the wind, which was keen, had dried it thoroughly.

"What are you doing?" asked Trigaud.

"What am I doing,—or rather what am I going to do?" replied the cripple. "I am going to make a glorious bonfire; and you can boast to-night, if the fire saves us, as I hope it will, that you never saw the like before."

So saying, he gave Trigaud several lighted bits of tinder, which the latter stuck into bundles of dried herbage, which he placed at intervals of ten feet among the heather, blowing each of them into a flame with his powerful lungs.

In fact ten minutes had not expired before ten columns of smoke were blended into one and formed a dense sheet stretching to right and left five hundred feet, while the flames roared sullenly behind them.

"We have no other guide than the smoke," said Courte-Joie. "Let us follow that boldly and it will take us where we want to go.

They walked for fifteen minutes without getting out of the smoke with their conflagration, spreading with amazing rapidity under the force of the wind, rolled up about them.

Suddenly Trigaud, guided by Courte-Joie, and utterly indifferent to where he went, stepped back abruptly. He had set his feet in water, which the smoke had prevented him from seeing, and he was now knee-deep in it. Aubin uttered a cry of joy.

"We've done it!" he said; "the smoke has led us as straight as the best-broken hound ever led a sportsman."

"Yes. Now for the island."

Trigaud took Courte-Joie in his arms and entered the pond. He walked thus till the water was up to his middle. It stopped, however, at the level of the giant's breast. He crossed the pond to a sort of island about twelve feet square, which seemed in the midst of that stagnant water to be nothing more than a vast duck's-nest. It was covered with a forest of reeds.

The flames were rolling onward with terrifying rapidity; they ran along the flowery tops of the broom and heather like gold and purple birds swept forward by the wind, as if they preferred to play among the twigs and branches before they seized upon the stems. Their mutterings, like the roar of ocean, increased in all directions round the fugitives, and the smoke grew denser and more suffocating.

But the steel muscles possessed by Trigaud were a match for the flames, and they were soon safe from all danger of fire. They turned obliquely to the left, and soon reached a dip in the valley which was almost free of the smoke which so far had been their main protection,—serving to hide the direction of their flight, and Trigaud deposited Courte-Joie to rest the latter.

Trigaud bent down as though he were going on all fours, and it was lucky for him he did so, for no sooner had he stooped than a ball, which he would otherwise have received in his breast, whizzed harmlessly through the air.

They now saw a file of soldiers posted at a hundred paces from each other, all the way from the dolmen to a distance of a mile and a half, evidently waiting, like huntsmen, till the quarry should reappear.

The comrades had scarcely advanced ten steps before six or eight successive discharges were heard; and one of the balls splintered the club which Trigaud was carrying in his hand. Happily for the fugitives, the soldiers hurrying on all sides to the help of their wounded companions, and coming up out of breath, had fired unsteadily. Trigaud was fortunate; and save for a ball which grazed his shoulder and added more rags to those he wore, he and his partner Courte-Joie got safely across the line.

"All right!" said the cripple; "and in twenty minutes, if we don't have a limb lopped off by those rascally Blues, we'll be in the fields; and once we are behind a hedge the devil himself can't touch us.

"No; and you, Trigaud? I thought I felt a sort of shudder on your hide."

The giant showed the gash the ball had made in his club; evidently, this misfortune, which destroyed the symmetry of the work at which he had fondly labored all the morning, troubled him far more than the damage done to his clothing or to his deltoid, which was slightly injured by the passage of the ball.

"Oh, be joyful!" cried Courte-Joie; "here are the fields."

In truth, not a thousand steps away from the fugitives at the bottom of a slope which was so gentle as to be almost imperceptible, fields of wheat were visible, their ears already yellowing and swaying to the breeze in their dull-green sheaths.

"Suppose we stop to breathe a minute," said Courte-Joie, who seemed to feel the fatigue that Trigaud felt.

The latter, to relieve his lungs, gave vent to a sort of bellow which a lusty Poitevin bull might have envied him, and then with a single stride he jumped an enormous stone which lay on his way.

The giant had just concluded this feat when the horsemen appeared at the top of the slope and dashed down in pursuit of the Chouans at full gallop.

Nevertheless, all hope was not lost. Trigaud and Courte-Joie were scarcely fifty steps from a hedge beyond which they would be safe from horsemen; and as for the foot-soldiers, they appeared to have relinquished their pursuit.

But a subaltern officer admirably mounted pressed them so hard that Courte-Joie felt the hot breath of the animal on his legs. The rider, determined to end the matter, rose in his stirrups and aimed such a blow with his sabre at the cripple's head that he would certainly have split it in two; but the horse, which he did not have well in hand, swerved to the left, while Trigaud instinctively flung himself to the right. The weapon therefore missed its mark and merely made a flesh wound on the cripple's arm.

"Face about!" cried Courte-Joie to Trigaud, as though he were commanding a company. The latter pivoted round, absolutely as though his body were riveted to the ground with an iron screw.

The horse, passing beside him, struck him in the breast, but did not shake him. At the same instant Courte-Joie, firing one barrel of his little gun, knocked over the subaltern, who was dragged to some distance by the impetus of his horse.

"One!" counted Trigaud, in whom the imminence of danger seemed to develop a loquacity which was not habitual with him.

During the moment that this affair lasted the other horsemen were rapidly approaching; a few horse's-lengths alone separated them from the two Vendéans, who could hear, above the tramp of their galloping steeds, the sharp cocking of their pistols and musketoons. But that moment had sufficed Courte-Joie to judge of the resources offered him by the place in which he found himself.

They were now at the farther end of the moor of Bouaimé, a few steps from a crossway whence several roads diverged. Like all such open spaces in Brittany and La Vendée, this crossway had its crucifix; and the cross, which was of stone, and dilapidated on one side, offered a temporary refuge which might soon become untenable. To right were the first hedges of the fields; but there was no chance whatever of reaching them, for three or four horsemen, forestalling their intention, had obliquely advanced to thwart it. Opposite to them and flowing to their left was the river Maine, which made a bend at this place; but Courte-Joie knew it was useless to even think of putting the river between himself and the soldiers, for the opposite bank was a face of rock rising from the water; and in following the current to find a spot to land, the two Chouans would have been simply a target for the enemy.

It was, therefore, the refuge of the cross on which Courte-Joie decided, and in that direction Trigaud, under his master's orders, proceeded. But just as he reached the column of stone and turned it to put its bulk between the soldiers and themselves, a ball struck an arm of the cross, ricochetted, and wounded Courte-Joie in the cheek, —not, however, preventing the cripple from replying to it in turn.

Unfortunately, the blood which poured from the wound fell on Trigaud's hands. He saw that blood, gave a roar of fury,—as though he felt nought but that which injured his companion,—and charged madly on the soldiers like a wild-boar on its hunters.

In an instant Courte-Joie and Trigaud were surrounded; a dozen sabres whirled above their heads, a dozen pistol muzzles threatened their bodies, and one gendarme seized Courte-Joie. But Trigaud's club descended; it fell upon the leg of the gendarme and crushed it; the hapless rider uttered a terrible cry and fell from his horse, which fled across the moor.

At the same instant a dozen shots were fired; Trigaud had a ball in the breast, and Courte-Joie's right arm, broken in two places, hung helpless at his side. The giant seemed insensible to pain; with his trunk of a tree he made a moulinet, which broke two or three sabres and warded others.

"To the cross! to the cross!" cried Courte-Joie. "It is well to die there."

"Yes," muttered Trigaud; hearing his master speak of dying he brought down his club convulsively on the head of a horseman, who fell like a log. Then, executing the order he had received, he walked backward to the cross—to cover as much as possible of his friend with his own body.

"A thousand thunders!" shouted a corporal; "we are wasting time and lives and powder on those beggars."

So saying, he spurred his horse and forced it with one bound upon the two Vendéans. The horse's head struck Trigaud full in the chest, and the shock was so violent that it brought the giant to his knees. The soldier profited by the chance to strike Courte-Joie a blow which entered his skull.

"Throw me at the foot of the cross and escape if you can," said Courte-Joie, in a failing voice. "It is all over with me." Then he began the prayer: "Receive my soul, O God!"

But the colossus no longer obeyed him; maddened with blood and fury, he uttered hoarse, inarticulate cries, like those of a lion at bay; his eyes, usually dull and lifeless, cast out flames; his lips drew up, exposing the clenched and savage teeth ready to render craunch for craunch with a tiger. The gallop of the horse had carried the soldier who wounded Courte-Joie to some distance. Trigaud could not reach him; but he measured the space with his eye, and whirling the club above his head, he flung it hissing through the air as if from a catapult.

The rider forced his horse to rear, and avoided the blow; but the horse received it on his head. The creature beat the air with his forefeet as he fell over backward, and rolled with his rider on the ground.

Trigaud uttered a cry of joy more terrible and horrible than a cry of pain; the rider's leg was caught beneath the animal. He flung himself upon him, parried with his arm, which was deeply gashed, a sabre-cut; seized the soldier by the leg; dragged him from the body of the horse; and then, twirling him in the air, as a child does a sling, he dashed out his brains upon an arm of the cross.

The byzantine stone shook to its base, and remained bent over to one side, and covered with blood. A cry of horror and of vengeance burst from the troops, but this specimen of the giant's strength deterred the soldiers from approaching him; they stopped where they were, to reload their guns.

During this time Courte-Joie breathed his last, saying, in a loud voice:—

"Amen!"

Then Trigaud, feeling his beloved master dead, and utterly ignoring the preparations the chasseurs were making to kill him,—Trigaud sat down at the foot of the cross, unfastened the body of the Courte-Joie from his shoulders and laid it on his knees, as a mother might handle the body of her child;

he gazed on the livid face, wiping with his sleeve the blood that blurred it, while a torrent of tears—the first that being, indifferent to all the miseries of life, had ever shed—flowed thick and fast from his eyes, mingling with the blood he was piously and absorbedly removing.

A violent explosion, two new wounds, and the dull thud produced by three or four balls striking the body which Trigaud was holding in his arms and pressing to his breast, roused him from his grief and his insensibility. He rose to his full height; and this movement, which made the soldiers think he meant to spring upon them, caused them to gather up the reins of their horses, while a visible shudder ran through their ranks.

But Trigaud never looked at them; he thought of them no longer; he was seeking a means of not being parted from his friend by death; was he searching for a spot which promised him a union throughout eternity?

He walked toward the river. In spite of his wounds, in spite of the blood which flowed down his body from the holes of several pistol-balls and left a rivulet of blood behind him, Trigaud walked firm and erect. He reached the river-bank before a single soldier thought of preventing him; there he stopped at a point overlooking a black pool of water, the stillness of which proclaimed its depth. Clasping the body of the cripple still tighter to his breast, and gathering up his last remaining strength, he sprang forward into its depths without uttering a word.

The water dashed noisily above the mighty mass it now engulfed, boiling and foaming long over the place where Trigaud and his friend had disappeared; then it subsided into rings, which widened ever till they died upon the shore. The soldiers had ridden up. They thought the beggar had thrown himself into the water to reach the other bank, and pistol in hand they held themselves ready to fire the moment he came to the surface of the stream.

But Trigaud never reappeared; his soul had gone to join the soul of the only being he had loved in this world, and their bodies lay softly together on a bed of reeds in a pool of the river Maine.

Louis XIII

Louis XIII., who was born Thursday, September 27th, 1601, had a long, sad face, with black mustachios, and brown complexion. Not a feature of his recalled Henry IV., no more than did any trait of his character. Nothing French was about him, no gaiety, not even in youth.

With some probability, the Spaniard says he was offspring of Virginio Orsini, Duke of Bracciano, Marie de Medicis' cousin. In fact, on leaving home for France, Marie, twenty-seven then, received from her uncle Ferdinand (who had poisoned his brother Francisco and his sister-in-law Bianca Capello to rise to the Tuscan throne) the following advice:

"My beloved niece, you are going to wed a monarch who repudiated his first wife because she had no children, You have a month to make the journey in, and three handsome blades in your train: Virginio Orsini, your cicisbeo's one, t'other's Paolo Orisini and Concini is the last. Just arrange matters so that you need not fear being rejected after you get in France."

The Spaniard goes on to say that Marie had punctually carried out her uncle's counsel. She spent ten days in passing from Genoa to Marseilles only. Henry IV., though not impatient to see "his fat money-changer," as he styled her, fancied the journey a bit too long; but Malherbe the poet had looked for a reason for the delay and found one good or bad. He asserted that the hindrance came from the passion Neptune had conceived for the betrothed of the crown of France.

Two weeks he has enjoyed
    The pleasure of regarding her,
And greedy still to gaze
    Continues in retarding her.

Maybe the excuse was not very logical, but Queen Mag of Navarre had taught her husband not to be hard in overlooking conjugal shortcomings. [You can see the lazy ship surrounded by Nereides in Reuben's fine picture at the Louvre.]

In nine month's time, Grand-duke Ferdinand was set at ease. He heard of the birth of the Dauphin Louis, immediately dubbed "the Just," because born under the sign of the balance.

From childhood Louis evinced the sadness inborn in the Orsini's, at the time he had all the tastes of an Italian of the Decline. In fact, a muscian and a passable composer even, a mediocre painter, he was, handy at many a little work, though he never knew king-craft, notwithstanding his prodigious worship of royalty. Weak constitutionally, he had been outrageously physiced in his youth and, on coming of age, he was so sickly a creature that three or four times already he had been on the very verge of expiring.

A journal, kept for eight-and-twenty years, by his physician Herouard, day by day records all he eats, and hour by hour all he does.

From his first days up, he had little kindness, was dry and harsh, sometimes cruel. Henry Fourth twice flogged him with his own hands; first time because he had manifested so much aversion to a gentleman that, to pacify him, they had had to fire an unloaded pistol at the man, and make the dauphin believe he had been shot, the second because he had crushed a tame bird's head with a hammer.

Only once had he a kind thought, and that once only did not act it. The day of his coronation, as the sceptre, very heavy, made of gold and silver and weighty with precious stones, was held out to him, his hand trembled under it. Prince Condé, near him by reason of his station, was going to support his arm and thus aid him to uphold the wand.

But he turned sharply and frowned and said:

"No! I'll bear it alone, and want no sharer!"

His greatest childish sport was to turn bits of ivory, tint engravings, make cages, build card houses, and make magpies and a yellow parrot chase lit-tle birds around his room. In all his actions, says Etoile, "for a child, most childish."

But his most deeply-rooted and ever-moving loves were for music and hunt-ing. In Herouard's journal, nearly, if not quite unknown to historians, we must gather these and other still more curious details.

"At noon (saith the leech) he goes to play in the galerie with Patelot and Gresette his dogs. At one, he comes back to his room, sits in his nurse's chair, calls Ingret his lute-player and makes music, a-singing himself, for he's fond of music to great excess."

Oftimes, to distract himself, he rhym-ed on trifles, on popular sayings, max-ims and all that, and when he had the whim seize him, would have others ver-sify with him. Once he asked Herouard to "put this prose into rhyme: 'I want those who love me to love me long, or if they love me little, to leave me to-morrow.' "

The good doctor, better courtier than poet instantly hammered out this dis-tich:

"Love me no little but love me long, Or you I'll renounce like an old song."

Like all melancholy characters, Louis wonderfully dissimulated and at the very moment when he dug the pitfall for another it was that he showed his teeth in his sweetest smile.

Year of our Lord, 1613, a Friday, March the second, at the age of twelve, for the first time making use of the phrase frequent with Francis the First, he swore: "by my gentleman's faith!"

It was this time that Luynes was brought to him by the marshal d'Ancre. Until this, the only feeder and keeper of his birds had been a simple peasant, "a flat-footed clod-hopper from Saint Germain, named Pierrot." says Etoile. Luynes was appointed head falconer and the previously all-powerful Pierrot was bade obey him. Next the falcons, gerfalcons, hawks, pies and parrots were styled "cabinet birds" in order that Luynes might always be near Louis. From that epoch dates such a friendship for him in the king that, not only would he not let his head falconer leave him from dawn to dewy eve, but even in a-bed he would dream out aloud of him, says Herouard, "calling out his name in slumber and fancying him away."

If Luynes could not amuse him (we shall see presently that the monarch never was delighted but twice in his life) he at least contrived to keep his mind busy, by developing his fondness for the chase as much as the little liberty allowed to royal children would permit.

We know that Louis set parrots upon birds in his rooms. Luynes taught him to course hares with little hounds in the moats of the Louvre and to hawk on Grenelle Plain. It was there, on New Year's Day (all dates being important in such a sovereign's life) that he brought down his first heron, and at Vaugirard, the eighteenth of the same year's April, he shot his quail number one. Lastly, at the head of the bridge near the Louvre, he had his first man-hunt and was the death of Concini.

Let us interleave a page from Herouard's diary, the page being curious to philosopher and historian, to show what Louis XIII, did this Monday (April 24th, 1617) when he hunted man instead of bird and beast.

Line for line, we copy.

"MONDAY, *April 24th*, 1617,—Up at half after seven; full, even pulse; slight ly heated; gay and lively face, had his hair dressed and was clothed; prayed. At half after eight, breakfast, four plates, no drink save a little pure wine much diluted. *Ye marsshale d'Ancre kil'd on ye brydg of ye Lourvre betwixte tenne and eleven hours of ye morninge.* Dined at noon. Sported at half after seven. Sported again at half after nine. Drank bitters, was undressed and put a-bed. Pulse full, even; slightly heated; prayed. Asleep at 10 to sleep till seven."

Be easy about this poor royal child. You or I might have feared that the murder of his mother's lover, of his brother Gaston's father (more than likely), of a constable of France, the most mighty dignitary in the realm next to him, even before him, would have taken away his appetite and gaiety, and made him hesitate to pray with bloody hands.

Not he.

His dinner was an hour later, that's true, but he could not be regaling at eleven and also viewing through the ground floor window, Vitry slaying the Marshal d'Ancre. He sported at seven, and still again at nine a repetition whose single was not in his habits.

In the eight-and-twenty years that Doctor Herouard's watched him, only these two times did he DISPORT himself.

Moreover, into bed with an even pulse and only a little warm. Prayed at ten and slept till seven in the morning, a nine hour's slumber.

Poor boy!

The next day he awoke, a king. The long rest had endowed him with strength and, after having acted a man's if not a manly part the eve before, he performed a kingly deed that day.

The queen-mother was not only disgraced but exiled to Blois. She was forbidden to see her daughters, her well-beloved son Gaston d'Orleans. Her ministers were dismissed and the bishop Lucon (the future great cardinal) was alone permitted to follow her into exile.

But, monarch though he was, Louis was not man as yet. Two years wedded to the Infanta of Spain, Anne of Austria, he was only her husband in name. Durand, provincial war contractor, fruitlessly invented ballets, in which the king represented the Demon of Flames and sang the most touching verses to the queen, but his gallantry went no further than:

"Beautiful orb! in whose rays,
I would linger all my days,
    Behold where I'm led
Upon your luminous ways;
I will be all I've said!"

Louis wore a dress all fire, but at bed-time off went the flames with the coat.

As the Deliverance of Rinaldo Ballet had had no effect, another was tried under the title of Tancred's Adventures in the Enchanted Forest. Porchere's choreography a little pricked the monarch, and his curiosity rose into wanting to know what real man and wife did of a wedding-night. M. d'Elboeuf and Mlle de Vendome went through a rehearsal of the piece not yet played, but the king, after a couple of hours' sitting on their couch, coolly walked away into his bachelor's room.

At last, Luynes, tormented by the Spanish ambassador and the papal nuncio, saddled himself with this affair, not concealing from those who egged him on that he was "running the risk of losing his credit in that quarter."

The day was fixed for January 29th, 1619, for which we recur to Herouard again.

That day, the king, unaware of what the next twenty-four hours was to bring forth, rose in excellent health, rather light spirited relatively. He took breakfast at a quarter after nine; heard mass at the Tower Chapel; presided over the Council; dined at noon; paid a visit to the queen; went to the Tuileries by water; returned at half past four to the Council by the same way; went to Luynes' rooms; supped at eight; again visited the queen, leaving her at ten, returned to his own chamber and went to bed. But hardly had he lain down than Luynes came in and begged him to rise. The king stared at him as if he had been asked to go see the Man in the Moon. But Luynes insisted, saying that Europe was restless at the French throne having no heir, and that it would be a shame for his sister Christina who had just espoused Prince Amadeus of Savoy, to have offspring before the queen.

But, as none of the reasons, though approved with a nod, appeared sufficient to decide the king Luynes took him up and bore him away to the place of destination.

Now, if you should in the least doubt this, because no historian has noted it and a romancer does, only read the despatch, dated January 30th, 1619, at this conclusive paragraph:

"Luynes tooke him upp arounde ye bodie and bore him somewise *per forsse* to ye bedde of ye Queene."

Though Luynes did not lose his credit, on the contrary gaining the post of Lord High Constable, he lost his trouble at all events, or it was repaid very long after. The dauphin which ought to have outstripped the Duchess of Savoy's first-born only came to life, however ardently reclaimed, nineteen years after in 1638, and Luynes who was not fated to have the happiness of seeing that bear fruit which he had planted, died only two years after in a scarlet fever.

Death of Mirabeau

About the end of March, 1791, Dr. Gilbert was hurriedly called to his friend Mirabeau, by the latter's faithful servant Deutsch, who had been alarmed.

Mirabeau had spoken in the House on the question of Mines, the interests of owners and of the State not being very clearly defined. To celebrate his victory, he gave a supper to some friends and was prostrated by internal pains.

Gilbert was too skillful a physician not to see how grave the invalid was. He bled him and the black blood relieved the sufferer.

"You are a downright great man," said he.

"And you a great blockhead to risk a life so precious to your friends for a few hours of fictitious pleasure," retorted his deliverer.

The orator smiled almost ironically, in melancholy.

"I think you exaggerate and that my friends and France do not hold me so dear."

"Upon my honor," replied Gilbert laughing, "great men complain of ingratitude and they are really the ungrateful ones. If it were a most serious malady of yours, all Paris would flock under your window; were you to die, all France would come to your obsequies."

"What you say is very consoling, let me tell you," said the other, merrily.

"It is just because you can see one without risking the other that I say it, and indeed, you need a great public demonstration to restore your morale. Let me take you to Paris within a couple of hours, my dear count; let me tell the first man on the street corner that you are ailing and you will see the excitement."

"I would go if you put off the departure till this evening, and let me meet you at my house in Paris at eleven."

Gilbert looked at his patient and the latter saw that he was seen through.

"My dear count, I noticed flowers on the Dining-room table," said he; "it was not merely a supper to friends."

"You know that I cannot do without flowers; they are my craze."

"But they were not alone."

"If they are a necessity I must suffer from the consequences they entail."

"Count, the consequences will kill you."

"Confess, doctor, that it will be a delightful kind of suicide."

"I will not leave you this day."

"Doctor, I have pledged my word and you would not make me fail in that."

"I shall see you this night, though?"

"Yes, really I feel better."

"You mean you drive me away?"

"The idea of such a thing."

"I shall be in town; I am on duty at the palace."

"Then you will see the Queen," said Mirabeau, becoming gloomy once more.

"Probably; have you any message for her?"

Mirabeau smiled bitterly.

"I should not take such a liberty, doctor; do not even say that you have seen me: for she will ask if I have saved the monarchy, as I promised, and you will be obliged to answer No! It is true," he added with a nervous laugh, "that the fault is as much hers as mine."

"You do not want me to tell her your excess of exertions in the tribune is killing you."

"Nay, you may tell her that," he replied after brief meditation: "you may make me out as worse than I am, to test her feelings."

"I promise you that, and to repeat her own words."

"It is well. I thank you, doctor—adieu!"

"What are you prescribing?"

"Warm drinks, soothing, strict diet and—no nurse-woman less than fifty——"

"Rather than infringe the regulation I would take two of twenty-five!"

At the door Gilbert met Deutsch, who was in tears.

"All this through a woman—just because she looks like the Queen," said the man; "how stupid of a genius, as they say he is."

He let out Gilbert who stepped into his carriage, muttering:

"What does he mean by a woman like the Queen?"

He thought of asking Deutsch, but it was the count's secret, and he ordered his coachman to drive to town.

On the way he met Camille Desmoulins, the living newspaper of the day, to whom he told the truth of the illness because it was the truth.

When he announced the news to the King, the latter inquired if the count had lost his appetite.

"Yes, Sire," was the doctor's reply.

"Then it is a bad case," sighed the monarch, shifting the subject.

When the same words were repeated to the daughter of Maria Theresa, her forehead darkened.

"Why was he not so stricken on the day of his panegyric on the tricolor flag?" she sneered. "Never mind," she went on, as if repenting the expression of her hatred before a Frenchman, "it would be very unfortunate for France if this malady makes progress. Doctor, I rely on your keeping me informed about it."

At the appointed hour, Gilbert called on his patient at his town house. His eyes caught sight of a lady's scarf on a chair.

"Glad to see you," said Mirabeau, quickly as though to divert his attention from it. "I have learnt that you kept half your promise. Deutsch has been busy answering friendly inquiries from our arrival. Are you true to the second part? have you been to the palace and seen the King and Queen?"

"Yes; and told them you were unwell. The King sincerely condoled when he heard that you had lost your appetite. The Queen was sorry and bade me keep her informed."

"But I want the words she used."

"Well, she said that it was a pity you were not ill when you praised the new flag of the country."

He wished to judge of the Queen's influence over the orator.

He started on the easy chair as if receiving the discharge of a galvanic battery.

"Ingratitude of monarchs," he muttered. "That speech of mine blotted out remembrance of the rich Civil List and the dower I obtained for her. This Queen must be ignorant that I was compelled to regain the popularity I lost for her sake: but she no more remembers it than my proposing the adjournment of the annexation of Avignon to France in order to please the King's religious scruples. But these and other faults of mine I have dearly paid for," continued Mirabeau. "Not that these faults will ruin them, but there are times when ruin must come, whether faults help them forward or not. The Queen does not wish to be saved but to be revenged; hence she relishes no reasonable ideas.

"I have tried to save liberty and royalty at the same time; but I am not fighting against men, or tigers, but an element—it is submerging me like the sea: yesterday up to the knee, to-day up to the waist, to-morrow I shall be struggling with it up to my neck. I must be open with you, doctor; I felt chagrin first, then disgust. I dreamt

of being the arbiter between the Revolution and monarchy. I believed I should have an ascendancy over the Queen as a man, and some day when she was going under the flood, I meant to leap in and rescue her. But, no! they would not honestly take me; they try to destroy my popularity, ruin me, annihilate me, and make me powerless to do either good or evil. So, now that I have done my best, I tell you, doctor, that the best thing I can do is die in the nick of time; fall artistically like the Dying Gladiator, and offer my throat to be cut with gracefulness; yield up the ghost with decency."

He sank back on the reclining chair and bit the pillow savagely. Gilbert knew what he sought, on what Mirabeau's life depended.

"What will you say if the King or the Queen should send to inquire after your health?" he asked.

"The Queen will not do it—she will not stoop so low."

"I do not believe, but I suppose, I presume——"

"I will wait till to-morrow night."

"And then?"

"If she sends a confidential man I will say you are right and I wrong. But if on the contrary none come, then it will be the other way."

"Keep tranquil till then. But this scarf?"

"I shall not see her, on my honor," he said, smiling.

"Good, try to get a good quiet night, and I will answer for you," said Gilbert, going out.

"Your master is better, my honest Deutsch," said he to the attendant at the door.

The old valet shook his head sadly. "Do you doubt my word?"

"I doubt everything since this bad angel will be beside him."

He sighed as he left the doctor on the gloomy stairs. At the landing corner Gilbert saw a veiled shadow which seemed waiting: on perceiving him, it uttered a low scream and disappeared so quickly by a partly opened door that is resembled a flight.

"Who is that woman?" questioned the doctor.

"The one who looks like the Queen," responded Deutsch.

For the second time Gilbert was struck by the same idea on hearing this phrase: he took a couple of steps as though to chase the phantom, but he checked himself, saying

"It cannot be."

He continued his way, leaving the old domestic in despair that this learned man could not conjure away the demon whom he believed the agent of the Inferno.

Next day all Paris called to inquire after the invalid orator. The crowd in the street would not believe Deutsch's encouraging report but forced all vehicles to turn into the side streets so that their idol should not be disturbed by their noise.

Mirabeau got up and went to the window to wave a greeting to these worshippers, who shouted their wishes for his long life.

But he was thinking of the haughty woman who did not trouble her head about him, and his eyes wandered over the mob to see if any servants in the royal blue livery were not trying to make their way through the mass. By evening his impatience changed into gloomy bitterness.

Still he waited for the almost promised token of interest, and still it did not come.

At eleven, Gilbert came; he had written his best wishes during the day: he came in smiling, but he was daunted by the expression on Mirabeau's face, faithful mirror of his soul's perturbations.

"Nobody has come," said he. "Will you tell me what you have done this day?"

"Why, the same as usual——"

"No, doctor, and I saw what happened and will tell you the same as though present. You called on the Queen and told her how ill I was: she said she would send to ask the latest news, and you went away, happy and satisfied, relying on the royal word. She was left laughing, bitter and haughty, ignorant that a royal word must not be broken—mocking at your credulity."

"Truly, had you been there, you could not have seen and heard more clearly," said Gilbert.

"What numbskulls they are," exclaimed Mirabeau. "I told you they never did a thing at the right time. Men in the royal livery coming to my door would have wrung shouts of 'Long live the King!' from the multitude and given them popularity for a year."

He shook his head with grief.

"What is the matter, count?" asked Gilbert.

"Nothing."

"Have you had anything to eat?"

"Not since two o'clock."

"Then take a bath and have a meal."

"A capital idea!"

Mirabeau listened in the bath until he heard the street door close after the doctor.

Then he rang for his servant, not Deutsch but another, to have the table in his room decked with flowers and "Madam" invited to sup with him.

He closed all the doors of the supper-room except that to the rooms of the strange woman whom the old German called his bad angel.

At about four in the morning, Deutsch who sat up, heard a violent ring of the room bell. He and another servant rushed to the supper-room, but all the doors were fastened so that they had to go round by the strange lady's rooms There they found her in the arms of their master, who had tried to prevent her giving the alarm. She had rung the table-bell from inability to get at the bellpull.

She was screaming as much for her own relief as her lover's, as he was suffocating her in his convulsive embrace.

It seemed to be Death trying to drag her into the grave.

Jean, the servant, ran to rouse Dr. Gilbert while Deutsch got his master to a couch. In ten minutes the doctor drove up.

"What is it now?" he asked of Deutsch, in the hall.

"That woman again and the cursed flowers! Come and see."

At this moment something like a sob was heard; Gilbert ran up the stairs at the top step of which a door opened, and a woman in a white wrapper ran out suddenly and fell at the doctor's feet.

"Oh, Gilbert," she screamed, "save him!"

"Nicole Legay," cried the doctor; "was it you, wretch, who have killed him?" A dreadful thought overwhelmed him. "I saw her bully Beausire selling broadsides against Mirabeau, and she became his mistress. He is undoubtedly lost."

He turned back into his patient's room, fully aware that no time was to be lost. Indeed, he was too versed in secrets of his craft still to hope, far less to preserve any doubt. In the body before his eyes, it was impossible to see the living Mirabeau. From that time, his face assumed the solemn cast of great men dying.

Meanwhile the news had spread that there was a relapse and that the doom impended. Then could it be judged what a gigantic place one man may fill among his fellows. The entire city was stirred as on great calamities. The door was besieged by persons of all opinions as though everybody knew they had something to lose by his loss.

He caused the window to be opened that he might be soothed by the hum of the multitude beneath.

"Oh, good people," he murmured: "slandered, despised and insulted like me, it is right that those Royals should forget me and the Plebs bear me in mind."

Night drew near.

"My dear doctor," he said to him who would not leave him, "this is my dying day. At this point nothing is to be done but embalm my corpse and strew flowers roundabout."

Scarcely had Jean, to whom everybody rushed at the door for news, said he wanted flowers for his master, than all the windows opened, and flowers were offered from conservatories and gardens of the rarest sorts. By nine in the morning the room was transformed into a bower of bloom.

"My dear doctor, I beg a quarter of an hour to say good-bye to a person who ought to quit the house before I go. I ask you to protect her in case they hoot her."

"I leave you alone," said Gilbert, understanding.

"Before going, kindly hand me the little casket in the secretary."

Gilbert did as requested; the money-box was heavy enough to be full of gold.

At the end of half an hour, spent by Gilbert in giving news to the inquirers, Jean ushered a veiled lady out to a hackney-carriage at the door

Gilbert ran to his patient.

"Put the casket back," said he in a faint voice "Odd, is it not?" he continued, seeing how astonished the doctor looked at its being as heavy as before, "but where the deuce will disinterestedness next have a nest?"

Near the bed, Gilbert picked up a lace handkerchief wet with tears.

"Ah, she would take nothing away—but she left something," remarked Mirabeau.

Feeling it was damp he pressed it to his forehead.

"Tears? is she the only one who has a heart?" he murmured.

He fell back on the bed, with closed eyes; he might have been believed dead or swooning but for the death-rattle in his breast.

How came it that this man of athletic, herculean build should die?

Was it not because he had held out his hand to stay the tumbling throne from toppling over? was it not because

he had offered his arm to that woman of misfortune known as Marie Antoinette?

Gilbert was going to try upon him the elixir of life.

The patient had opened his eyes.

"Nay," said he, "a few drops will be vain. You must give me the whole phial. I had the stuff analyzed and found it was Indian hemp; I had some compounded for myself and I have been taking it copiously not to live but to dream."

"Unhappy man that I am," sighed Gilbert, "to be dealing out poison to my friend."

"A sweet poison, by which I have lengthened out the last moments of my life a hundredfold. In my dream I have enjoyed what has really escaped me, riches, power, and love. I do not know whether I ought to thank God for my life, but I thank you, doctor, for your drug. Fill up the glass and let me have it."

Gilbert presented the extract which the patient absorbed with gusto.

"Ah, doctor," he said after a short pause, as if the veil of the future were raised at the approach of eternity; "blessed are those who die in this year, 1791! for they will have seen the sunny side of the Revolution. Never has a great one cost so little bloodshed up to now, because it is the mind that was conquered: but on the morrow the war will be upon facts and in things. Perhaps you believe that the tenants of the Tuileries will mourn for me? Not at all. My death rids them of an engagement. With me, they had to rule in a certain way, I was less support than hindrance. *She* excused herself for leaning on me, to her brother: 'Mirabeau believes that he is advising me— I am only amusing myself with him.' That is why I wished that woman, her likeness, to be my mistress, and not my Queen.

"What a fine part he shall play in History who undertook to sustain the young nation with one hand and the old monarchy in the other, forcing them to tread the same goal—the happiness of the governed and the respect of the governors. It might have been possible and might be but a dream; but I am convinced that I alone could have realized the dream. My sorrow is not in dying, but in dying with work unfinished. Who will glorify my idea left mangled, an abortion? What will be known of me will be the part that should be buried in oblivion—my wild, reckless, rakish life and my obscene writings.

"I shall be blamed for having made a bond with the court out of which comes gain for no man; I shall be judged, dying at forty-two, like one who lived man's full age. They will take me to task as if instead of trying to walk on the waters in a storm, I had trodden a broad way paved with laws, statutes, and regulations. To whom shall I league my memory to be cleansed and be an honor to my country?

"But I could do nothing without her, and she would not take my helping hand. I pledged myself like a fool, while she remained unfettered. Be it so—all is for the best; and if you will promise one thing, no regret will trouble my last breath."

"Good God, what would I not promise?"

"If my passing from life is tedious, make it easy? I ask the aid not only of the doctor but of the man and the philosopher—promise to aid me. I do not wish to die dead,—but living, and the last step will not be hard to take."

The doctor bent his head towards the speaker.

"I promised not to leave you, my friend; if heaven hath condemned you —though I hope we have not come to that point—leave to my affection at the supreme instant the care of accomplishing what I ought to do. If death comes, I shall be at hand also."

"Thanks," said the dying one as if this were all he awaited.

The abundant dose of cannabis indicus had restored speech to the doomed one: but this vitalism of the mind vanished and for three hours the cold hand remained in the doctor's without a throb. Suddenly he felt a start: the awakening had come.

"It will be a dreadful struggle," he thought.

Such was the agony in which the strong frame wrestled that Gilbert forgot that he had promised to second death, not to oppose it. But, reminded of his pledge, he seized the pen to write a prescription for an opiate. Scarcely had he written the last words than Mirabeau rose on the pillow and asked for the pen. With his hand clenched by death he scrawled:

"Flee, flee, flee!"

He tried to sign but could only trace four letters of his name.

"For her," he gasped, holding out his convulsed arm towards his companion.

He fell back without breath, movement or look—he was dead.

Gilbert turned to the spectators of this scene and said:

"Mirabeau is no more."

He rapidly departed from the death chamber.

Some seconds after the doctor's going, a great clamor arose in the street and was prolonged throughout Paris.

The grief was intense and wide. The Assembly voted a public funeral, and the Pantheon, formerly Church of St. Genevieve, was selected for the great man's resting-place. Three years subsequently the Convention sent the coffin to the Clamart Cemetery to be bundled among the corpses of the publicly executed.

It was claimed to have discovered a contra-revolutionary plot written in the hand of Mirabeau later, and Congress reversed its previous judgment and declared that genius could not condone corruption.

Anne of Austria

ANNE of Austria was pretty rather than handsome. She had small features, a meaningless nose, but the transparent, velvety skin of that fair Flemish dynasty from whence sprang the Charles Quints and Philip Seconds. A coquette towards all men without distinction, she never wanted to miss a point even on her brother-in-law, Gaston of Orleans.

As this evening he had an appointment with her, she reclining upon a luxurious couch adjusted several locks of hair disarranged, regulated the folds of the long silken wrapper which enveloped her, supported herself on her elbow to try in what attitude she looked best, returned the reflector to her maid of honor and motioned her, with a thankful smile, to go to her own rooms.

Isabelle the maid laid down the glass and the candlestick on the dressing-table, respectfully curtseyed and went away.

The apartment was now illumined by the double beams of the lamp and candle, so placed as to shed their rays upon the couch.

At length, at very nearly the same time two doors that the queen had seemed to question, opened. Through one entry walked in a youth of twenty, with ruddy, round face, black hair, and hard eye which looked false to its nature when a mild expression was given it. He was splendidly arrayed in white satin and a cloak of cherry-color embroidered with gold. The collar of the Order of the Holy Ghost was worn round his neck. In his hand he held his white felt hat adorned with twin plumes of the cloak color. This was Gaston of Orleans, generally designated as the "My Lord," and asserted by the scandal-lovers in the Louvre to be so loved by his mother only because he was the son of the handsome favorite Concino Concini. In support of this, whoever will compare (as we may in the Blois Museum) the portraits of Marshal d'Ancre and of Marie de Medicis' second son will understand that the extraordinary likeness existant between them might well throw credit upon the serious accusation.

By the other door, almost simultaneously, had entered a woman of fifty-five or six, royally appareled, wearing a small gold crown on the top of her head, and a long mantle of purple and ermine falling from her shoulders on a white satin robe laced with gold.

She had been fresh-looking at one time, but had never been distinguished for her beauty; as an excessive *embonpoint* had imparted to her such a vulgar appearance as to call forth for her, from the mouth of Henry IV., the appellation of the *Grosse-banquiere*.

Inferior in genius to Catherine de Medicis, she far exceeded her in debauchery. If common report was to be believed, only one of the children said to be Henry IV.'s were his indeed. This was Henrietta. Gaston only she loved of all. She had taken the much desired death of her eldest son, King Louïs XIII., for granted regarding it as inevitable and consoling herself beforehand. Her fixed idea was to behold Gàston on the throne, as the fixed idea of Catherine had been to see Henry III. thereon.

But a still graver accusation than these weighed upon her and caused Louis XIII. to scorn her as strongly as he hated her: she was said, if not to have put, to have left in the hands of Ravaillac, the attempted assassin of the king, the knife that she could have dashed aside.

Sworn testimony asserted that Ravaillac had named her and d'Epernon when on the rack. The Justice Hall had been fired to burn up all traces of those two names.

The night before mother and son had been told Anne had letters for them. Handing them the missives, she spoke a few words and dismissed them.

The queen-mother, Marie de Medici, took leave of her daughter-in-law and, being come to her own room, dressed for the night and gave leave to her tiring women.

On being alone, she pulled a bell-cord hidden in a curtain.

A few seconds after, a man of forty-five or fifty, with a yellow but strongly-marked visage, black hair, brows and moustache, entered in response to the summons by a passage under the tapestry.

This was the queen's musician, physician and astrologer.

Sad to say, he was the successor of Henry IV. and of Vittoria Orsino, of Concini. Vaultier, who, to better govern the body, had become a doctor, and to better soften the brain had become an astrologer. If Richelieu should fall, his place would be contested by Berulle, a fool, and Vaultier, a mountebank; and many who knew the latter's influence over the queen-dowager, averred that Vaultier had as much of a chance as his rival for the premiership.

Vaultier had come into this sort of ante-chamber preceding the bed-room.

"Quick, quick! run!" exclaimed she, "and give me, if you have compounded it, that liquor with power to render legible writings that are invisible."

"Yes, madame," replied Vaultier, drawing a phial from his pocket; "your Majesty's desire is too precious for me to ever forget it. Here it is. Your Majesty has then received a letter?"

" 'Tis here," she said, producing the paper from her bosom, "a few lines merely, almost meaningless, from the Duke of Savoy; but it is clear that he would not have written so confidentially to me and sent it by one of my husband's fondlings only to tell me such stuff."

She had held out the letter to Vaultier, who unfolded and perused it.

"In fact, there must be more in it," he remarked.

The apparent writing, truly by Charles Emanuel, of Piedmont, was at the top of the page, which with the standing orders for all missives to be experimented on for all not evident in the text, confirmed the queen in the idea of this being the time to call in the aid of the chemical preparation commanded to be made by Vaultier.

It seemed to be certain that if any unseen advice was innate on the Duke of Savoy's epistle it ought to come to life under the concluding line, on the blank, say three-quarters of the page.

Vaultier dipped a brush in the liquid and lightly washed the paper, from the last line downwards.

As the brush was drawn to moisten the spotless surface, up started letters here and there, hastier than their mates, next lines ran out their length, and lastly, after five minutes' soaking, the following could be read:

"Simulate a quarrel with your son Gaston, the cause for which might be his hot love for Maria of Gonzago; and if the Italian Campaign is settled spite your opposition, obtain for him, under pretence of sending him away to cure his foolish passion, the command of the army. The Cardinal Duke, whose whole ambition is to pass for the leading general of the age, will not put up with the affront and will hand in his resignation. The only fear is that the king would not accept it."

Marie and her councillor looked at one another.

"Have you anything better to propose?" she asked.

"Nay, madame," he answered. "I have noticed that the duke's advice was always good to follow."

"Let's obey it, then," said Marie with a sigh. "We cannot be in a worse position than the present. Have you consulted the stars, Vaultier?"

"This evening I spent all of an hour on top of Catherine de Medicis' observatory in studying the orbs."

"Well, what do they augur?"

"They foretell complete triumph over your Majesty's enemies."

"Amen!" rejoined Marie de Medicis, giving the star-gazer a hand, somewhat plump but not so unfair, which he kissed with ardour.

Business was completed for the evening.

On being alone in her couch, Anne of Austria had successively listened for the steps to die away of Gaston of Orleans and of her mother-in-law. When all sound had been completely extinguished, she quietly rose, ran her small Spanish feet into blue satin slippers studded with gold, and went to sit down at her dressing-table. From one of its drawers, she took out a little bag, containing (instead of her favorite perfume of Florence) some pulverized charcoal. With this dust, she powdered the second page, blank, of a letter from Don Gonzalez of Cordova and—in like manner as to result though diverse in method as to the practices of the heated and the bathed scrolls—writing was revealed on the queen's epistle.

This was from King Philip IV., himself.

It was thus couched:

"SISTER:—Our friend, Lady Fargis, tells me that in case of King Louis XIII.'s decease, you propose to wed Gaston, his brother and successor. But it will be much better if, at the period of that death, you should be with child.

"French queens have the advantage over their husbands of the dauphin coming only from them, with or without the consort.

"Study this incontestable truth, and, as you will not need my letter to study by, burn it.   "PHILIP."

After the queen had read the royal letter a second time, in order to more deeply engrave it on her mind, she took it by one corner, put it in the candle light and there held it till the flame ran up to lick the rosy tips of her lovely hand. Then, and only then, she let go the fragment, which was ashes as the sparks fell to the floor. But at the same instant, she transcribed the whole letter from memory upon a paper, afterwards shut up in a secret drawer of a little writing-desk.

She returned slowly to her bed, let her satin wrapper fall from neck to waist, from waist to the carpet; so that she seemed to rise like Venus out of the silvery wave, lay slowly down and, sighing as her head pressed the pillow, murmured:

"Oh! Buckingham! Buckingham!"

Thenceforward all that troubled the stillness in the royal chamber were some smothered sobs.

A Black Pearl

IN A domestic crisis once chance came to my assistance. Mind, I am not so conceited as to say *Providence*; I leave that to the crowned heads.

Chevet, to whom I owed a bill of 113 francs, having heard say I was starting for a voyage round the world, thought he would like to see the amount of his little account paid up before I left Saint-Germain.

He appeared, therefore, one morning in person, his bill in his hand. This settled, I asked if by any chance he knew of a good servant who would be willing to accompany me abroad.

"Why, sir," he exclaimed, "how aptly that falls out; I have a perfect pearl to offer you—a negro."

"A black pearl, it seems."

"Yes, sir, but a true pearl nevertheless."

"The deuce, Chevet! I have a negro already, a ten years' old one, who is, off his own bat, as lazy as two negroes of twenty—if they grow to twenty."

"That is just his age, sir."

"He will be as lazy as two negroes of forty then."

"Sir, he is not a true negro."

"What, he is dyed!"

"No, no, sir; he is an Arab."

"Ah, the deuce! but that is a find for any one going to Algeria—unless indeed he talks Arabic the same way Alexis talked Creole."

"I don't know, sir, how Alexis talked Creole; but I do know an officer of Spahis came to the house the other day, and they jabbered away together, Paul and he."

"He is called Paul?"

"Yes, he is called Paul for us, that's his French name; but for his compatriots, he has another name, an Arab name that means *Benzoin-Water*."

"You would be answerable for him?"

"As I would for myself, sir."

"Very well, then, send me your Benzoin-Water."

"Ah, sir, you will soon see what a treasure you have got! A *valet de chambre* as elegant as a man could wish, of a fine olive tint, speaking four languages, not counting his own, a good walker and a good rider. He has only one fault; he invariably loses whatever you trust to his care. But then, you understand, one never trusts him with anything——"

"Good, Chevet, good; thank you, thank you!"

By the four o'clock train I duly saw Benzoin-Water arrive. Chevet had not deceived me; the man showed no sign whatever of the low brow, flat nose, and thick lips of the natives of the Congo or Mozambique.

He was an Abyssinian Arab, with all the elegant shape and limbs of his race. As Chevet had told me, his complexion was of the very tint to have delighted Delacroix. Being anxious to test his boasted linguistic talents, I spoke a few words to him in Italian, English, and Spanish. He answered me quite correctly, and as he also spoke French very fluently, I came to the same conclusion as Chevet, that he knew four languages besides his own.

Now how this drop of fragrance named Benzoin-Water had come into existence on the slopes of the Samen Mountains, between the shores of Lake Ambra and the sources of the Blue Nile, is a matter on which Benzoin-Water could never afford me any information, and so I cannot tell you. All that one could make out amid the obscurity of his earliest years was that an English gentleman, a globe-trotter, returning from India by way of the Gulf of Aden, had chosen to ascend the River to Naso and pass by Emfras and Gondar, had halted at the latter town, had there seen the little Benzoin-Water, a lad of five or six, and, taking a fancy to his looks, had bought him of his father in exchange for a bottle of rum.

The boy followed his new master, crying bitterly for three or four days after his lost parents. Then, under the influence, so powerful with all and especially with children, of change of scene and surroundings, he grew pretty nearly reconciled in the course of a week, by which time the caravan reached the sources of the river Rahad. The English traveller descended that river to the point where it discharges its waters into the Blue Nile; then he followed down the latter stream to where it joins the White Nile; he halted a fortnight at Khartoum, then resumed his journey, and two months later arrived at Grand Cairo.

For six years Benzoin-Water remained with his English master. During that time he went all over Italy, and learnt a little Italian; Spain, and learnt a little Spanish; England, and learnt a little English. Finally he settled down in France, and acquired a really sound knowledge of French.

The child from Lake Ambra took very kindly to this nomad life, which recalled that of his ancestors the Shepherd Kings—for Benzoin-Water had so proud a carriage, so aristocratic an air, that I have always maintained, and do so still, that he must have been descended from those conquerors of Egypt. If it had depended on him, he would never, despite the ancient saw of good King Dagobert, have left his English master; but, alas! his English master left him. He was a great traveller, this Englishman; he had seen everything—Europe, Asia, Africa, America, and even Oceania. He had seen all this world, and determined to visit the next. Every morning at seven o'clock he was in the habit of ringing for Benzoin-Water. One morning he did not ring. At eight o'clock Benzoin-Water went into his room, to find his master hanging from the ceiling, the bell-rope round his neck—which sufficiently explained why he had not rung.

The Englishman was generous; he had even taken the precaution, before hanging himself, to leave a rouleau of guineas to Benzoin-Water. But the poor lad was not of a saving disposition; like a true child of the tropics, he loved everything that glittered in the sun; provided it glittered, what matter to him whether it were copper or gold, green glass or emerald, tinsel or ruby, paste or diamond. So he spent his guineas in buying whatever glittered, purchasing now and again by way of variety sundry drinks of rum, for the fellow was very fond of rum—a fact, by the bye, which Chevet had omitted to tell me, no doubt because I was sure to find it out very soon for myself.

When Benzoin-Water had, I won't say eaten up—he was but a small eater, the poor lad—but scattered to the winds his last guinea, he realised the time was come to look out for another place.

As he was good-looking, pleasant, and obliging in all his ways, with a clear eye, an open smile, and flashing white teeth, he was not long in finding a new master. This was a French colonel, who took him with him to Algeria, where Paul found himself as it were *en famille*. It was his native language the Algerians spoke, or, to be strictly accurate, he spoke the mother-tongue of the Algerians with far more purity and elegance than they did themselves, for his Arabic is borrowed from the primitive source of that beautiful speech. He stayed five years in Algeria, in the course of which time, the grace of the Lord having touched him, he had himself baptized under the name of Pierre, doubtless to safeguard himself the right, like his patron saint, of thrice denying God.

Unfortunately he had forgotten, when he chose the name, that it was his master's too. The end was that the Colonel, not wishing to have a servant called the same as himself, unbaptized Benzoin-Water and changed his name from Peter to Paul, deeming it would not fail to please him to exchange the patronage of the Apostle who holds the keys for that of the one who holds the sword.

At the end of these five years Paul's Colonel was retired. He came back to France to appeal against the order, but to no purpose. So the Colonel being reduced to half-pay, had to inform Paul that to his great regret he was forced to part with him.

There was one disagreeable difference between the Colonel and the Englishman, to wit, that the former being still alive and needing his money to end his days with, gave Paul just what was due to him for wages and no more. The amount came to thirty-three francs and a half, which promptly vanished between Paul's brown fingers.

However, in the Colonel's service, that officer being very fond of good living, Paul had made one very useful acquaintance, Chevet's namely. We have seen how the latter had recommended him to my notice, telling me he was a capital servant, with one great fault, however, that he always lost whatever was entrusted to his keeping.

I stated a little above, somewhere, that Chevet had omitted to warn me that Paul had another fault, a decided predilection for rum; I added that this was probably because Chevet felt sure I should soon find out this fact for myself.

Well, Chevet had formed too exalted an opinion of my powers of observation. True, I saw Paul from time to time getting to his feet as I went by to salute me, and rolling big eyes which had turned from white to yellow; I noticed that he held his little finger desperately to the seam of his trousers, a pleasing military posture he had learnt in the Colonel's establishment; I heard how he mixed up confusedly English, French, Spanish, and Italian. But, buried in my work, I paid small heed to these superficial changes, and continued to be very well satisfied with his behaviour. Only, in accordance with Chevet's advice, I never trusted anything to Paul's charge—except the key of the cellar, which, contrary to his general custom, he never lost.

Thus I remained in blissful ignorance of this fatal failing of Paul's until one day an unexpected incident revealed it to me. After starting for a shooting party, intending to remain away a week, I came back next day unexpectedly, and as I usually did on returning home, called for Paul.

But there was no answer. Then I called Michel; but Michel was in the garden. So I called Michel's wife, Augustine; but she was out marketing. I made up my mind to go upstairs without more ado to Paul's bedroom, fearing he might have hanged himself like his former master the Englishman.

A single glance reassured me on this head. For the moment Paul had entirely forsaken the vertical posture for the horizontal; fully dressed in complete livery, the fellow was lying on his bed, as stiff and still as if he were embalmed; I did not think he was this, but I own I thought he was pretty near gone to another world. I called him by name, but could get no answer. I shook him, but he never stirred; I lifted him by the shoulders, just as Pierrot lifts Harlequin; not a joint gave. I set him up on his legs, and seeing a point of support was absolutely necessary to enable him to stay there, I planted him against the wall.

During this latter operation Paul had at last vouchsafed some tokens of life. He had tried to speak, opened his eyes very wide, showing only the whites. At last his lips managed to articulate some almost unintelligible sounds, and he asked peevishly—

"Why are they disturbing me?"

At that moment I heard a noise at the bedroom door. It came from Michel, who had heard me calling from the bottom of the garden, and had come at last.

"Halloa!" I asked him, "is Paul mad?"

"No, sir," he answered me, "but Paul is drunk."

"What! Paul drunk?"

"Alas, yes, sir. The instant Monsieur's back is turned, Paul has a bottle neck between his teeth."

"Why, Michel, you mean to say you knew this, and you never told me!"

"I am here to be Monsieur's gardener, not to play the informer."

"True, Michel; you are in the right. Well, and now, what are we to do with the fellow? I cannot spend all the day holding him up against the wall."

"Oh, if Monsieur wants to sober Paul, it's easily done."

Michel possessed a recipe to meet all embarrassing circumstances whatsoever.

"What must we do to sober Paul, eh, Michel?"

"Heavens and earth, man! try to keep upright against the wall, do!" (this parenthetically to Paul).

"Monsieur has only to take a glass of water, drop into it eight or ten drops of alkali, and force Paul to drink it off. He'll give a great sneeze and be sober in an instant."

"Have you any alkali, Michel?"

"No; but I have a supply of ammonia."

"That comes to exactly the same thing. Put some ammonia into a glass —not too much—and bring it me here."

Five minutes later Michel came back with the required mixture. We unclenched Paul's teeth with a paper-knife; then we slipped in the edge of the glass and tilted it gently. The contents followed two main directions— down Paul's throat and down his necktie. Though the latter certainly got the lion's share, still the patient imbibed some, and as Michel had foretold, presently gave so terrific a sneeze that I fled, leaving him unsupported. He staggered for a moment, sneezed a second time, opened great staring eyes and looked about him, uttering only a single word the while, though that seemed to express his thoughts quite adequately—"Faugh!"

"Well, now, Paul," I said to him, "now that you are sober again, lie down, my fine fellow, and go to sleep, and directly you wake, bring me your account; I do not like drunkards."

But, whether it was that Paul was of exceptional nervous susceptibility, or that his brain was overstimulated by the ammonia, instead of dropping off to sleep as I advised him, or presenting me with his claim for wages, as he was entitled to, he fell to throwing his head back, writhing his arms and making the faces of a demoniac. Paul had a violent nervous seizure, and amidst, or rather in the intervals between, his wild contortions, he kept crying out—

"No, I don't want to go away; I am happy here, and I want to stay! I only left my first master because he hanged himself; I only left my second because he was put on half-pay. M. Dumas has neither been retired nor hanged himself—and I want to stay on with M. Dumas."

www.ingramcontent.com/pod-product-compliance
Lightning Source LLC
Chambersburg PA
CBHW032150020726
47496CB00003B/813